Last Chance
CALIFORNIA

Brian Price

BUCKY B.
PUBLISHING

An Imprint of Brian Versus the World

For the groovy soul who convinced me California was a good idea.

Last Chance California

Brian Price

The Irish Exit

March 19, 2020

California was over.

I gave one last yank on the rope that pinned my suitcases to the roof of my car. The rope wasn't as tight as I would have liked, but that's why I put the least valuable of my things in the suitcases.

I squeezed inside the car. My front seat was so close to the dash that I was practically fucking my steering wheel. No matter how hard I pushed my back against the boxes crammed behind me, they refused to budge.

I took a deep breath and brought the engine to life.

A few recovering addicts waved goodbye from the sidewalk as they lit panic cigarettes. I cranked up the window when their smoke invaded my car. That's right. Cranked. I couldn't afford automatic windows.

I glided down Seventh Avenue past a halfway house, two decaying hotels, a few closet-size apartments with rent prices well over two thousand dollars, a bail bond office, a dirty rotten law school, a homeless encampment, and the largest Scientology center in the city. There was nothing beautiful about the neighborhood. Except that it was mine.

I stopped at the last traffic light before the I-5 South ramp. That's when a breaking news alert interrupted the music on the radio.

"Governor Gavin Newsom issues the first-ever lockdown in response to the outbreak of COVID-19 in the state of California."

I muted it.

There was no point in listening to what I already knew.

The traffic light turned from red to green.

Everything I could ever want was in California.

I turned left to leave it all behind.

The tarp covering the suitcases whipped through the air as I accelerated onto the highway. The suitcases stayed firm. I pushed harder on the gas.

Silhouettes of palm trees raced by me in the darkness. Even now, I couldn't help but smile.

My phone ruined the moment.

I didn't want to answer the call.

But I did.

"What took you so long to pick up?" my father asked.

Most people say hello.

"I've been a little busy."

"You wouldn't be rushing like this if you left days ago. Like I said."

Helpful, as always.

"I've planned it all out," I said.

"Like your plan to move to California. How'd that one work out?"

No one could have predicted this.

"I should be home in a few days. I'll call you when I get to Arizona."

"You need to listen to me," my father said. "There's going to be more lockdowns. People are acting nuts. This is serious."

"I'm going to focus on the road."

"Wyatt. No. Listen."

"Gotta go. There's a lot of traffic. Bye."

I hung up and looked ahead of me.

Minus a few electric-powered cars, the freeway was empty.

My phone danced in my cup holder.

My father.

Of course.

I let it ring to voicemail.

He called back.

Three.

Four.

Five.

Six times before finally giving up.

I'd deal with him soon enough.

Three days to be exact.

But I wasn't sure if I had that much time.

9

What if the cell phone towers stopped working?

What if I couldn't rely on technology?

I-10 to I-20 to I-30 to I-40 to I-81 to I-95.

Commit the route to memory.

Just in case.

I-10 to I-20 to I-30 to I-40 to I-81 to I-95.

Arizona to Texas across middle America before landing in the country's armpit, New Jersey. All other routes took me through Ohio, which already had strict travel restrictions. I didn't want to take a chance driving through there.

I-10 to I-20 to I-30 to I-40 to I-81 to I-95.

What if things got worse?

What if I got stuck in another state because of a new lockdown order?

Where would I stay?

I couldn't afford living at a hotel.

I-10 to I-20 to I-30 to I-40 to I-81 to I-95.

What if I got sick?

The medical bill would kill me.

I-10 to I-20 to I-30 to I-40 to I-81 to I-95.

My phone startled me when it screamed to life.

My father refused to quit.

I had to give him that.

But it wasn't him calling.

The word "Leah" lit up my screen.

I thought I could avoid her until I got back to Jersey.

Wrong again.

My phone continued to ring.

Without Leah, I would have never made it to California.

And now, she was calling to convince me to stay.

I couldn't answer.

Because I wasn't ready to say goodbye.

Luxardo Maraschino Cherries
May 18, 2018

The tops of palm trees danced in the cloudy, gray sky. Eco-friendly boxes on wheels and six-figure convertibles flew around the asphalt that surrounded the airport. Friends, families, and lovers reconnected with warm embraces, excited screams, and tears of joy.

I let out a loud burp.

A few heads turned and looked at me disgusted.

Like I could give a fuck.

My trip consisted of three beers and two rum and cokes. It would have been more if Boundary Airlines allowed more than one drink per hour on their flights.

My phone buzzed.

It was my father asking if I arrived safely.

I didn't bother to answer.

I found an open spot by the curb to wait for my ride. Summer said I would know which car was Noah's without her having to describe it. And she was right.

The roar of an expensive engine powered around the airport's ramps. A few travelers stopped pulling their luggage, wowed by Noah's red sports car, as it slammed to a halt in front of me.

Noah shot me a big, attractive grin. His muscles exploded out of his T-shirt when he reached over the passenger's seat to open my door. I threw my suitcase in the back and slid into the smooth black leather passenger's seat.

"Welcome to San Diego," he said.

"I haven't seen you since . . .?" I asked.

"It wasn't Christmas, was it?"

Noah always brought up his Christmas trip to Jersey.

He was very proud.

"I get sick thinking about that night," I said.

"You still throwing back old-fashioneds?"

I hadn't sniffed the cocktail since Noah drank me sick.

"It's all I drink," I lied.

"You were the only one keeping up with me."

I didn't keep up with Noah.

"Two-day hangover after that one," I said.

We exited the airport and raced down a highway decorated with palm trees. The city's skyline was in perfect view, sitting across a bay that fed into the Pacific Ocean. The sun fought through the dull sky and lit up the world. Smiling people walked around looking healthy and beautiful. No beat-up cars dared to grace the roads.

Nothing about California reminded me of home.

It was perfect.

California always was.

Noah drove us through the city, pointing out his favorite bars, while reliving his college glory days. He was the type of guy who got things done. He never asked permission. It's how he convinced Summer, the most stubborn person I knew, to leave Jersey and move across the country. I felt like Summer when Noah and I arrived at a small brewery on the outskirts of the city. It was a new joint that Noah wanted to try, but it didn't open until one.

"Sometimes a man needs a beer at eleven," I said.

Like on the weekend of his cancelled wedding.

"I know a place."

The joint Noah knew was a retired firehouse that transformed into a brewery. There was an old fire truck parked in the back and all the beers were named after firefighting jargon and movies. I ordered a Backdraft IPA and a few other similarly named beers for my flight. The burly bartender filled each glass three-quarters full.

Triple the standard pour.

"Enjoy, bro," the bartender said.

We didn't bother to find a table; we stayed right at the bar.

"What's your plan for the weekend?" Noah asked.

"Get drunk enough to forget it."

Noah avoided my eyes.

"Don't worry, I'm a happy drunk." I took a sip of my beer. "Usually."

Noah let out a nervous laugh.

"There's plenty of girls out here to make you forget all about her."

"Here's to hoping."

I lifted my beer and tapped Noah's glass.

"Too bad I won't be around to help you out," he said. "I'm flying to Sacramento for a last-minute business deal tomorrow."

Working on a weekend.

Sounded like a real bummer.

"I won't see you at all?" I asked.

"I'll be back Sunday night." Noah started on his second beer. "I almost didn't make it to pick you up today."

"Why?"

"I just got back from a month-long assignment in Virginia. When I got home, I dropped my bags off at the condo and headed to the garage. When I got there, my car was running."

"What the fuck?"

"Who knows how long she left it on," Noah said.

"Summer?"

"Yeah."

"How does that even happen?" I asked.

"We have two parking spots. Summer must have moved my car to get hers out, but she left mine running. It could have been running all morning . . . or all week."

"Good thing it wasn't stolen."

Noah gulped down his Extinguisher No. 9.

"I barely had enough gas to make it to the gas station."

"She's never been a morning person," I said.

He laughed.

"You're not wrong there."

Honestly, Summer was a real asshole before noon.

Noah caught me up on his job, his stock market portfolio, and his future rental investment ideas. The guy understood money. He could afford to live a little. And in California, that cost a lot.

Noah finished his beers before I sipped my last drink.

"Want to check out some places downtown? Summer won't be done working until six or seven."

I chugged my Firehouse lager, and we left the brewery.

The bartender followed behind us.

"Hey, bro," the bartender said. "Is it cool if I check out your car? It's so fucking sick, bro."

Noah gave the bartender a tour of his car. He explained the car's specifications, modifications, and details like a proud parent.

"Can I sit in the front seat?"

"I'm afraid not," Noah said. "Only I sit there."

"Totally get it, bro," the bartender said. "I'd be the same way if I had a car like that. I appreciate you letting me take a look."

"No problem," Noah said.

The bartender returned to the brewery.

"This happens more often than I like to admit," Noah said. "He must have seen my car when we pulled up."

That's why he gave us that extra pour.

We drove to another brewery, one that had demonic gargoyles flying on the walls. The monsters kept Noah and me company in the empty tasting room. We each had two beers and a sandwich to soak up some of the alcohol. Both beers were IPAs, but one was a tangerine beer, Noah's favorite.

After we took down those drinks, Noah and I walked to a different brewery a few blocks away, but I never caught the name. We stopped for a beer.

"They only have one good brew," Noah said.

It was good enough to wash away the hints of tangerine and pineapple that polluted my mouth.

"I'm going to drop my car off," he said. "I can't drive."

I swallowed the rest of my beer in a gulp.

"I haven't been able to drive since the second brewery."

Noah remembered to turn the engine off when he parked his car in his building's garage. We walked back outside to the sidewalk without stopping inside Noah's home.

"We can scooter over to the bars," he said.

"Scooter?"

Abandoned motorized scooters and rentable bikes were wrecked on the surrounding sidewalks. There were dozens of them lying in the street, hugging the curb. Some were green and yellow. Others black and white.

"You download an app, put in your credit card, and ride these bad boys. They're fast." Noah swiveled in circles around me on a goddamn scooter. "They showed up a few months ago. Makes life way easier."

I downloaded the app, signed my life away, and unlocked the nearest scooter by scanning a barcode on the machine. I pushed off the sidewalk with one leg and pounced on the scooter. The machine lurched forward when I pulled back on the accelerator, nearly tossing me onto the street. I gathered myself, gripped the handlebar, and flicked my wrist to make the wannabe bike move.

"Follow me," Noah said.

He shot like a missile down the crowded city street, then maneuvered on and off the sidewalk, finding openings to speed around slow people in his way.

"Watch where you're going!"

"Asshole!"

No one seemed to like Noah's moves.

Too afraid to pull the throttle hard, I paced behind Noah, apologizing to everyone I wobbled past.

Noah led me to a corner bar called Complex Brewing. The joint welcomed guests with the words BREW PUB decorating the center of a black awning outside the entrance. Inside reminded me of a classic bar. No gimmicks. No theme. A bar, stools, tables, and tons of beers on tap.

No longer drinking in our own conversation, Noah and I listened to the chatter of happy-hourers, finally awake drunks, and eager tourists. Noah suggested a fruity beer. I ordered a pale ale. I had drunk enough fruit for the day.

"The aroma hits different on this one," Noah said. "And the aftertaste? Perfection."

All I tasted was cold and delicious.

Our young, attractive blonde waitress returned with the next round of drinks. I handed her my empty glass. When she leaned towards me, I caught a whiff of her perfume. Our hands briefly touched on the glass. She gazed into my eyes as she held her hand on top of mine, before taking the glass away. She bounced away from our table.

"Say something to her when she comes back," Noah said.

"We'll see," I said, knowing I wouldn't say a word.

Erin ruined blondes for me.

I was finished with them.

But a quick glance at the waitress's round ass as she headed for the bar made me reconsider.

Noah downed all of his beers before I sipped my third.

"Should we head back to meet Summer?" I asked.

Between the plane ride and booze, I needed sleep.

And a break for my liver.

Noah and I didn't steer any scooter.

We stumbled by foot back to his place.

* * *

He called it "The Palace." The penthouse in the heart of the city reeked of new money. The Palace featured two large bedrooms, two bathrooms, two showers, and a luxury bathtub. The bathrooms alone had more square footage than any place I'd ever lived. Outside, there was a deck with a hot tub and a perfect view of the city skyline.

Noah flashed on the LED lights that were above and under the kitchen cabinets. He showed me six shade changes. Noah installed those. Using an app on his phone, he turned on a brand-new fake fireplace. He built that as well. Noah changed the temperature of the apartment and locked the front door. All from his phone. He hired a professional for those amenities.

"I'll make us a drink," Noah said.

The white puffy couch in the living room caught me.

My eyelids grew heavy.

Finally, some rest.

Metal clanked against glass, bringing me back to this reality. Noah stirred together two cocktails in the wall-less kitchen.

"These cherries are practically twenty bucks a pop," he said. "That's why good bars charge a lot for old-fashioneds. That's when you know they use the good stuff."

Until a minute ago, I didn't even know there were more than one type of cherry.

"What are they called?" I asked.

Noah handed me a drink.

"Luxardo maraschino cherries."

Before I could take a sip, The Palace front door opened. Tall and stunning, Summer hadn't aged since college. I was glad to see her. And not just because she saved me from a fruit lecture.

"I told you to keep his mind off of things," Summer said. "Not get him wasted."

"I did both," Noah said.

"We're not that drunk," I said.

Summer let out a fake laugh.

"Have you ever said that sober?"

"Once."

"I can't get drunk with you guys if you're already drunk."

Noah handed Summer his drink.

"I made this for you," he said.

"You're full of shit. That was yours."

Summer shoved the drink back at Noah. When he grabbed the glass, she threw two fingers and a thumb into it. She pulled out his two expensive cherries. He was too drunk to stop her.

"I'll take these," Summer said. "It's asshole tax."

And just like that, two twenty-dollar cherries were gone.

I hid my drink, peeled myself off the couch, and squeezed Summer.

"How the hell are you?" I asked.

"Not as good as you're feeling."

"Happy to see you. And that's not the booze talking."

"I can't believe you're actually out here," Summer said.

"My other plans fell through," I said.

Noah laughed.

"Did you at least get any of your deposits back?"

"Noah!" Summer yelled. "That's not appropriate."

"Some," I said. "The owner of the venue was a real dick."

"Are you okay?" Summer asked.

I wasn't.

My heart ached worse than my wallet.

"It's impossible to be sad out here," I said.

* * *

The three of us headed to a dimly lit restaurant a block from The Palace. I'm surprised the hostess let me in.

Noah ordered two old-fashioneds, a glass of red wine, an exotic salad, and a few rolls of sushi for the table. Something at the restaurant reminded Summer of a distant memory, but in my drunken state I didn't know what she meant.

"Come on. You remember Doug's party in high school," Summer said.

"Which one?" I asked.

"The one we got into that big fight," Summer said. "I went full bitch mode."

"I am familiar with that side of Summer," Noah said.

"Shut up," Summer said. "Wyatt did something extra stupid that night, I'm sure of it."

I wanted to remember.

But I was too drunk to care.

"I took a bunch of shots when I couldn't find him," Summer said. "Remember Wyatt? But the vodka didn't calm me down. Nope. Not at all."

"I've definitely seen that from her," Noah said.

"Why do you have to do this while I'm telling a story?"

"Imagine if I left your car running all morning," Noah said. "Or all week."

"Really? You want to do this now?"

"You'd be pissed if it was your car."

I grabbed my chair and squeezed the wood.

Arguing always brought me back to my parents nearly murdering one another during their late-night arguments. Almost every night they'd scream at each other. My father would wake me up to play judge in his disagreements with my mother. My mother would plead with him to not drag me into the fray. My father would say I needed to be a man. The only thing was, if I didn't take my father's side in his marital issues, he'd beat me for my disloyalty the next time he had me alone.

"I said I'm sorry," Summer said.

I twisted the seat in my palms.

It wasn't normal.

My childhood.

I never realized it until I dated Erin.

And witnessed a functioning family.

But she was gone now, too.

Because of me.

"It's my car, Summer," Noah said.

My grip tightened on my seat.

It was PTSD.

I knew that.

I just didn't know how to stop it.

"Can we just drop it?" Summer asked. "I fucked up. I'm sorry. Let's move on."

Noah bit his lower lip.

Summer never told the rest of her story.

The waitress returned to our table.
"The food will be out soon. Anybody need anything?"
I asked for another drink.

The (Almost) Wedding Night
May 19, 2018

Car alarms boomed. Horns shrieked. A homeless man preached about the Lord damning everyone to hell. A dozen ambulances screamed by on the streets below.

Outside the bedroom door, I heard Summer and Noah.

"Don't wake him up," Summer said.

"You think he's hungover?" Noah asked.

"He might be dead."

I came out of the bedroom, stinking like yesterday.

Noah wore a fresh shave with a tailored gray suit.

"Feeling alright?" he asked.

No man should be that cheery after drinking that much booze. I grunted as I passed Noah. I found the bathroom. The wall behind the toilet prevented me from face-planting while I pissed. It was a long one.

When I came out of the bathroom, Noah stood behind a sizzling stove, scorching slices of a dead pig.

"Want some breakfast? I made a fruit smoothie, eggs, and bacon."

Summer handed me three aspirins. I thanked her and downed the drugs before crawling back into bed.

After most of the morning passed, the lack of moisture in my mouth forced me from under my covers. I didn't bother to get dressed. I threw on some shoes, grabbed Summer's spare key, and left.

I walked outside the building and onto the street. The sun melted my skin. My sweat reeked of old-fashioneds. Each time my foot hit the ground, a painful strike shot up my leg, vibrating my skull.

Somehow, I made it half a block to a convenience store, where a small bag of cashews and a twenty-ounce soda set me back fifteen bucks.

I finished the bag at The Palace.

Then, I dove onto my pillows.

Figured if I was asleep, I wouldn't think of Erin.

Or the almost significance of the day.

I slept for another few hours before I treated myself to a hot shower. Not long after, Summer found me dazed on the couch when she came home from work.

"You look like shit," Summer said.

"I was really feeling myself today too."

She threw her purse on the counter and laughed.

"What the fuck is wrong with you?"

"Do I really need to tell you?"

"Get a shower," Summer said. "I know the perfect place to cure your hangover blues."

That's how bad I looked.

Summer didn't even realize I already showered.

* * *

Boarded up houses covered the blocks where the dispensary was. Bars locked all the windows of every shop. There were unkempt rock lawns with weeds as tall as humans. Summer parked across the street from the biggest garage on the block. People strolled inside while others snuck out with sealed black bags.

Two booming men with guns guarded the entrance. Bulletproof glass protected the woman checking IDs. A locked door prevented anyone from leaving the lobby once they entered the building.

I emptied my pockets, placing everything in a dish.

"Arms up," a clean-cut giant said.

Summer picked up a piece of old paper that must have fell from my wallet. She went to place it in the trash.

Wait.

No.

I lunged at her.

"Don't throw it away," I said.

The security guard grabbed me.

"Relax."

"That's something my grandfather gave me. It's all I have left."

The security guard released me from his grasp. Summer handed me the last piece of my grandfather's California postcard. I clutched it in my hand.

"Sorry," I said. "It's really important to me."

"What is it?" Summer asked.

I showed Summer the delicate piece of scrap.

"My grandpa wrote me this when I was a kid. A postcard from California. My grandpa said I'd love it out here."

"Seems like he was onto something," Summer said.

I put the old, torn postcard back into my wallet.

It was more than an heirloom.

The guard waved an electric paddle over my body before motioning me to enter the dispensary.

The door opened, and I knew exactly how the children in *Charlie and the Chocolate Factory* must have felt. Every type of weed someone could imagine filled the shop's walls and counters. Weed in special cases. Different colored weed treats in packages. Weed gummies hanging like fruit on a tree. Weed chocolate stocked in displays. Cooking oil weed. Candy-infused weed. Lotion weed. Regular weed. Oil weed. Weed that made Oompa-Loompas appear.

Three college-aged weed enthusiasts worked the joint, allowing stoners a sniff of the various marijuana strains upon request. All the weed was in stench-proof containers, making the dispensary reek of incense instead of marijuana.

I bought a pack of pink-and-blue-striped weed-infused fruit snacks covered in chunks of sugar. I didn't bother to learn about THC percentage or whatever else the guy—I mean, the budtender—tried telling me.

On our way back to The Palace, Summer and I stopped at the grocery store for essentials. We bought a bottle of wine, two bags of chips and two chocolate bars.

* * *

Summer poured two glasses of wine back at The Palace. Her phone rang before she could sit down on the couch.

"You serious?" she said to whomever was on the line.

Summer ran into her bedroom.

I took an edible.

There was nothing good on TV, so I left on whatever Marvel movie was playing. Summer reemerged fifteen minutes later. She brought the wine and took an edible when she joined me on the couch.

"Work going well?" I asked.

"Fucking great." Summer took a swig of wine. "Seventy hours a week. I'm a secretary, salesperson, and social media expert. Three people's fucking jobs. And I'm only paid for one."

"That's some bullshit."

Summer gulped down her glass of red.

"Some weeks I don't even get fucking paid."

"How is that legal?" I asked.

"Last month I got two free surgeries instead of a check."

"Can't you report that to someone?" I asked.

"Who? Who would listen? Even if anyone did, I'd lose my job. Can't afford that. Especially not out here."

Summer poured out her frustration with work.

She opened another bottle of wine when she finished.

"At least you've got Noah," I said to change subjects.

"I moved across the fucking country for that guy." Summer twirled her empty ring finger. "Least he could do is buy me a diamond."

"What's he waiting for?"

"I have no fucking idea. We've done this city thing for three years. Two years too long, if you ask me. It's all for Noah. He wanted this. A last hoorah before settling down."

I drank some of the dry wine.

"You're leaving the city?"

"If Noah wants to stay with me."

Summer poured some wine.

"If not?" I asked.

"Back to Jersey."

"Any excuse to get back there," I said.

"It's amazing here. I know. I'm lucky. Beyond lucky."

"But?"

Summer sighed.

"I check flights to fly back once a week."

"Why?"

"Babies. Birthdays. Anniversaries. Holidays. I'm missing everything. And for what? Is Noah ever gonna marry me? Or am I just wasting my time out here?"

"Noah loves you," I said.

"It's not even about that. My biological clock is fucking ticking. I don't have time for Peter Pan to grow up."

"You can't think like that."

"Noah needs to shit or get off the pot." A frown cracked through Summer's face. "Why can't he just move to Jersey?"

"You'd miss seventy and sunny all year round."

"There's no seasons out here!" Summer shouted. "I never know what fucking month it is. It'll drive a person mad."

"You were mad before you moved."

I poured us another glass of red.

"Enough about me," Summer said. "Tell me about you."

"I'm good."

"Don't make me ask."

I tasted the wine.

"Ask what?"

"Come on."

I knew what she wanted to know.

"I really don't know what you mean."

"Have you talked to her?"

I took some more wine.

"Erin."

"Yeah," Summer said. "Erin."

"Was this your plan? Get me drunk and ask about her?"

"I also bought you weed. I know you're into that."

"Good luck getting me to talk about Erin."

Summer sighed.

"You can't keep this stuff inside."

I drank the remaining wine in my nearly full glass.

"She moved to New York. Lives with her new boyfriend."

"A new boyfriend?"

"Yeah."

"Already?"

"She's a quick healer, I guess."

"How long after did she start dating him?"

"Two months."

"Target has a longer return policy than that." Summer grabbed my wrists. She turned red and laughed. "I'm sorry. I don't mean to . . . I think the edible is working."

"Yeah, yeah," I said.

Summer wiped her eyes dry.

"That tells you all you need to know. No way she could have loved you."

I didn't know about that.

"Sure," I said. "But I'm the one who ended it."

"You never told me what happened."

I still hadn't processed my breakup with Erin.

It was the worst moment of my life.

"Pour me another glass."

Summer emptied a second bottle of wine.

"That sounds healthy."

"I wanted to move to California. Erin didn't. I couldn't get past it."

It wasn't a lie.

But it wasn't the whole truth.

"That wasn't your only issue," Summer said.

I glanced at my phone for the time.

"I'd have been married by now."

"She wasn't the one."

I wasn't so sure.

"You don't know that."

"I do," Summer said. "She was wrong for you."

I clanked my wine glass against Summer's.

"Happy Wedding Day to me."

"I'm celebrating the fact you didn't marry her. I'd have to be wasted to watch you pledge your life to that woman."

I finished my wine.

"Tell me how you really feel."

"I know today is hard. But you know how she acted. Especially when you both came out to visit. I'll never like that woman."

Erin was jealous of Summer.

And Erin didn't hide it when she met her.

"You're not wrong," I said.

"Are you okay?"

"Nah," I said. "But I'm working on it."

"I know how to cheer you up."

"More booze, please."

"My best friend out here is single. She's amazing. And just your type."

"My type?"

"Blonde," Summer said.

"No more blondes," I said.

"Shut up."

I downed some more wine.

"I'm trying new things."

"I'll see it when I believe it," Summer said. "We're doing brunch with her tomorrow."

I wasn't ready to meet someone.

But I was excited to meet a California girl.

More than I admitted to Summer.

We took another edible and put on an old movie from the 2000s. I recommended an old Schwarzenegger flick, but Summer vetoed that real quick. Both too high, drunk, and exhausted to make it to bed, we passed out on opposite ends of the couch before the movie ended.

California Blondes and Molly
May 20, 2018

S he was exactly how I imagined. A perfect smile formed on her lips. Her blue eyes lit up her platinum blonde hair, which fell past her neck and rested on the biggest fake boobs I'd ever seen.

She handed me a crumpled napkin when Summer left the table. I peeked inside to find a small chunk of a broken blue pill.

"Don't be so obvious," Leah said. "One of my friends got busted here."

I hid the napkin under the side of my plate.

"What is it?"

"Molly."

Shit.

I never tried molly.

Or any other hard drug.

Just booze and weed for me.

I blame the fear tactics instilled in me from DARE public school takeovers. Apparently, the Drug Abuse Resistance Education program was a massive failure against the war on drugs, but it worked on me. So much so that as a teen, I volunteered to scare elementary school children on the dangers of alcohol and narcotics. I even gave out DARE stickers and coloring books.

"I'm doing mine now," Leah said, as if it weren't the first time. She washed down her pill with the melted ice from her oversize margarita. "Are you going to take yours?"

A police officer with DARE volunteers would visit every classroom. They'd give a presentation and show the downside of drugs.

"Not yet," I said.

"I gave Summer some. She's doing hers in the bathroom."

"You gave some to Summer?"

After I had learned about the devastation drugs cause, a cop taught my classmates how to say no to drugs. That was the slogan. SAY NO TO DRUGS.

That's all I had to do.

Tell Leah no.

"There's nothing to worry about," Leah said. "It's good stuff."

I couldn't just say no to drugs.

Who does that?

I swirled around my empty margarita.

"I'm flying from the tequila."

"It's not even noon."

I was afraid the drugs would make me breakdown over Erin. But I was also terrified to discover my reaction to narcotics. Because I knew I'd chase the high.

"I want to. I really do. But I don't want to miss my flight tomorrow. It's an early one."

Leah grabbed my hand.

"I need an excuse to get fucked-up."

DARE didn't prepare me for this.

"Well," I said.

"Honestly, I'm just using you to get fucked up."

I smiled.

"I've never been used before."

"Let me tell you," Leah said. "It's a real treat."

How could I lose the pill without Leah noticing?

I looked around for a place to ditch the molly. I could act like I swept the drug into my hand. Let the pill fall to the floor while pretending to catch it. Fake toss the imaginary molly in my mouth.

No.

She would know when I wasn't high.

"I can be the sitter," I said.

"What if I want to get fucked-up with a cute Jersey boy on his last day in California?"

It's easy to understand why DARE failed.

"Um."

Leah caressed my thigh.

"It could be a lot of fun."

"I'm not sure if I want this to be my first time."

She leaned into my ear.

"Why not have your first time in California?"

Before I could respond, Summer stormed back to our table. Leah pulled herself away from me.

"Do I look like a shady motherfucker?" Summer asked. "Two waitresses at two different times came in while I was in there. What if I was taking a shit?"

"Nothing but narcs here," Leah said.

And one right here, too.

"We all poop, people!" Summer yelled. She stabbed her margarita with a straw before an exaggerated sip.

"Did you take it?" Leah asked.

"Yeah. And the waitresses didn't see a damn thing." Summer looked at my drug napkin. "Did you?"

"My hangover is really wreaking havoc," I lied. "I don't know if molly is a good chemistry experiment right now."

"It'll help with your hangover," Leah said.

"You'll be fine," Summer said.

The classroom DARE cops had told students that people will use peer pressure to force them to do drugs. "People who do that aren't your friends," they'd say.

"If you don't want to do it, give it back," Leah said. "Can't be wasteful."

What would Leah think if I handed the drug back?

Probably that I was a fucking narc.

"Let me think about it," I said.

We ordered another round of drinks when our server came back. I switched to beer. Summer and Leah told war stories about their old job where they met. Their former boss enjoyed strippers and cocaine a little too much for a responsible business owner. One morning Summer and Leah found naked women passed out all over the office. It disgusted them. But the story made me smile. Snorting cocaine off strippers at the business he owned sounded like the American Dream to me. Or at least a good one.

The molly sat on the table.

Daring me with a good time.

Or sending me into a mental breakdown.

Death could be in the cards.

According to DARE.

I considered taking a stroll on the beach and burying the pill in the sand. With my feet. Obviously. I'd tell Leah and Summer I already took the molly if they asked.

But what excuse could I have for wanting to walk on a dreary beach? And with my luck, some kid would find the pill and shove it in his mouth. A child high on molly would be absolutely hilarious. If it didn't kill the little bastard first.

"Crazy you're here," Summer said. "It doesn't feel real."

"Why?" Leah asked.

"Life," I said.

"Or that prissy thing you almost married."

"Almost married?" Leah asked.

I needed more booze.

Or mind-numbing drugs.

"Today would have been the first day of our honeymoon," I said. "Starting in Italy. I'd still be flying right now."

"But not flying like this?" Leah asked.

I smiled and drank more beer.

"What happened?" Leah asked.

"Don't open that can of worms," Summer said. "He won't even tell me."

I knew how to get rid of the pill.

And change the conversation.

DARE fails again.

"I'd rather open this can of worms." I unfolded my drug napkin. "Go easy on me. It's my first time."

A swish of booze washed down the molly.

"This is gonna be a lot of fun, Jersey boy."

Summer took more drugs from Leah's hand on her way back to the bathroom.

"Tell me about your ex," Leah said.

"No."

"Well, I used to be married."

"Looks like you got me beat. I didn't get to that level."

Leah laughed.

"Tell me about her."

"I'll talk about anything but that," I said.

Leah stayed silent for a few seconds.

"How much would you let someone poop on you for?"

"Did you just say poop?" I asked.

Leah took a sip of Summer's margarita.

"Some people are into that."

"Are you?"

"What if I am?"

"No way am I letting someone piss out their asshole all over me."

Leah laughed.

"Piss out their asshole? That's disgusting."

"There's no guarantee you're going to get solid shit," I said. "Explosive shits. You don't have those here? I wouldn't be surprised."

"You're so strange."

"Says the person who just asked a stranger how much money they'd take to let someone shit on them," I said.

"We're not strangers anymore. We're drug buds. And I'd do it for a hundred."

"Thousand?"

"A hundred dollars," Leah said.

"That's fucking gross."

"What about you?"

"If I could guarantee solid poop? A grand. At least."

Leah reached for my knee and clawed her way up my thigh. "What if I asked you to do it?"

"Am I getting shit on in this situation?"

Leah grabbed Summer's margarita.

She took her time with it.

"Yeah. I poop on you."

"A hundred bucks."

Leah buried her face in her cleavage as she laughed.

In between laughs, she gasped for air.

She squeezed my shoulder with her hand.

"You good?" I asked. "It wasn't that funny."

"I'll be okay."

Her chest sucked in while her nails dug into my skin.

I don't remember DARE teaching me about drug overdoses. Worthless fucking program.

"You should probably get that checked out," I said.

"It's a food allergy," Leah said. "I'm fine. If not, I have my pen."

I'd let someone die before stabbing them with an EpiPen.

She pulled her hand away from her chest and grabbed the nearest glass of water. She chugged it, then tossed the empty glass on the table. I handed her another drink. Water leaked from her mouth right to her giant funbags. Little drops splashed when it hit her bare skin.

Summer returned to the table but didn't sit.

Leah wiped her eyes with a napkin.

"I asked the waiter for the check on my way back," Summer said. "I blew up that bathroom. There was a girl waiting to use it. Let's get the fuck out of here before she smells what I did."

* * *

The three of us walked along the beach to the next bar. Herds of people waddled down the narrow path that separated the sand from civilization. Leah's ass swayed in front of me. Side to side with every step. Her hips dipping and swinging. Dip and swing. Dip and swing. Dip. Swing. Swing. Dip.

"ID."

The loud voice of a large, tattooed man woke me from my trance. I grabbed my wallet from my back pocket. As I pulled it out, my wallet flew out of my hands and hit the bouncer in the nose. He wasn't pleased.

Leah picked up my wallet from the ground, pulled out my driver's license, and handed it to the bouncer in one smooth motion.

"Sorry, he's with me," she said.

Leah fixated on me for a moment before her eyes found the bouncer's. "But not with me."

He handed her back my ID and waved us in.

"Go ahead."

Leah rubbed his arm as she entered the bar. She reached back and gave me my wallet. I checked to make sure my grandpa's postcard didn't fall out. It was still there.

We headed up a flight of steep stairs to a joint that reminded me of a frat house, but with more women. White. Black. Tan. Hispanic. Asian. Every race and color. Blondes. Brunettes. Black hair. Dyed hair. Highlighted hair. No hair.

There wasn't an ugly person there.

I smiled at all the pretty people.

Fuck.

I was messed up.

It felt groovy.

Leah led me by the hand through the bar's two wooden rooms to an outdoor roof-deck. Elevated tables, benches, and a bar parallel to the ocean were jammed with people drinking booze. As soon as we got near the edge of the patio, a group of four left their seats that faced the beach. Summer used her hips to block another woman from sitting down. I sat next to Summer, with Leah on my other side. It was quite a view.

"You think we'll get a good sunset?" I asked.

"The clouds should clear by the afternoon," Summer said.

A waitress approached us.

"We'll do three Red Bull vodka slushies, three waters, and a Diet Coke," Leah said.

"You're going to love this drink," Summer said.

"It's frozen booze," Leah said.

The waitress returned with three clear chalices filled with what looked like a yellow-tinted snow cone. Summer, Leah, and I cheered our drinks. The alcohol chilled my throat on its way down.

"It tastes like college," I said.

Leah reached her hand toward mine. She put something in my palm. Leah closed my hand into a fist.

"We should take more. It's kind of wearing off."

The molly wasn't wearing off.

But I swallowed another piece of a pill.

* * *

When the sun finally escaped the clouds, everyone pulled down their sunglasses to shield their eyes. Leah's face glowed in the fading light. She was the most beautiful woman I had ever seen. I smiled at her.

My parents.

Friends.

Their parents.

The law.

Society.

DARE.

Liars.

All of them.

Drugs were awesome.

"What are you doing?" Leah asked.

"I . . . um . . . I don't know."

"You're so fucked-up," she said.

"You're not?" I asked.

"Not totally," Leah said. "It's called 'rolling' by the way."

"Rolling?"

"When you get high on molly, you're rolling. And you're definitely rolling."

"I'm fucking jealous," Summer said.

Leah handed me my untouched cup of water.

"Make sure you drink up."

I tasted a sip.

Next thing I knew, I was out of water.

"I've taken two fucking pills and nothing," Summer said. "I didn't even take my meds today."

"What are you taking?" Leah asked.

"Zoloft."

Leah sighed.

"The molly won't work with that."

"What do you think about me trying another pill?" Summer asked. "I'll pay you."

Leah and Summer went to the bathroom together. I protected their seats and ordered more booze.

By the time they returned, three new drinks arrived.

Leah and I ignored Summer for most of the day.

But not on purpose.

We were lost in our own little slice of the world.

Laughing, flirting, and saying nothing of importance.

We were rolling.

And happy.

But time moved quicker than I realized.

The sun began to set.

Everyone on the beach below and at the bar stopped in the middle of what they were doing and appreciated the beauty of the moment. The giant fireball lit up the sky every color imaginable before it silently fell into the ocean, out of sight.

We left the bar after one last round.

"You coming back to my place?" Summer asked. "Noah would love to see you."

"Noah's back?" I asked.

"He got in an hour ago."

34

"I have work tomorrow," Leah said.

"It's my last night in California."

"I don't know."

I grabbed Leah's hand.

"Honestly, I'm just using you, Cali girl."

Leah's face told me she changed her mind.

"As long as you don't ever call California 'Cali' again."

* * *

Noah waited in The Palace hot tub. Summer stripped to her bikini and joined him.

"They're wasted," Summer said. "I'm just a tad tipsy."

"No drugs?" Noah asked.

Summer didn't want Noah to know we did molly.

What a narc.

"Booze slushies," I said.

"And margaritas," Leah said.

"You guys all looked pretty banged up," Noah said.

I tossed off my shirt and pants before sliding into the water in my boxers.

"Last day of vacation. Gotta make it count."

Leah unstrapped her sandals. Her eyes caught me staring. I hoped for a bikini. She took her time when she slithered out of her jean shorts and launched her ass high in the air. Leah smirked before she pulled off her tank top, flaunting her modest one-piece suit.

"See something you like?" Leah asked.

"Everything," I said.

Leah shook her enormous breasts before hiding them in the water.

"You don't have to stare, Noah," Summer said.

At least I wasn't alone.

The jet streams soothed me in and out of consciousness.

Drunk, tired, and relaxed, I felt weightless in the water.

"Did Wyatt tell Leah about how I met him?" Noah asked.

I awoke from my trance.

"The time we met?"

"Christmas," he said.

"Oh right. Christmas."

"Here we go," Summer said.

"Summer made me spend a Christmas in New Jersey to meet all her friends and family," Noah said.

Summer splashed at Noah.

"I made you? Like I could make you do anything."

"We visited New Jersey for Christmas," he said.

"That's better."

"Summer's friends challenged me to a drinking contest. They didn't think a 'Cali boy' could out drink the tough men of the East."

Leah sprang awake.

"I hate when people call California Cali."

"I drank them all under the table," Noah said. "Well, all except one."

"It was the first time in a decade I puked from drinking," I said.

"And that's how Wyatt met Noah," Summer said.

"Such a gremlin," Leah said.

"Gremlin?" I asked.

"If you move out here, I'll tell you what it means," Leah said.

"Or he could just look it up on his phone," Noah said.

Summer splashed him again.

Leah got out of the water to lie on The Palace deck.

She sighed before placing her arm over her head.

"Are you okay?" I asked.

"I'm going to go home."

Leah dried off with a towel.

I sat in the hot tub.

She gathered her things.

I sat in the hot tub.

Leah put on her shorts and slipped on her sandals.

I sat in the hot tub.

"See you later, yeah?" Leah said.

I nodded.

Leah left.

I sat in the hot tub.

"Go after her," Summer said.

I pulled my jaw from the floor and hurried to the elevators. Without getting dressed. Or drying off. I caught up with Leah on the sidewalk outside the building. She waited for me to say something. Nothing came from my mouth.

Leah broke the silence.

"You're in your underwear. And you forgot to dry off."

A trail of water glistened on the sidewalk all the way to the building's entrance.

"I had somewhere to be."

"Where's that?" Leah asked.

"Right here."

I pulled Leah by her hips and kissed her.

She grabbed my face and returned the favor.

Her pants vibrated against my leg.

Leah checked her phone.

"My ride's here."

"Take my number," I said.

"I can't risk falling for visitors."

I kissed Leah's cheek.

"I'm moving here."

"Don't make me a promise you can't keep," she said.

"Promise."

Leah took my number.

I smiled the whole time as she typed it.

She gave me back my phone.

I sent her a text right there.

You're cute.

Leah smirked when she read it.

We walked across the street to her ride.

"You're a romantic," Leah said. "And a gentleman."

"Only for the first three months."

"And so honest."

Right before Leah got into the car, she kissed me again.

I certainly wasn't finished with blondes.

Hungover on a Jet Plane

May 20, 2018

Noah and Summer were already in bed when I came back inside. I changed into dry clothes and wrapped myself in the six blankets Summer left on the couch for me. Still, I shivered. My jaw throbbed. When I went to readjust my chin, I noticed my teeth chattering. Had they always been? For how long? Is that why my jaw hurts? How much molly did Leah give me?

I texted her.

I'm freezing. Is this normal?

Leah sent a photo of a Bible, which sat next to her in the back seat of her ride.

She fired off a bunch of messages in a row.

Is this a sign that I need Jesus?

You're not cold. It's the molly. You're coming down.

Take a hot shower and listen to music.

My comedown music is usually Bob Dylan.

The first California girl to ever speak to me sent a music playlist titled Folk Comedown that featured Bob Dylan, Cat Stevens, and John Denver. I knew most of the artists but never listened to any of their songs. Folk music kinda sucked.

I messaged Leah.

I can't wait to listen.

She responded.

Home.

I haven't had that much fun in a really long time.

Night Jersey Boy.

I typed a good night message but erased it.

The words didn't fit.

I tried again.

That wasn't it, either.

I needed the perfect lines.

My thoughts went blank.

The drugs clouded my mind.
I typed nothing back to Leah.
Instead, I sprawled out on the couch and fell asleep.

May 21, 2018

S hit.
My flight.
I awoke in a panic, searching for my phone.
1:30 a.m.
One.
Two.
Three.
Four hours until my flight.
A sigh escaped my mouth in relief.

I turned on the TV, but almost fell back asleep flipping through all the streaming services. My eyes caught a notebook on top of my suitcase. I forgot I even brought the damn thing with me to California. I couldn't even remember the last time I wrote anything that wasn't work related.

I placed the notebook on The Palace's glass coffee table and clicked a pen ready. The first page of the notebook was blank. Fresh. Clean. Perfect. A new beginning. Magic filled The Palace and rushed through my body. Time to show the world your way with words, Wyatt.

I wrote the first thing that came to mind.

You're a hack, Wyatt Lewis. Everyone will know you're a fraud if you write. Can't even string together a text message to a woman you're infacutated with. It's infatuated, dumbass. Don't prove your stupidity by writing shit down. That's permanent. Can't take it back once it's out there. Don't be a goddamn fool.

I shut the notebook on my pen.
The Resistance.
Steven Pressfield named the son of a bitch.
The Resistance.
Forgot about him.
It takes down creatives daily.
But not me.

39

Not tonight.

I walked to the kitchen and filled a glass with water from the tap. Noah left a bottle of aspirin on the table, so I took three pills.

The Resistance waited for me.

Attempting to stop the words from flowing.

I let out a laugh.

Writers are our own worst enemies.

Sometimes the Resistance was harsh criticism.

Other times it was distractions.

Work.

Women.

Bullshit social obligations.

Anything that took me away from sitting my ass in a chair and writing. But the Resistance hurt me most when it asked, "What if you're crazy, Wyatt? You're going to embarrass yourself. You know it. You're not special. You're nothing."

It was a goddamn war in here.

More determined, I sat back down to write.

But the only thing I could think about was the girl I almost married.

Erin,

Some believe that your dreams are often the last thing you think about before falling asleep. When I'm awake, I can deliberately avoid thinking about you. Or numb myself drunk or stoned. But when my guard is down, right before bed, you always make your move.

Every night, I dream about you. I wish it was an exaggeration. It's funny because I used to never remember my dreams. That is, until we broke up. Now? It's a fucking double feature every night with you making an appearance in both showings. The dreams feel like a window giving me a little taste of what could have been. But every morning, my heart rebreaks as I settle into the reality with the choice I made.

And I'm not sure if it was the right one.

But you deserve more than me.

Someone who appreciates you.

And isn't fucked up and broken.

Looking back at everything, it's funny what I miss. Talking with you as you'd clean the dishes after dinner. Morning coffee dates on the porch. How good you were at keeping surprises a secret. Winter nights on the couch snuggled up with the softest blanket in the world. How excited you'd get over the littlest things – a tasty new wine, the funniest thing you saw that day, or the perfect outfit.

A part of me wishes we never went to California. I never told you what California meant to me. I kept that from you. A huge part of me that I never told you about. That I've never told anyone. I don't know how. Or if it even matters. But I needed California. To at least try. The more you told me no, the more resentful I became. And angry. And I became a monster.

You deserve someone who won't ever leave you.
Someone who wouldn't even entertain that thought.
No matter what.
I think we all deserve that.
Whether we get it or not, is up to us.
You deserved more than I could give.
You always have.

The pen stopped in its tracks.
It didn't matter.
That chapter of my life was over.
I read the words again through tears. I ripped the letter from the notebook and threw it in the trash. I sat back down and wrote the beginning of something new.

There was something special about falling in love with a Jersey girl. Carrying themselves with elegance or arrogance, rarely anything in between, Jersey girls could make a man forget all about his silly dreams. But California girls made him chase them.

Shit.
I was still high.
How much molly did I take?
The notebook and pen went back into my suitcase, along with all of my clothes and belongings. I called for a ride to the airport, figuring I'd rather get there early than risk falling asleep again.
It was early in the morning, or late at night, depending on one's view of time. Boundary Airlines didn't have any staff working at the kiosk in the airport lobby. I couldn't hand over my suitcase, leaving me stuck in the part of the airport before the TSA check. I slouched in an uncomfortable metal chair. That's when my body began to ache. I bought two bottles of water from the only joint

open, a retail chain coffee shop, but my throat remained dry. My brain bashed against my skull like a beat. Hangover or comedown, I didn't get a lick of sleep before I boarded my flight.

* * *

If the plane crashed, I'd have to be the person to open one of the aircraft's doors. I traded extra leg room for responsibility. I told the attractive blonde flight attendant that I agreed to fulfill whatever duty I didn't read about. If we were going down, knowing how to open the emergency door probably wouldn't matter.

I tried not to invade the space of the person sitting next to me as I attempted to get comfortable. He was a bigger fellow who was a manspreader with his legs farther open than a woman giving birth. The selfish prick took my armrest, too.

I stretched my legs out as far as I could. The side of the plane supported my throbbing head. I passed out before the plane took off.

A sudden jolt shook me awake. Passengers gasped in horror. I clutched the armrests. Realizing I grabbed the man's hand next to me, I pulled away. The plane rocked back and forth. People squealed with each jerk.

I hunted for flight attendants.

A pretty blonde flight attendant smiled in her seat as we rattled through the air. She was either an Oscar-winning actress or there was nothing to fear. I made one last glance at her to ensure she wasn't pretending.

She was fine.

We were fine.

The plane gave one last quake before stabilizing.

After a few minutes of relief chatter, the plane went silent. Even the little kids had their eyes glued to their electronic devices with headphones zapping sounds into their brains.

When the adrenaline subsided, my head felt like it was going to explode. Somehow my body hurt more. I stretched my stiff legs. Hungover while coming down from drugs is no way to fly.

"What's that? My favorite new ride? Glad you asked," a drunk mom said, breaking the plane's silence.

Her young son, who sat right beside her, hadn't said a word. Like his mother, the boy's clothes featured a famous capitalist-mouse.

"It's impossible for me to pick a favorite new ride," she said. "Um. Maybe . . . no! I always forget about that one." She finished her drink. "It's so hard! They're all incredible in their own unique way. It's the little details about each one that makes them special for me."

Between her and my hangover, I was at peace with dying in a plane crash.

Put me out of my misery.

Please.

Spotting a flight attendant collecting trash down the aisle, the mom made her move by waving her female mouse visor.

"Excuse me," she said. "I'll have another vodka soda!"

I sensed the Jersey in her drunken plea.

"I will be back around," a flight attendant said.

She didn't bother to look into the mom's soulless eyes when she passed her. She glided to the next row.

"Trash?"

The crinkling of the plastic bag startled the sleeping middle-aged man in the row a few feet in front of me. I don't know how he slept through the mother's screaming explanations of her favorite rides. After regaining his consciousness, he asked, "When are we going to be in Philadelphia?"

"In about three hours," the flight attendant said.

"Does that mean last call?" the Jersey princess asked.

"We can get you one more, ma'am." The flight attendant's smile turned to a frown as she moved to my row. "Like she needs another."

The Jersey woman continued to scream about every pop culture thing she loved. Apparently, her interests only included the parks, films, and shows of one company. I looked out the window to distract myself. The world was always beautiful a few thousand miles up. I never appreciated it for too long. Because I'd realize I was in the air, riding in an aluminum tube depending on wind and technology I'd never understand.

Two Goddesses of the Air, one blonde and one brunette, swayed as they went row to row with a bar cart, asking passengers if they wanted a beverage. Not one guy turned down the beauty queens' offers. A few teenage boys ordered sodas at the dismay of their mothers.

You know, I've never seen an ugly flight attendant. There are supposedly laws that prevent "men will want to have sex with her, they'll buy what she sells" hires, but they were easy to circumvent.

Clearly.

"Cold beverage, sir?" the blonde flight attendant asked.

"Whiskey on the rocks," I said. "And a water."

"What kind, sir?"

"Which."

"Huh?"

The English language died with good rock and roll.

"Which. The word 'what' implies I can pick any liquor in the world. The word 'which' tells me I can choose from only a specific selection. Given we're in the air, I imagine you only have a few choices of whiskey."

"Sorry," she said.

I write a few sentences, and now I'm a pretentious asshole.

"No. I'm sorry. I didn't mean it. It's been a rough night. Just get me the cheapest."

Hangovers really bring out the best in me.

Miserable prick.

She looked through the alcohol bottles on the bottom of the cart without pulling any booze for me.

"That whiskey is on the other cart. We'll bring you your drink in a few moments, sir."

She was going to spit in my drink. Probably somewhere in the back of the plane where I couldn't see. I deserved it.

A different flight attendant brought me my whiskey. I didn't bother to check for saliva before I took a sip. The airline temptress smiled when I took another drink.

I closed my eyes and tried to sleep after I finished the booze.

"This is a vodka tonic, not a vodka soda," the drunk mom said.

I didn't know there was a difference.

I reached into my bag to find something to drown her out. Pushing aside an extra water bottle, a bag of beef jerky, and my notebook before finding my earphones. I cranked them up and played the folk music playlist Leah sent me. She said it helped her relax during comedowns, but Bob Dylan's screechy voice made my brain bleed.

I turned it off and fell asleep.

* * *

I woke up sweating.
Drool leaked out of my mouth.
I bet I snored.
I always did on flights.
The poor bastards around me.
I pulled my phone from my pocket and found my way to my messages with Leah.

Fuck.

I never responded back to her. I couldn't afford in-flight Wi-Fi, but I could write my thoughts down and come up with something smooth to say when we land. With no pullout tray in front of me for my notebook, I typed my thoughts using a phone app.

The last thing I expected on this trip was to meet someone like Leah. I wish I had more time.

The hangover made me soft.
The comedown didn't help.
The plane dropped altitude. I flexed my jaw open as far as I could, causing my ears to pop. Former Miss Americas collected trash one last time. I buckled my seat belt and waited. A flight attendant scolded me for playing with my phone while we were landing. I put it back in my front pocket.

"Flight attendants, please prepare for landing," the pilot said over the loudspeaker.

I braced for impact.
The plane hit the runway rather harshly.
It always did.

A collective sigh of relief rushed through the cabin when the plane settled on the ground.

"Welcome to Philadelphia. The temperature is seventy degrees, and the weather is perfect," the pilot said.

A couple of dorks, including souvenir-buying, drunk Jersey mom, clapped. The brunette flight attendant made announcements about luggage, airline credit cards, and God knows what else. I didn't know how long she had been talking. I wasn't listening.

Nobody was.

As soon as the plane parked, a bunch of the clappers stood up to hunt for their overhead luggage. Like every flight in the history of commercial airlines, airplane purgatory plagued our foreseeable future. It's why the luggage rush made no sense.

I pulled my phone out. Whoops. Forgot to turn on airplane mode. It was a wonder we even landed. I texted my father and let him know he could pick me up in a half hour.

He was already waiting in one of the airport's lots.

My father was never late.

* * *

I tossed my suitcase into the trunk of my father's car and sat in the passenger's seat.

"How was your trip?"

"Exactly what I needed," I said. "Got any aspirin?"

"Check the glove box."

I took two pills from a small bottle and washed it down with one of the water bottles from my book bag.

"How's Summer doing?" he asked.

"She's having the time of her life. You should see her place. It's this gorgeous penthouse suite right in the middle of the city. And—"

"Got it out of your system?" my father asked.

"What?"

My father exited the airport and hit the freeway.

"California," he said. "Got it out of your system?"

Not saying anything was the smart move.

The right way to avoid confrontation.

But California changes a man.

"I'm thinking about moving there."

46

My father shook his head.

"Always the dreamer."

Always the same response to anything I said.

"We'll see."

"You'll pay taxes out the ass," he said. "Live among all the goddamn liberals, too. Why would you want to do that?"

My father couldn't see the smile on my face.

We drove in silence for a few minutes before making small talk about the upcoming Philadelphia Eagles football season. When we reached my mother's house, my father unloaded my suitcase from his trunk.

"Don't tell your mother about this California idea of yours," he said. "It'll break her heart."

My father gave me a handshake and got back into his car. I walked toward my childhood home's front door, pulling my luggage. When my father drove out of sight, I stopped walking and grabbed my phone.

I finally knew what to text Leah.

I have a lot of reasons to move to California, but I think you're my favorite. See you soon.

Jersey

May 21, 2018

Hank whimpered behind the front door. I opened it. Hank's ass pivoted back and forth at the hips. I dropped to my knees. Hank used his front paws to climb my legs and coat my face with his tongue. I rubbed his belly.

"I missed you too, bud."

I wrestled Hank on the floor until he calmed down. My rescue pup followed me and my suitcase into the kitchen. Onions, garlic, and sizzling meat engulfed the air. My sister, Kayla, stirred a boiling pot of pasta. Her husband, Zane, cut an onion.

"Welcome back, dude!" Kayla said.

"How was your flight?" Zane asked.

"Terrible," I said. "I thought I was going to die."

"Turbulence?" Kayla asked.

"It was the most hungover I've ever flown."

They laughed.

"How's Summer? And California?" Kayla asked.

My mouth spread wide.

Before I could answer, Zane spoke.

"You're right. He's moving."

I caught them up on my trip.

Never mentioning the sad parts.

Just the good stuff.

Can't let anyone worry about me.

"Mom coming to eat?" I asked.

"She's asleep," Kayla said.

"What about Mike?"

Zane nearly choked.

"He's at happy hour," Kayla said. "Or working late. Or on a date. Who the fuck really knows with him?"

Zane made three plates of meat pasta. I was happy to be a test eater. Our conversation was minimal during dinner. None of us wanted to ruin the intimacy of a human devouring a damn-good meal. I twirled the last bit of spaghetti with my fork.

"Now that was a dish," I said. "What was it?"

"We just threw together some of the old meat we had to get rid of. Six different types. I couldn't believe it came out like that," Zane said.

"I hope you wrote it down."

"He's not that kind of cook," Kayla said.

Zane tapped his head.

"Steel trap. I won't forget something that tasted like that."

As the two cleaned up the kitchen, Mike stumbled into the house, smelling like a bar.

"Look who's back," Mike said. "Moving out yet?"

He caught himself on the wall.

"Work hard, fall hard," I said.

Mike rolled his eyes.

"Shut the fuck up, loser."

He disappeared upstairs and slammed his bedroom door.

"I thought there was some progress," I said.

"He did say something to you," Kayla said.

"When's he moving out?" I asked.

"Whenever his house is done," Zane said.

Kayla took my plate.

"Not soon enough."

My mother found her way down to the kitchen.

"Welcome home," she said.

"Thanks."

"How was your trip? How's Summer?"

"You missed the debrief," I said.

"I was sleeping," she said.

"I'll tell the story another time. I'm tired."

Before I could leave, Mike returned in sweatpants and a hoodie.

"The whole family is here," my mother said. "Don't go."

That wasn't true.

The whole family wasn't there.

I sat back down at the kitchen table.

"Have fun in California?" Mike asked as he ate meat straight from the pot.

"I'm moving there."

Kayla looked shocked that I said the words aloud.

"What?" my mother asked.

"Yeah."

"Why?" my mother demanded.

"Seems like heaven to be able to go to the beach every day."

"Why do you want to be so far from your family?" my mother asked.

It's like my childhood didn't happen.

"The lack of palm trees here is a real sticking point."

"Don't be a dick," Mike said.

"How will you even afford California?" my mother asked.

"He won't," Mike said. "They kill you on taxes."

Mike was his father's son.

"The cost of living is too high," my mother said. "I see it on the news. You'll go broke."

"Only one way to find out," I said.

"Why not find a nice Jersey girl and settle down here?"

"I tried that."

"Always so dramatic," Mike said.

"If he wants to move to California, he should," Kayla said.

"Just don't be too hard on yourself if it doesn't happen," Mike said. "I know how you get."

I rose from the table.

"I'm going to bed. It's been a long weekend. And an even longer day. Nice to see everyone."

I headed for the stairs. Hank chased behind me.

"What does your father think of all this?" my mother called. "Did you tell him?"

When I reached the top of the steps, I answered.

"He knows better than to try to talk me out of California."

Beat Me to California

March 8, 1995

Allison, a curly-haired high school soccer player, picked Mike and me up from school and took us to her parents' house. She was also babysitting her little cousin, Alex, who was a year younger than me. Allison gave us a tour of the house, and that's when I saw her Nintendo. Any chance to play video games felt like Christmas morning. The Lewis house was video game free. At least for Mike and me. My father had a Gameboy, but only he was allowed to play that.

I snuck a peek at Allison's Nintendo game collection.

Super Mario Bros. 3.

Yes!

I could finally be Mario.

As the younger brother, I was forever delegated to be Luigi. But not today. Alex was younger than me.

Mario was mine.

I just had to beat Mike to the system.

"Want to play Mario?" I asked Alex after the tour. "Cool if I go first?"

"I don't know," Alex said.

"My brother is right," Mike said. "Luigi is way better. Have you ever played as him?" Alex shook his head. "You're missing out. He's awesome. He jumps higher. Plus, green is way cooler than red."

"Can I be Luigi?" Alex asked.

"I'll be Mario." Mike picked up the first controller. "Wyatt, you can play after us."

No.

Wait.

How?

Alex snagged the second controller.

I sat down and watched Mike play as Mario.

After what was certainly hours, Mario fell to his death.

"Can I play now?" I asked.

Mike pointed at the screen.

"When I get a game over."

"When we get a game over," Alex said.

They both laughed.

A fireball killed Luigi.

A turtle shell ended Mario's next life.

Neither Mike nor Alex would give up their controllers.

I spent an eternity watching them.

They were on the third world with two lives left each.

"Let me play!" I yelled after a cannonball killed Mario.

"Quiet down or I'm telling your parents," Allison screamed from another room. She returned to her phone call.

"Next time," Mike said.

Luigi fell into lava.

"I was close," Alex said. "I swear, next time."

I fantasized about pulling the Nintendo out of the outlet and smashing Mike over the head with it. Then I'd pivot, swing, and strike Alex in the face.

"We're going to play a different game soon," Mike said.

"I'm over Mario," Alex said.

"After this life," Mike said.

Rather than murder a Nintendo, I yanked the cords for the controllers out of the system and stepped in front of the TV.

"Let me play!"

Bowser killed Mario.

"What the fuck!" Mike yelled.

Allison ran into the room.

"Who said that?"

I was bright red, panting in front of Mike and Alex.

My fists were clenched.

"It was Wyatt," Mike said. "He kept hogging the games, and when I finally got to play, he got all spazzy. He pulled the cords out and yelled . . ." Mike paused for effect. "He yelled the worst word. The . . . um . . . f-word."

Give the kid a fucking Oscar.

"Yeah," Alex said. "He's crazy."

I stomped my feet on the floor.

"They're lying! That's not what happened! They were hogging and didn't let me play!"

"It seems like you've been in front of the TV for too long," Allison said. "Calm down."

I flapped my arms.

"I didn't get to play!"

"I'm telling your parents," Allison said. "You're out of control."

Allison grabbed me by the arm and escorted me from the room. Alex snickered as she did. Mike smiled and waved goodbye. Allison stuck me in her father's office.

I hated Mike.

He tortured me.

Constantly.

If he wasn't beating me up, he was breaking my toys.

I searched for something to entertain me in the boring old person's office. On the shelf, a book with palm trees on the cover called me. It was called *The History of California*. It helped me pass the rest of the afternoon.

* * *

When six came, it was my father's green car that pulled up in the driveway.

My life was over.

Mike and I gathered our book bags and went to the door. Mike said hi cheerfully to my father, when he entered the house. I didn't bother. I was dead.

Allison pulled my father aside.

He waved at Mike and me to go into the car without him. I dove into the back seat. No way was I sitting in the front.

Allison and my father talked for a while. My father looked calm, but his face was red. He exploded when he entered the car in a boiling rage.

"Wyatt, when we're home, go straight to your room. Do nothing but think about what you said. No laying down. Or sleeping."

Eight years is more than some people get to live.

"Use your words, you disrespectful, little asshole," my father said.

I swallowed.

"Okay, Dad."

"Sorry you had to hear that word, Mike," my father said. "Don't be like Wyatt. I know you won't be, but just don't pay any mind to what he says or does."

I hated Mike.

We drove the rest of the way home in silence. No radio. No talking. No one moved. I tried to figure out a way to tell my father what really happened. I needed to tell him it was Mike. But my father hated tattletales. I didn't know what to do.

* * *

I went right to my room, shut the door, and sat on my bed. My father could come in at any moment. I needed to be awake and alert. Or face his fury.

Stop.

I'd be fine.

He'd believe me.

He had to.

The truth was on my side.

Mike cursed.

He would tell the truth.

And so would I.

I didn't need to worry.

I just needed to make sure to be awake and sitting when my father came into my room. If I fell asleep or did anything besides sitting in silence, I'd be in trouble. Obedience or pain. It's how my father ruled.

It was taking my father longer than usual to punish me.

I always hid a stash of emergency stuff in my pillowcase. A notebook, pencils, books, and a bag of cheese curls.

Crushed cheese curls were better than no food.

I learned that the hard way.

I dumped out my supplies onto the bed.

A creak outside my door made me stuff all my things back into my pillowcase.

I sat up straight.

Waiting for the door to open.

It never did.

I took out my notebook and a pen from my pillowcase. Inside my notebook was a postcard. It was from my grandpa.

Dear Wyatt,

Me and your grandma miss you very much! But California sure is beautiful. You should see the beaches and palm trees. You'd love it out here. We will see you soon!

Love,

Grandpa

Footsteps approached my door.

I threw everything back into my pillowcase.

Another false alarm.

I pulled out the postcard, notebook, and pen again.

The palm trees on the front of the postcard inspired me to write a story about a young boy named Wyatt Jones. He needed to hunt down treasure in California while battling an evil organization trying to control the world. I loosely based it on the Indiana Jones films, but only in name, costume, and concept.

The writing took a lot out of me.

Before long, I fell asleep.

* * *

My father was sitting next to me when I awoke.

He tapped my California postcard on his fist.

"I thought I told you not to fall asleep," my father said.

I put my head down in shame.

"I'm sorry."

"What happened today?"

My emotion got the best of me.

"I didn't do anything! Mike. He cursed."

"You're not talking you're way out of this. What happened?"

"Mike and Alex wouldn't . . ."

"What did you do, Wyatt?" my father snarled.

"It wasn't me! They wouldn't let me play!"

My father made a fist.

His hand went red.

"What curse did you say, boy?"

"I didn't curse."

He grabbed me by my shirt.

"Tell me what you said."

Tears fell from my eyes.

Why wouldn't he listen?

"I'm telling the truth!" I yelled.

My father slapped me across my face.

I grabbed where it hurt.

"Don't you lie to me!" he yelled. "What did you say?"

"It was Mike!"

My father pulled me toward his nose.

"Don't you fucking lie to me, boy!"

"I didn't—"

He threw me against my headboard.

It made a loud thump.

The wood rattled my brain.

"Tell me what you said."

Why didn't he believe me?

"I'm telling the truth!"

My father pretended to swing at me.

I ducked into my arms, making myself small.

My father laughed.

"Not such a tough guy now, huh? Big bad boy who lies and curses but flinches like a little girl."

My father pretended to throw a strike with a right.

When I moved my body to protect myself, his left hand caved in my defenseless right side. My father struck me with another fist to the right temple. I fell back into the headboard with another loud thump. But I didn't feel a thing.

My father raised his hand and wound it up.

Shaking it.

Taunting me.

"What curse did you say?"

My father was going to kill me.

I pulled my arms down and crossed them.

I closed my eyes and shook my head.

"I didn't curse."

I thought it was the last thing I'd ever say.

My father cocked back his right fist and struck me harder. He followed it with another open palm with his left. I shut my eyes and threw my hands up. But I couldn't protect myself. I shrieked in pain. The blows caused me to fall out of my bed.

My father grabbed me by the top of my shirt and pulled me up to his face.

"Fuck! I said fuck," I lied.

"Anything else, you little bastard?"

I cried and used my arms to cover my head.

"I'm sorry. Please stop. Please."

He dropped me on the floor.

"You better not go cry to your mother about this. This is man stuff. Be a man for once in your life."

He grabbed the California postcard on my bed.

"Lying, cursing little boys don't make it to California."

My father ripped the postcard in half.

Despite the throbbing head pain, I reached for it.

My father was too quick.

He struck me with an open palm to my left temple.

I fell back onto the floor.

My ears rang.

He tossed the ripped scraps of my grandpa's postcard at me before gently closing my door behind him.

It hurt to cry.

But the tears didn't stop.

I picked up the biggest piece of what remained of the California postcard.

West Coast Crushed

August 17, 2018

For three months, I'd stay up too late texting Leah. With both of us working over seventy hours a week and the time difference, I sacrificed sleep. Work in the morning be damned. I'd be quitting the joint soon, anyway.

Leah sent me playlists, and really pushed folk music. I still didn't get the appeal of Bob Dylan. Lord knows I tried. We'd also swap shows to watch. She always recommended true crime documentaries. Except one time she told me to watch some British tea show or something. That was a little out there. Even for me. Leah always talked about love. She loved love but could never find it. It was something I could relate to.

I'd send her a few of my writings here and there. Since California, I couldn't stop jotting things down. Like a maniac. Scribbling during work meetings and writing on napkins during dinners. I kept a journal by my bed to write down anything I thought important before drifting off to sleep.

I also applied for tons of jobs in San Diego. Hundreds of applications. Not one response. For three months. Nothing.

But finally, I got a lead.

Keith Curtis was the human resources director of a hip advertising firm called Crowne Advertising. After a brief email exchange, Keith gave me a ring.

"We were impressed with your cover letter," Keith said. "We could tell you took the time to craft a specific message for us."

"Thanks," I said. "I was really impressed with your website and what I found online about your company. You deserved my best."

We talked for an hour on the phone.

The whole thing felt more like a conversation than an interview. He didn't care that I lived in New Jersey, as long as I planned to move to San Diego if I was hired. At the end of our call, Keith let me know he liked what I brought to the table.

"The next step is going to be a chat with Amber Sullivan, an account manager with us," Keith said. "I'll email you with some times for a discussion with her. Let's try to get this done next week."

August 20, 2018

I spoke with Amber for two hours. Amber would be my supervisor if I was hired. She asked a lot of the same questions as Keith. But Amber had a few of her own.

"What's your biggest weakness?" Amber asked.

"Sometimes I work too hard," I said. "I like to finish what I start. And by like, I mean I'm relentless about completing my work."

"Wow," Amber said. "That's a good answer."

I could hear her pen darting back and forth across her notepad. She was either multitasking or writing down my response.

"If you're stealing my answer for yourself, be sure to give me credit."

Amber chuckled.

Cue the fake laugh.

She asked a few more questions.

Nothing that stood out.

She told me she was impressed.

After our call ended, Keith emailed and told me Amber thought I'd make a great colleague.

He also scheduled my next interview.

August 21, 2018

I discussed the new job role at Crowne Advertising with Ellen Campbell, account director.

"Why do you want to leave your current company?" she asked.

It was the third time in three interviews I was asked the question.

"Winter," I said.

Ellen laughed.

Same answer.

Same reaction.

Every time.

"Seriously. I don't want to leave my company," I said. "It's a great job. The best I've ever had. I have a dream, though. And that's in California."

"Don't be too honest," Ellen said.

"I can't help it," I lied. "It's one of my weaknesses. I'm always too honest."

The call went smooth. Ellen told Keith that I was the perfect culture fit for the company. Keith put another interview on my schedule.

August 22, 2018

Tina Rose, senior vice president of Crowne Advertising, squeezed me in for a half-hour talk. She seemed rushed on the call, like she was doing other things, instead of focusing on the interview. I knew this because she lost her train of thought in almost every sentence.

But Keith told me I crushed that interview, too.

My next interview was with Julie Pinto.

The founder and CEO of Crowne Advertising.

August 24, 2018

Julie Pinto employed sixteen people. She considered them all family. I wasn't sure if it was fake or who she really was. Julie told me she liked to employ East Coast transplants.

"East Coasters work hard," Julie said. "You'll push your California colleagues to work a little harder. East Coasters always do."

She was progressive and present, but it felt aggressive. Almost like she was hiding fangs behind her kindness.

Julie spent forty minutes on the phone with me. I told her that I appreciated her time, considering how many things a CEO has to do in a given day.

Keith sent me a long email thanking me for my time after the call. He also let me know Julie loved my mindset.

I figured I had the job.

But no.

Keith wanted me to speak with a few more team members per Julie's request.

August 27, 2018

William Clay, account manager, spoke with me for twenty minutes. We mostly talked about the upcoming NFL season. The call ended. Keith sent me an email. He scheduled another phone interview.

August 28, 2018

Gabe Scott, creative director, told me he didn't think I needed to be interviewing with so many people.

"I appreciate the sentiment," I said. "But it's nice to chat with the team. I'll know everyone before I start. It'll be great."

Gabe laughed.

"You're good at this," he said. "You're going to do great here."

Keith sent me an email when I got off the phone.

He scheduled another phone interview.

August 30, 2018

Tanya Lopez, copywriter, commiserated with me for a half hour. We talked about how writers get all of the work and pressure but none of the praise. It was in a fun way, though. She ended the call by telling me that she was looking forward to working with me.

Keith assured me that I only had a few interviews left before a decision would be made on my hiring.

When I learned I'd be interviewing with a college intern, I nearly lost my shit. Ten minutes before my call with Kyle Phillips, I calmed myself. Fifteen minutes of my life were wasted talking to Kyle. The young man seemed nervous. He barely spoke.

Afterwards, Keith assured me Kyle would be offered a full-time role when his unpaid labor contract expired. I mean, internship. He also let me know I could potentially be Kyle's supervisor. I hated the thought of being in charge of someone. I pretended to be excited at the chance to manage Kyle.

There were no more interviews scheduled.

A final decision awaited.

I texted Leah.

California. Here I come.

Keith called me in the afternoon.

"We appreciate your taking a part in this," Keith said. "We know it's a grueling process, but it's why we have such a low turnover rate. We've been blown away by your interviews. We know you've spent a lot of time during this interview process, but there's one more person we want you to meet."

Another goddamn interview?

Wait.

"Meet?" I asked.

"Our East Coast office is in Manhattan. Would you be willing to take a drive to talk to McKenzie Smith, the director of our East Coast brand, this week?"

Interview after interview, groveling for a paycheck at some self-important advertising firm.

"I can't wait to meet her," I said. "What day works best for McKenzie?"

I'd sell my soul for California.

"She's a tough cookie," Keith said. "Not everyone gets along with her. But she does masterful work. I'll get back to you with some times to set this up. Thanks again, Wyatt."

I texted Leah after I hung up.

One more until California.

My boss wished me well when I emailed him some bullshit about having a stomach bug the day of my interview with McKenzie Smith. Since I was out of sick days, I burned a vacation day. Not like I had any choice in the matter. New York City was a two-hour drive from my job, and McKenzie could meet only during her lunch hour. On top of that, if I didn't schedule an interview within the next week, I wouldn't be able to meet with McKenzie for four weeks. She was leaving the country for a month-long boat trip around France.

Must be nice.

Crowne Advertising's East Coast office was located across the street from a forty-dollar parking lot, which wasn't bad for the city. Leah texted me good luck as soon as I entered the office building.

Crush it today. Can't wait until you live here!

Crowne Advertising was somewhere in the coworking space, but I never got a tour of the office.

"Let's just sit right here," McKenzie said.

She led me to a couch in the buzzing open kitchen during the noon lunch hour.

"Why do you want to leave your current company?" she asked.

Somehow, I knew the question was coming.

"Winter," I said for the ninth time.

McKenzie rolled her eyes.

"Okay. Why are you a fit here?"

"I have close to a decade of experience in the field. With various clients in every industry imaginable."

Two men sat down on the couch next to me. They ate their lunch and chatted. It wasn't distracting.

Not at all.

McKenzie grilled me for an hour. I yelled and repeated my answers over chatter and slamming dishes. McKenzie challenged everything I said, trying to see if I was full of shit.

She never showed any emotion. I didn't feel great when I left the interview, but I didn't feel terrible either.

***

On my drive home, I stopped by my college roommate's parents' house. Radek's folks lived an hour south of the Big Apple, and the family pool was still open.

The house was empty besides Radek, who floated in the backyard pool, drinking some European beer. I borrowed a pair of his shorts, grabbed a few beers, and joined him. I placed my phone on the side of the pool where I could reach it when it dinged. Keith would email me soon, and I was desperate to learn my California fate.

"How'd it go, broski?" Radek asked.

"It was the hardest interview I had, but I nailed it. I think."

"I know you got this." Radek chuckled to himself. "Cali suits you."

"What makes you say that?"

"That Cali girl you never shut up about."

I slammed the top of his beer bottle with the bottom of mine. Beer raced up the neck before exploding out. Radek caught most of the beer with his mouth. Some erupted into the pool.

"Her name is Leah."

"Leah. I know," Radek said. "Now you can chase her out there."

Radek and I drifted around the pool drinking beer and bullshitting about my future in California.

My phone chimed. I popped off my float and walked through the water to the edge of the pool. After finishing my beer, I opened a new email from Keith.

Wyatt,

The interview with McKenzie went wonderfully. She absolutely loved how you handled yourself in the chaos of that office without losing your composure. Well done!

I'll be in touch at the beginning of next week with the team's final decision.

—Keith

"Well?" Radek asked.

I stared at my phone with the biggest smile I've ever felt.

"Looks like I need to tell Leah I'm officially moving to California."

Radek shook up what was left of his beer and poured it all over me.

"Yeah, broski!"

California tasted better than I imagined.

September 14, 2018

I still hadn't heard from Keith. Or any of the dozen Crown Advertising employees I spoke with.

It didn't make sense.

I didn't have one bad interview.

Everything went amazing.

I sent an email to Keith asking him about the status of my application. My phone rang ten minutes after I hit send.

Keith.

"I was about to email you," Keith said. "I apologize for not getting back to you sooner. We had a lot of discussions about you. You were an incredible candidate. One of the most creative we've ever interviewed."

Here comes the pain.

"But we're going in another direction."

My first instinct was to curse the bastard.

I let out a loud exhale.

"What? Why? Can you tell me why?"

"We don't think you have enough SEO experience. If you get some more, you can reapply."

I wasn't sure how it took Crowne Advertising ten interviews to figure out that I didn't have enough SEO experience. No one ever asked me about search engine optimization. Not once in a dozen interviews. Fuck. A quick glance at my resume should have let the company's decision makers see all they needed to know about my SEO experience.

"It was a pleasure speaking with you," I said. "I'm sorry things didn't work out."

"I'm sorry too. If you get more experience, please reapply."

Crowne Advertising was a bust.

A waste of time.

I had no leads.
No hope for California.

Beach Burial

November 16, 2018

I turned down the heat that shot from my car's vents. There was no way to get comfortable while driving on a cold fall night. I wore my coat, thermal underwear, sweatpants, and hoodie because without them I'd freeze. I rolled down the window a bit to cool off, but I couldn't handle the bitter air for more than a few seconds. With no heat, my gloveless hands turned red. Shivers ran down my spine. I cranked up the window and fired up the heat.

After a few minutes, the heat was too much.

I turned it off and rolled down the window.

The car went frigid.

Up with the window and up with the heat.

Back and forth.

Hot and cold.

Switching the knob or cranking up the window.

It was too fucking cold.

I parked on a street in front of the deserted boardwalk. I left my phone in the car, grabbed my vices: a bottle of whiskey and my journal and headed for the ocean.

The sand was frosty on my ass.

A swig of whiskey warmed me up.

My journal sat closed on my lap.

I shut my eyes and listened to the waves.

It should have been a good day.

A promotion with a ten-thousand-dollar raise.

A steady paycheck.

I drank another sip of whiskey.

Five years trapped in a cube.

Now, I'd have my own office.

The view from my new cage featured a window.

It was more than the cube could say.

I gulped more booze.

Long hours.

Doing the same shit.

Every day for eternity.

I saw my future.

I'd get married to someone I'd met at a sales conference. We'd only enjoying life on weekends, weather permitting, while fattening 401(k) accounts and our bellies, hoping to be well enough to enjoy retirement in our eighties. Unlivable living expenses would most likely drown our relationship. We'd have a few kids to save our fading marriage. Maybe it would work. Maybe we'd fake it. Quite the American Dream.

The whiskey no longer burned when it went down.

The white tips of folding waves were all I could see in the distance. My face hurt from the bitter breeze. I opened my journal. The thing was empty a few months ago, but now it was filled with poems, jokes, things I heard, stories, and random crazy thoughts I had to jot down. California woke up the writer in me. But it was all for nothing.

I opened to a random page.

After I graduated from college, I remember applying for every entry-level writing gig I could find in California. I tailored resumes for every available job at major movie studios and Playboy magazine. I figured any type of employment at Playboy would get me into at least one party at the Mansion. A job at a movie studio wouldn't hurt my chances either. And who wouldn't want to live among the stars in LA?

Too bad nobody wanted to hire a fresh-out-of-college kid from Jersey. Especially a broke one with no relevant writing experience.

Next thing I knew I was fat, further in debt, on the wrong side of thirty, and still stuck in New Jersey. I made all kinds of excuses for not chasing California. I didn't have the energy. There was no time. I had bills to pay. Things to do. People to see. Jobs to waste away at. Dreams wither away, rarely do they die in a single moment.

The page tore away from the notebook without a problem. I didn't bother to read the next page before ripping it out.

I flipped through the journal.

Things to remember about Leah

- *Bob Dylan fan*
- *Loves hazy IPAs*
- *History buff*
- *Balboa Park (favorite place in San Diego)*

I pulled the list from the journal.
The words suffered the same fate as the rest.
More and more pages were lost forever.
"Erin."
I paused my execution when I saw her name.

There was so much about Erin to love, but my favorite was her patience. She wasn't patient with a goddamn thing, except with me. She'd erupt into pillows or scream to herself whenever I drove her mad. She never took out her frustration on me. Even when I deserved it. I'd get an eye roll or two, but only before a laugh and a kiss.

I chugged the whiskey before throwing the bottle as far as I could. I stood up and rushed the water, tearing more pages to pieces as I did.

"It's all fucking bullshit!" I yelled. "A pointless existence."

I launched what was left of the journal into the ocean. It landed with a splash. My knees fell into shallow water. I sobbed for longer than I'll ever admit.

When I couldn't feel my legs, I wiped my eyes dry, left the destroyed journal, and made my way back to my car.

I let the engine warm up a bit before blasting the heat.

It was time to admit the truth.

California was over.

Another fantasy of mine.

I'd break the news to Leah first.

I reached for my phone on the passenger's seat.

Two notifications lit up the screen.

A voicemail and a missed call.

From a San Diego number.

"Hi. This is for Wyatt. This is Chuck Reynolds with Reynolds Incorporated. You applied for a position back in May. We weren't quite ready for new staff, but we've had some new business come in. I'd like to talk to you a bit about an open position that I'm looking to fill by January."

Four-Hour Interrogation

December 3, 2018

The smell of the ocean seeped into the lobby. The joint had a marble white floor that was so clean that my reflection showed me where I missed shaving.

A hunched-over, older desk clerk in a well-fitting suit walked me to the bank of elevators and hit the eleventh-floor button.

"When you get off the elevators, turn left, and it's the fifth office," he said.

My stomach churned when the elevator doors closed.

I swallowed some spit to try to moisturize my throat.

My skull pounded against my brain.

Alcohol poured out of my pores.

A ding let me know I'd landed on the right floor.

I walked down the hallway, passing a few small offices. It didn't take me long to arrive at Reynolds Incorporated.

Inside, all I could see was a conference room, and a wall filled with photos of Chuck with athletes I didn't recognize. There was a desk for a secretary, but instead of a person there was a bell. Machines have been taking human's jobs since the Industrial Revolution. I refused to ring it.

"Excuse me," I said. "Ahem! Excuse me!"

An older, dark-haired woman hustled around the corner toward me.

"Welcome to Reynolds Incorporated," she said. "I'm Trish."

Trish led me to the conference room where puffy red chairs surrounded a sturdy wood table.

"Can I offer you a beverage? Water? Coffee?"

Could she see my hangover?

"Coffee. Black."

The aspirin was wearing off.

I pulled out a few paper copies of my resume. I rehearsed my talking points. The things I learned in my career that I could use at

Reynolds Incorporated. The bullshit excuses I made for being fired or quitting my previous jobs. And why I was looking for new employment. That was the easy one. My American Dream. To live, work, and die in California.

Trish returned with a coffee and a square water bottle.

"Chuck will be right with you."

She left the room.

My head throbbed.

It was a mistake scheduling my interview with Chuck the day after the Philadelphia Eagles played on Monday Night Football. I was so excited for an in-person interview in San Diego that I accepted the first date Chuck offered. I never consulted with my religion's schedule. Football. My religion. But the Monday night worship sessions were nothing but a pain in the dick. Especially for me. In this moment.

Seventeen Hours Earlier

S ummer had told me to meet her at the best Eagles bar in San Diego. The joint was called Pub and Pool, and it had dozens of massive TVs, Eagles flags, and decor plastered all over the walls. Connected to the bar was a roomful of smoke and a half a dozen pool tables.

The joint felt like Philly.

I tucked my suitcase under a high table and waited. With the time difference, the Eagles game started at happy hour, which was a dreadful combination for my sobriety. The Birds, aka the Eagles, played the unnamed team formerly known as the Washington Redskins. The Birds needed a win to keep their slim playoff hopes alive. I ordered a beer. I could do one. I had to. The Eagles always played better when I drank. Or at least were more tolerable to watch.

Summer and Noah walked into the bar a few minutes into the first quarter. Turns out the joint was only three blocks from The Palace. That's why it was their favorite Eagles bar.

The location.

The Eagles scored, and the bar erupted in cheers. Dozens of misplaced Eagles fans sang the Eagles fight song in drunken unison. I belted the words like I was at home. Bartenders ran around the bar offering half-price Bird Bombs, a drink that combined some sort of green booze and an energy drink into a drop shot.

Stay sober for a job interview in San Diego tomorrow?

Or drink the Eagles into the playoffs?

Noah ordered three Bird Bombs and three beers.

My interview was at noon.

Plenty of time to fend off a hangover.

Go Birds.

* * *

Chuck flung the conference door open. He was shorter than I expected with a clean-shaven, handsome face. The stress from running a business, I assumed, caused him to bald prematurely and get round in all the wrong places. He stuck out a giant paw.

"Pleasure to meet you," Chuck said. "In person."

He crushed my fingers.

"You too." I pulled my hand away. "The office is incredible. It looks brand-new."

"I've been here five years, believe it or not," he said. "What's your five-year plan?"

"Excellent segue, Chuck."

A steady beat played against my skull.

I hated Monday Night Football.

"My plan is to move to San Diego, but only with a position and company I can grow with. Settle with the same woman and same job. Start a family. God willing."

I swallowed some coffee in disgust.

"That's what this position is," Chuck said. "We're a family-orientated business. I have two kids myself. We're expecting our third in a few months."

"Congratulations. An exciting time for you. A new baby. It's reaffirming to hear that your company is a family-orientated business."

Reaffirming?

Who the fuck says reaffirming?

And it was oriented, not orientated.

But I couldn't correct my potential boss.

"Thank you," Chuck said. "We're very excited. I want to build a team here that stays with me for the long haul." He asked the same questions from our phone call a few weeks earlier. I gave the same responses.

Chuck disappeared into the office to grab some of my potential future coworkers.

My stomach bumbled.

I straightened up in my chair.

My shoes were tied.

My fly was up.

Focus.

Trish and a blonde woman wearing a scowl walked into the room. The angry woman moved away from Trish, who sat across from me. She huffed after she told me her name was Danielle.

"I was in retail six months ago," Trish said. "Chuck is giving me my first opportunity in the corporate world."

My stomach needed food.

My ass needed release.

"You must have shown a lot of potential," I said.

Trish read from a printout of questions.

"What are your goals for the next year and ten years?"

Not die?

"Find a company I can retire with, get promoted to the executive level, get married, and start a family," I said.

I hate myself.

"Why do you want to work here?"

Because this is the only place that will interview me?

"I did extensive online research about the company. Everything was glowing. I read client testimonials and saw some of the company's portfolio. It seems like an exciting place to work, where I can grow as a professional."

I threw up in my mouth.

The last of my coffee washed it down.

Trish jotted down vigorous notes as I fed her clichés.

"What was the worst thing about your last job?" Trish asked.

The hours.

"It stopped challenging me," I said. "My bosses are world-class, but I'm ready to expand my skill set. Tackle a new challenge. Figure San Diego seems like the best place to do that. Besides, it's hard to beat seventy and sunny all year round."

Trish looked up from her notepad.

"How honest are you?"

My hangover was on the verge of breaking me.

I squeezed my ass cheeks together.

"About as honest as the average person."

Danielle smirked.

I knew I'd get her with that one.

"What's your greatest weakness?" Trish asked.

I call them the six Bs.

Booze. Butts. Blondes. Brains. Boobs. Beer.

"Kryptonite," I said. "Obviously."

I let out a fake laugh.

Trish didn't get it.

Danielle scrolled through her phone when Trish asked me how I handled stress.

"Fresh air. Coffee. Or work through it."

Danielle startled me when she finally spoke.

"This place is nothing but stress. Chuck is always on top of you."

"What do you mean?" I asked.

"He asks you to do things, then trashes your work. He uses it, changes it slightly, and complains about how he has to do everything. And—"

Trish stood up.

"I think we should go get Chuck."

"Good luck," Danielle said as she left the room.

"It was nice meeting you," Trish said.

A giant pool of sweat rubbed against my dress shirt.

I needed a beer.

Chuck returned to the conference room.

"Is this position you're hiring for new or am I replacing anyone?" I asked.

"I'm hoping whoever we hire can integrate seamlessly into our current team dynamic."

He didn't bother to sit back down. He dialed a number on the conference room phone.

"Let's call Gary, really quick. He works in the office on Mondays and Fridays. Remotely on Tuesdays, Wednesdays, and Thursdays. To be with his kid."

Chuck left when Gary's voice echoed through the room. Gary told me about his career as a copywriter, and how he and his partner were looking to adopt their second child. I talked about my California dream and my career highlights. I tried to be friendly, but I was too hungover to answer the same questions for a fourth fucking time.

Chuck interrupted us after forty minutes of surface-level noise. The clock above the mounted television told me I had been in the same chair for three hours. If this didn't wrap up soon, I was going to shit myself.

"Now for the written part of the interview." Chuck put a laptop in front of me. "You have an hour to complete the writing test I sent to your email. Send your test back to me when you finish. Let me know if you have any questions."

"No questions. Thanks, Chuck."

My hangover went full assault after he left the room. I used my left hand to tighten my belt. That would stop the booze shits for long enough.

Too bloated to focus.

A fart would clear some room.

A few whiffs of air escaped.

A turd poked out of my ass.

Fuck this test.

The first part forced me to edit a news release.

My stomach ate itself as I finished that section.

Being hungry and having to shit is a feeling I'd never wish on my enemies. It's not unbearable, but I assure you it's close.

I completed the assessment forty minutes and six farts later. I rose from my seat and waved the conference room door a few times. When the air cleared, I emailed Chuck my test.

He returned.

"Eagles fan?" he asked.

"Die hard," I said.

"You catch that game last night?"

"Big win. The playoffs are still in play."

"Where'd you watch it?" Chuck asked. "I don't know any Philadelphia Eagles bars around here."

I curled my toes to prevent shit from falling out of my ass.

"My friend took me to a place in the city. It felt like I was in Philly."

"I want to make sure your sports needs are met out here. San Diego has been a terrible sports town for most of the time I've been here."

"Sounds like I should fit in seamlessly."

Chuck showed me out of the office.

"Thanks," I said. "I appreciate your time."

"We'll be in touch."

I walked straight to the floor's shared bathroom. It was locked. I couldn't go back and ask Chuck for the passcode. It wasn't proper etiquette. Thanks for the interview. Can I shit in your bathroom?

I let out another fart in the elevator.

Poop clawed farther out of me.

There was no bathroom in the lobby.

I grabbed my cheeks and called for a ride.

The bumpy drive back to Noah and Summer's penthouse made it hard to hold my shit inside. I dove out of the car when I arrived at the apartment building. The elevator was farther away from The Palace than I remembered.

I repeatedly smashed the button to go up.

A year passed before the elevator doors opened.

I stepped inside and closed my eyes.

The whole ride I held my ass cheeks together.

My legs were heavy.

Each lift of my leg felt like a hundred pounds.

It wasn't this long of a hallway yesterday.

Sweat poured down my body.

Finally, I reached The Palace door.

It opened.

Before I could step in, Noah handed me an old-fashioned.

"Round two tonight?"

A West Coast Christmas

December 3, 2018

Every year, some joint—Leah had told me the name a hundred times, Polite Provisions, that's it—turns their bar into a Christmas wonderland. It's one of the most popular bars around the holidays, so there's always a line. People flowed down the street, waiting to get into the joint

"I asked the bouncer," Noah said. "He said it's an hour."

"There's a liquor store across the street," Leah said. "Want to stay tipsy while we wait?"

I crossed the street and found a cheap bottle of red. I asked the cashier to paper-bag it. The four of us took swigs from the warm wine as we waited to enter the bar. Two women behind us wanted to share, so we gave them a few swigs. It was the holidays, after all.

I threw out the empty bottle as we entered the Christmas paradise. A giant pine tree sat in the center of the bar. Wrapping paper covered the walls, with fake snow and cotton all over the place. Taped Santa decorations, Christmas ornaments, and an entire little Christmas town were spread down the bar.

Leah handed me a menu listing seven Christmas specialty cocktails, including one called *"Yippie Ki-Yay, Motherf*cker."*

I showed Leah.

"You see, *Die Hard* is a Christmas movie."

"No."

"It's listed right here. On the menu of your favorite Christmas bar."

"I can't believe it," she said.

I ordered the *Die Hard* cocktail.

I'm not sure what Leah ordered.

She hated it.

I hated it too.

But I drank it.

Phones flashed every few seconds. People took pictures of the Christmas menu and all the decorations. Social media celebrities posed for dozens of photos, clogging up the bar. We did a lap around the joint—it wasn't a big place—before settling in a corner. I leaned into Leah to ask her if she wanted another drink. She said nothing. She pointed to the ceiling. We were under mistletoe.

"Merry Christmas, Jersey boy."

"A few weeks early," I said.

"I wanted to say it to you first."

She kissed me.

When she broke the kiss, I pulled her back in.

"We're still under the mistletoe."

I kissed her this time.

We didn't bother to order another drink. We couldn't if we'd wanted to. The joint was too crowded for any sane human. Noah called us a ride to The Palace.

We all grabbed an Uber home. On the way, we passed a pop-up Christmas tree farm.

"Look Christmas trees," I said.

"We should get one," Summer said.

"Right now?" I said.

"Excuse me, can you stop there? We want to get a Christmas tree," Noah said.

"Noah!" Summer yelled. "Not like this."

Leah stayed in the car. Mumbling on and on about something. Noah and I found a free hot chocolate Thermos by the Christmas tree lot's register. We loaded up on it and examined Christmas trees. Looking for the perfect one. I loved the smell of pine. It mixed perfect with that ocean scent.

Summer joined us, and I left the couple alone.

I stumbled around watching children, families, and couples pick their perfect Christmas trees. I wished I had some rum for the hot chocolate. I wandered around for a while. I wondered what the difference was between a California Christmas tree and a New Jersey one. Besides the obvious logistical differences.

Summer and Noah finally settled on a tree. Noah convinced the Uber driver to let us tie it on top of his car.

"This is not how we're supposed to get our first Christmas tree," Summer said.

I held Leah's hand during the silent and tense ride back to The Palace. Summer wasn't happy. Drunk Christmas tree shopping wasn't how she pictured getting her first "real" Christmas tree with Noah.

The couple disappeared into their bedroom as soon as we got back to The Palace, leaving me and Leah alone.

"I still have some time to kill before my flight," I said.

Leah started walking toward the door.

"I have work early."

"You want to stay over? With me?"

"Summer and Noah are in the next room."

"I'll be quiet," I said. "I can't speak for you."

Leah slapped my arm.

"You're still just a visitor. Even if you are a cute one. Get out here. Let's see what can happen."

She grabbed my face and kissed my lips. Then she disappeared down the hallway, away from The Palace.

Kayla's Letter

January 3, 2019

Kayla handed me a cigarette. "These will kill ya."

"Not if life does first," I said.

A pull from the cancer stick sent fire through my chest.

I coughed a deep one.

She laughed.

"Virgin lungs," I said.

"You're pretty hammered," Kayla said.

"I can't believe I'm drunk enough to be smoking a cig."

"I can't believe you're actually doing it."

"It's not my first time."

Kayla took a long drag.

"California, numb nuts."

"I'll be back. Maybe."

"It's crazy that you'll be gone," Kayla said.

I opened another can of beer.

"I'll be alright."

"Are you all packed?"

"Besides my laptop, Hank, and me? Yeah."

"There's one more thing." Kayla handed me an envelope. A few pages of a handwritten letter burst out of the flap. "Put this somewhere safe."

"I'm going to save this for when I'm missing home."

"Then you'll never read it," Kayla said.

I was afraid of what was inside the letter.

Something told me it would hurt in the best way.

I put out my cigarette.

Kayla and I hugged.

It always felt like Kayla and me versus the world growing up. We'd always keep an eye on one another. Sometimes checking battle wounds or ensuring neither one of us felt alone. Or starved. Now, the team was breaking up.

We held onto to each other.

The tears wouldn't stop.

Radek opened the back door.

"You gonna stay out here all night and freeze or have one more beer with me before you leave?"

I tucked the letter in my back pocket.

"Thanks for the smoke," I said. "You coming in?"

Kayla turned away from Radek.

"I'm going to stay out here for a minute."

I wiped my eyes before I joined Radek, Zane, and my friends Todd and Doug in my mother's family room. Doug had a beer waiting for me when I sat down.

"Last beer together in Jersey," Radek said.

"It doesn't feel real," I said.

"No way you last in California," Todd said.

"I don't think he's coming home," Doug said.

"He's coming home," Todd said. "How long do you think he'll last?"

"Forever," Doug said.

"You better come home," Kayla said as she came back into the house.

"I bet you he doesn't even make it a year," Todd said.

I sipped my beer.

"He won't miss it here," Zane said.

Doug smashed his beer into mine.

"He'll miss us, though."

"What time you leaving for Cali?" Radek asked.

"Seven."

"You sightseeing or stopping anywhere on your drive?" Doug asked.

"Nah. The Birds play Sunday. I'm not missing that."

"No way you make the game," Todd said.

"I mapped it out," I said. "Two and a half days is more than enough time."

"You'll never make it," Todd said.

Doug raised his beer.

"To safe travels."

Everyone cheered.

It was the final drink of the night.

Doug was the last to leave.

It was late.

I was drunk.

"Listen, man, don't worry about the bachelor party," Doug said. "I know how expensive California is. I can't be the guy to make you spend that type of money. You're gonna need as much as you can get your hands on."

"It's no big deal. I can—"

"That's your pride. This is your dream. I'll send you the date, but it's gonna be on the East Coast. And only one night. I can't do that to you. Just be there on my wedding day."

"I wouldn't miss it for the world."

"I'm proud of you for chasing this, man."

Doug and I hugged goodbye.

I stumbled upstairs to my bed. I pulled Kayla's letter from my pocket and held it against my chest. Tears poured down my face. I didn't realize how sad I'd feel leaving Jersey.

No One Likes Driving with Their Parents
January 5, 2019

I glanced at the GPS hanging on the dash. Only seven more hours until we reached San Diego.

"Fucking Democrats," my father said as he scrolled on his phone.

I wasn't sure if I could survive the next seven hours.

"What is it now?" I asked.

"I don't know why you're moving to the Land of the Liberals." He readjusted his seat. "At least with Republicans, I have a job. I have security."

He spouted more propaganda.

My father called it news.

"It's unbelievable what they're doing . . ."

I regretted letting him tag along.

". . . trying to impeach our president because they're pissed off that he's not one of them."

A light drizzle hit the windshield.

"One of them?" I asked.

"He's one of us."

"Um . . . who?"

"Pay attention! The man saving our country from the socialist bastards," my father said. "Donald J. Trump."

"Uh."

"He's delivered on everything he's promised," my father said.

Trump was no different than any other career politician. Trump, corporate executives, and elected officials all made their fortunes the same way. Scamming the American people.

"So far," I said hoping it would end the conversation.

"He shouldn't tweet like he does, but I enjoy it. He talks like you and me."

A gigantic beast on the side of the road caused me to swerve the car.

"The fuck was that?" I asked. "Those were the biggest antlers I'd ever seen."

"A big friggin' deer," my father said.

In his defense, it was dark with a steady rain, making it hard for the old man to see.

"I think it was a moose."

"It was a deer. Trust me. I know what a deer looks like."

"Moose," I said.

"You think you know everything. Always have."

"Clearly."

My father shook his head.

"Knock it off."

The rain came down harder as the road took us farther up a mountain.

"Are you going to turn on your wipers, or would you prefer not to see?"

Turn off the mountain and kill the bastard in a fiery grave. Dammit. I'm no hero.

I pressed a little firmer on the gas.

We continued to climb.

"Democrats want to take our guns. Did you see that on the news?"

"What did those bastards do this time?"

He ranted about guns and then something else. Impeachment again? I think. I don't know. I nodded along.

The rain transformed to sleet. It came down thick and fast. Before my father could get to the radical left, the sleet changed to snow.

"Just go slow," my father said.

I blazed through the whiteout at ten miles per hour.

The wipers were switched to warp speed.

It barely helped.

"Focus on what you can see."

It was terrible advice.

I couldn't see a fucking thing.

"Slower."

The snow blanketed the windshield.

I flipped on the radio.

"After this, let's check your stuff on the roof."

I turned up the volume.

It was a Bob Dylan song.

"Turn off this hippie shit," my father yelled. "I'm not doing this with you again. You're on your own when you move back."

Hank slept in the back.

The ignorant fool.

I pulled my seat closer to the windshield, praying it would somehow help me see. I squinted harder at the snow.

"Slower," he said.

I wasn't even hitting the gas.

"Slower, Wyatt."

My father wasn't wearing his seat belt. If I slammed the brakes, it would eject him from the car.

Actually.

No.

We weren't going fast enough.

The worst I could do was give him a nice bump from him hitting his head against the windshield.

Best case?

A concussion.

But what about Hank?

Slamming the brakes could end up hurting him.

The potential collateral damage wasn't worth it.

We drove on in terrified silence.

Inching our way to California.

"Go slow here," my father said.

We stopped climbing and started picking up speed. I pumped the brakes as we slid down the mountain.

"Slower."

I hit the brakes.

"Don't be a smart-ass."

The snow became rain.

"I don't know why you do this shit," my father said. "You nearly killed us."

I ignored him and sped toward civilization.

My father reached for the cooler in the back seat when we made it to the bottom of the mountain. He pulled out a piece of apple pie and a bottle of water.

"You still have that?" I asked.

"I take my time eating it." My father took a bite. "Want a piece?"

"I'm good."

My father chuckled.

"This is the last piece."

There's not a soul on this planet who's ever enjoyed driving with their parents.

"Not like you'd share it," I said.

"Why would I? It's made just for me."

Every time we visited my grandmother, she baked my father an apple pie. It was grandpa's favorite, and after he died, I guess she started making them for him.

"Yeah, yeah," I said. "That's over a week old anyway. I don't want it."

He licked his fingers clean.

"I didn't know it snowed in Arizona. Isn't it a desert?"

"I don't know," I said. "I probably should have paid more attention in geography class."

"Probably. But who really gives a shit about Arizona?"

* * *

We stopped at a small gas station to fill up. I grabbed a large coffee and some beef jerky inside the mini mart. I bought two Arizona lotto tickets from one of those automatic ticket machines. My father wanted to buy lotto tickets in every state we drove through, which sounds silly, but if you knew my father, you'd find it romantic.

The only state he had left to collect was California.

When I returned to the car, my father hopped out to take a leak. I ate some beef jerky with Hank until a blinking orange light behind the steering wheel caught my eye . . . CHECK ENGINE LIGHT. I scanned the car like I would find exactly what was wrong and fix it in an instant. I pulled the car manual from the glove box. Surprised I still had it. There was nothing in there that helped.

Maybe something damaged the car during the snowstorm.

I walked outside and pressed down on my tires. All firm. The trunk and hood were both latched and closed. Nothing seemed frozen. There wasn't any smoke coming out of the engine. I got back into the car and skimmed through the manual again.

My father returned to the passenger's seat.

"What's going on?"

"I have no idea what's fucking wrong with the car."

"Relax."

"The 'check engine light' is on. I don't know what it is."

My father searched around. Just like I had. He left and inspected the outside of the car. He checked the tires, the trunk, and the hood. I heard him twist and slam something closed.

"The gas cover wasn't shut," my father said. "Is the light still on?"

The CHECK ENGINE LIGHT turned off.

"No."

He fell back into his seat.

"And you think you can make it on your own in California?"

When we got back on the road, my father passed out.

I threw back my extra-large coffee in less than fifteen minutes. I didn't feel any increased alertness.

My phone brightened in my lap.

A text from Leah.

Are you in California yet?

I was surprised she was awake this late.

I took my eyes off the road to respond.

A few more hours. Why aren't you asleep?

Leah texted.

Fucking insomnia.

I wish I had insomnia.

My eyes barely stayed open, but I drove on.

Time didn't move.

The miles came slower.

Leah stopped texting.

It was too much.

I wasn't going to make it.

"I gotta piss."

My father's voice shook me awake.

The car jerked to the other side of the road.

"What the fuck!" my father yelled.

Hank barked.

"You scared me!" I yelled. "Fuck."

"Pull over at the next gas station," my father said. "I'm driving. I'm not dying for this shit."

I didn't bother to get another coffee when we stopped. My father and I switched seats. I pulled the last water from the back seat cooler before I propped up my pillow on the passenger's seat window.

"Wake me up before we get to California," I said.

"Will do."

I fell asleep within seconds of shutting my eyes.

When I awoke, the rising sun lit up the palm trees that guided the highway.

"Let me finish her out," I said.

We stopped one last time to fill the gas tank.

My father handed me the keys.

"You made it."

Half-asleep, I drove us into San Diego.

Home Sweet Shithole
January 6, 2019

We were parked right outside a sleazy hotel. My new home was sandwiched between a run-down apartment complex and a parking garage built during the Carter presidency. My father waited in the car with Hank while I went to meet the property manager.

"Welcome home!" Isabelle said.

Too excited for eight in the morning.

Isabelle unlocked the metal front door and led me inside.

She showed me the lobby, which was a row of mailboxes, an elevator, and a staircase. There was no room for anything else.

"Do I have a mailbox?" I asked.

"You share one with your neighbor."

That didn't seem legal.

Isabelle unlocked, opened, closed, and relocked my mailbox before handing me the key.

We took two steps, and we were in what Isabelle called the garage. A rancid, empty dumpster sat next to the entrance of the eight-car parking lot.

"You better hurry," she said. "These spots fill up quickly. Right now, we only have one left."

Of course, there was only one.

"How much?"

"It only costs an extra three hundred dollars a month."

Street parking it was.

Another two steps into the garage led me to a metal door. Inside was a small, musky room with a hot-water heater, two washers, and two dryers. The coin slots meant laundry wasn't free. A wash cycle cost three bucks. A drying cycle? Three seventy-five.

"Are there any laundromats around here?" I asked.

"There's one fifteen blocks away."

Looks like I'd be spending seven bucks a week for wash.

89

We took four steps and made it back to the lobby.

"Stairs or elevator?" Isabelle asked.

It was the type of place where I didn't trust the elevator.

We walked four flights of stairs, where Isabelle opened my future apartment door. The joint didn't smell like mildew, but it should have. The room had dull white walls. Lights that were too bright hung from the ceiling. A two-seat couch, TV, and table wouldn't all fit in the wood-floored living area.

"It's . . . ah . . . really . . . um . . . homey," Isabelle said. "It's so close to everything you could want."

She walked behind me with a clipboard, writing down the things I noticed wrong with the place.

The wooden planks stopped at the edge of the living space and led to a cold concrete floor. The kitchen and hallway were the same. The hallway side was a half-painted, half-concrete wall with electrical panels. On the other side, a stove, an oven, a sink, a microwave, and a refrigerator. A few cabinets hung on the wall, but they were all chipped, unable to fully open, or held together by duct tape.

I wasn't surprised there wasn't a dishwasher.

Water dripped from the sink when I turned on the faucet. The fridge let out a whiff of putrid air when I opened it. The freezer didn't smell, and it was cold. At least there was that.

The hallway ended at a closed white door. On the right, was the bathroom. The door opened a little more than halfway, then it didn't budge. I pushed my shoulder into it. Some splinters chipped off when the door slammed into the front of the toilet bowl.

"Put that on the walk-through sheet," I said. "Chipped door that won't open all the way."

The sink mirror was large, but all four corners were missing. I wasn't sure how I'd fit in the stall Isabelle sold as a shower.

The bedroom wasn't much better.

It wasn't a square or a rectangular space. Part of the wall jutted out, creating a tiny nook in the left corner. An air conditioner and window found their home there. The window faced a tan building. The stench of piss overtook the room when I opened the only window in the joint. I couldn't tell if it was sunny or cloudy outside from the view.

"What do you think?" Isabelle asked.

Convicts got more sunlight.

And had bigger showers.

The apartment was a shithole.

But it was the only affordable shithole in San Diego. "Where do I sign?"

* * *

Before my father and me completely unloaded the car, I set up the TV and internet to make sure we could watch the Eagles play the Chicago Bears. I hadn't missed an Eagles game in my entire life. I refused to start my life in California by missing the team's first-ever title defense.

I bought some snacks and a six-pack of beer from a liquor store around the corner. My father organized the kitchen. I turned on the Birds.

The beer was gone before the second half.

Despite the tragedy, the Birds held on to beat the Bears 16–15. California was off to a solid start.

My father and Hank slept in the bedroom. I passed out on an air mattress in the living room. For eighteen hours we slept.

January 7, 2019

We woke up starved. I left Hank some peanut butter slathered on a bone to distract him while my father and I headed out for food. I found a burrito joint ten minutes from my place. Both of us ordered a California burrito.

We were romantic like that.

It was the quickest I'd ever seen my father eat, and this was the man who used to conduct food races with his sons at dinner when my mother wasn't home.

* * *

We drove to a cheap retail store, where my father offered to buy me a couch. I found the best one in the joint, and one of the store's employees held the imitation black leather two-seater at the front of the store until we finished shopping.

Between the gas, food, and couch money, my father helped me get started in California with a little more coin in my pocket than I'd expected.

My father headed to grab paper towels, and I found my way to the frozen food section for some middle-of-the-night snacks. A little girl waving some sort of boxed doll at her father stomped her feet in front of the fridge with mozzarella sticks.

"Daddy! I want this!"

"If you don't knock it off, you won't get a goddamn thing," the khaki-wearing father said.

The little girl flung herself onto the floor in a violent cry.

"Get off the damn floor!"

The father grabbed his little girl by pinning her wrists together. She dropped the doll. He pulled his daughter off the ground.

"Daddy, that hurts!"

"Behave, you little shit," the father said.

"Ouch! Daddy, stop! Ow!"

Fuck this guy.

"Hey, buddy," I said. "Relax. She's just a kid."

"Mind your business."

He flung his daughter's wrists out of his grip.

It should have ended there.

"The future of my species is my business," I said.

The man clenched both fists and walked toward me.

I've been knocked out before.

This one felt worth it.

My father stepped between me and the violent man before he could strike. The irony almost ruined the moment.

"I apologize about my son."

The man went back to his daughter, shoving my father's hand away from him on his way.

"Your son's a punk bitch."

I went to charge the bastard.

"Take it easy," my father said as he pushed me in the opposite direction of another abusive man.

The short-tempered father grabbed his daughter by the hand and picked up his basket filled with groceries. The doll remained on the floor.

"Let's go, sweetie."

They left the aisle.

As they did, everyone else around us pretended like they weren't watching the drama unfold.

"What was that?" my father asked.

"Fuck him."

"Why do you have to do shit like that? What's wrong with you? What are you going to do when you're out here on your own?"

"I'd handle it."

"And get knocked the fuck out. For what?"

The little girl reminded me of Kayla.

I clenched my fist and said nothing.

* * *

Before dinner, we walked Hank around the neighborhood. More people than usual rode rentable scooters on the streets and sidewalks, causing us to have to dodge a few unskilled cyclists. My father looked confused at the scooters littered all over the streets.

"I've been meaning to ask, what are those for?"

"To ride," I said.

My father's eyes rolled.

"You can rent 'em and ride 'em through the city."

"Don't end up dead," he said.

We walked another block before Hank, who had never stepped a paw in a city until our move, squatted down on the sidewalk outside the main entrance of a giant Scientology center. A Scientologist glared at my pup. Hank locked eyes with the geek in a robe. Hank squatted and took a shit right in front of the worship center. I couldn't even pick up the poop because it smeared into the sidewalk every time I tried to scoop it. Brown goo fell into cracks and spread across the pavement with every wipe. I held in a laugh until we were a few blocks away from the scene.

"That's not funny," my father said. "Those people will hunt you down."

It would have been just as funny outside a Catholic church. Or any other cult. But I couldn't say that.

We dropped Hank off at the apartment, and I drove my father to the beach. I wanted to show him a California sunset. We stood on the stone walkway right before the sand and watched it unfold.

For a guy who rarely uses his phone, my father couldn't stop taking photos.

"This is incredible," my father said.

"It's my favorite part about the place."

"It's absolutely incredible," my father said. "Wow."

He kept repeating the word "incredible."

I understood the feeling.

* * *

It was late when we finally got back to the apartment.

My father stared at the uncompleted display cabinet that sat in the living room. It was the last piece of furniture I needed to build. He couldn't stand leaving things unfinished.

"You want me to put together this thing before I go?"

"I'll do it tomorrow," I said.

"It won't take long."

"You've done enough. Really."

My father ignored me.

He grabbed a hammer and went to work on the cabinet.

I headed for the bedroom while he banged away.

"This stupid fucking fuck!"

Hank ran into the bedroom.

"This cheap piece of shit from China," he screamed.

Hank and I snuggled. Nearly falling asleep before my father barged into the bedroom.

"We need more nails."

"Why?" I asked.

"They didn't give you enough."

"They?" I asked half-asleep.

His face showed a familiar flair of frustration and rage.

"The bastards who manufactured that cabinet."

I climbed out of bed. I found the instructions lying on the living room floor. Unopened.

My father reached for the instructions.

"You don't need that—look at the back of the cabinet."

I ignored him and continued to read the manual. I counted the nails hammered into the back of the cabinet.

"The cabinet comes with the exact number of nails needed," I said.

"We need more nails."

"If you followed the instructions, we wouldn't."

"I know what I'm doing," my father said. "Your cabinet would be flimsy if I didn't do it this way. Trust me. They cheat you on the nails. Your cabinet falls apart if you don't do it like this."

"The directions are lying?" I asked. "Why would they do that?"

"What you know, I can fit in a shoebox with a pair of shoes still inside."

"I'll get the nails tomorrow. I'm going to bed."

I turned off the lights, forcing him to abandon his project. I pushed the cabinet against the wall. My father headed to the bedroom without saying good night.

January 8, 2019

We passed palm tree after palm tree, coasting down the Pacific Highway, with a bay on our left and the airport approaching ahead on our right.

"Think the Eagles will beat the Saints?" my father asked.

Football small talk.

To avoid any real conversation.

"Anything is possible with Nick Foles."

"They play hard for him. I hope they keep him. Win or lose."

"I mean, he's the man, but Carson has way more talent. It's hard to pass that up."

"It'll be a mistake losing Foles," my father said. "When do you start work?"

I turned my car into the airport.

"Friday," I said.

"Friday? That's stupid to start work on a Friday."

"That's exactly what I said."

"They're only good on payday."

"What is?"

"Jobs," my father said.

I pulled up to his terminal and threw on my flashers.

"I'll come out and visit sometime."

We both knew it was a lie.

"Sounds good," I said.

I got out of the car and hugged him goodbye.

"I'm proud of you," my father said. "I love you."

It felt good to hear the words.

He grabbed his suitcase from the trunk and walked into the airport. For the first time in my life, I felt free.

Shipping Container Speakeasy

January 11, 2019

The first day of work always sucks. It doesn't matter if the job is good or bad. Office tours, corny jokes, filling out mystifying tax documents, company trainings, staff meetings, and awkward lunches.

Trish greeted me when I arrived at work.

"The rest of the team will be here soon," she said. "Chuck usually rolls in around ten."

She led me to the kitchen, where doughnuts and fruit were spread across the counter. We drank hot caffeine as she took me around the joint. It was a large space, too big for the number of employees currently on staff, with five conference rooms and sixteen offices. Each employee had their own separate workspace, no cubicles, but the walls surrounding each office was see-through glass. At the end of the row of offices was a giant open space with couches, motivational posters, and beanbag chairs. The giant windows overlooked the Pacific coast. That's where Chuck's office was, in the corner with a million-dollar view of the ocean. His office was surrounded by frosted glass. The type where he could see out, but no one could see in.

"Does Danielle usually come in at ten?" I asked.

Trish sighed.

"She quit."

That was a red flag.

Or maybe she was just a bad employee.

I didn't ask anything more about Danielle.

The rest of the staff came into work a little after nine. Without Danielle, my new colleagues were Trish, Gary, and Jessica. The staff, minus Chuck, and I got acquainted for an hour. Chuck showed up twenty minutes after ten. He gave me my second tour of the office. Afterward, I learned about Reynolds Incorporated by reading over the company's handbook. It took thirty minutes. The rest of the morning, I read articles about the upcoming Eagles and Saints playoff game. I also tested out the bathroom. And tried to understand tax forms.

Around noon, Chuck called an "all-hands" meeting. The staff met in the conference room for a team-building lunch. Chuck made everyone reintroduce themselves, but this time we had to roll two dice before we talked. Whatever number we rolled correlated with a question on a sheet of paper Chuck held in his hands.

We weren't a team.

We were a family.

Pizza arrived halfway through the meeting.

"Best pizza in SoCal," Chuck said. "Just as good as the East Coast."

I wasn't sure if Chuck ever ate East Coast pizza. The pie he ordered tasted like burned cardboard, canned spaghetti sauce, and sliced orange cheese.

Still, I appreciated the gesture.

"Wow," I said. "I can't believe how good this is."

He also signed my paychecks.

I did "additional market research" in the afternoon before an end-of-day huddle. Chuck wanted to pump up his new team for when we returned to the office on Monday.

Chuck let everyone leave at four.

* * *

That night, Noah and Summer met me at some fancy restaurant a few blocks from The Palace.

"You'll be over tomorrow for the game?" Summer asked.

"Yeah, but if the Birds start losing, I'm out."

"Be positive," Summer said. "I got a good feeling."

"I don't," Noah said.

"Don't be like that," Summer said.

The three of us downed a round.

I bought the next.

Noah got the round after that.

That's when Leah finally showed up.

Two hours late.

And she looked every second worth it.

She rushed toward me.

"I can't believe you live here!"

Leah wrapped herself around me in a leap. She kissed my cheeks, using her hands to flip my face side to side. When she'd had enough, she climbed down.

"I could get used to that," I said,

"Christ, you two," Summer said.

Leah settled in at the table.

"Tell me about the job. What are you doing out here?"

"The Devil's work," I said. "I call it copy writing."

"Tell them about the salary negotiations," Noah said.

"Here we go," Summer said.

"Wyatt's boss flew him out to California on his own dime," Noah said. "Then he offered him the job two days after his interview. That guy was desperate."

"He paid for your flights?" Leah asked.

"Yeah," I said. "But the salary offer still felt low."

"Because it was," Noah said. "I told him to take him for all he's got."

"You're such a hero," Summer said.

"Chuck bumped up the offer by a few thousand dollars, included vision and dental with my regular health insurance, and included a ten-thousand-dollar bonus after ten months of employment," I said.

"I might have to hit you up," Leah said.

"Put away some money," Noah said. "Look for other jobs. Only ones with a bigger salary and potential for growth. Take every networking event. This job isn't long-term. After ten months, get out of there."

Leah downed her drink.

"Boring!"

"Enough with the shoptalk," Summer said.

"It's what's paying for these drinks. And your wardrobe. Like all those shoes you left all over our bedroom."

"Can't a girl have a hobby?"

Noah motioned for the waiter.

"Not if it's hoarding."

"It's been a long fucking week."

I lifted my drink.

"To Noah, master of negotiations and finance."

"Let's not inflate his ego too much," Summer said.

We touched our glasses together.

"To Wyatt getting a job," Noah said.

"To my best fucking friend moving to California," Summer said.

"Welcome home, Wyatt."

I loved when Leah called California home.

We each took a long gulp.

Leah wanted to know all about my road trip with my father. There wasn't much to tell, but I made it sound interesting.

Maybe.

I don't know.

After another round of drinks, Summer and Noah called it a night. The two were touring open houses early the next day. Summer refused to let either of them be hungover for that.

"So lame," I said to Leah after the couple left.

"It's sweet," Leah said. "They're growing up."

"Sounds terrible."

"I know where us kids can go," Leah said. "But you can't tell anyone about it."

* * *

Leah and I arrived at a parking lot filled with shipping containers. I heard music and people but couldn't see behind the silver metal fortress. Leah led me through the massive outdoor entrance, and the lot transformed into a secret garden of fine dining and booze. Each massive metal shipping unit featured a restaurant, shop, or brewery. White lights hung from the tops of the containers, creating an illuminated pathway through the maze of giant boxes.

"You can't tell anyone about this, yeah?" Leah said. "It's my secret."

Leah pulled me by the hand toward her favorite container. The joint occupied the smallest space in the lot. It was split in two. One half, with bright green-and-red walls with a few hipsters sitting on old brown couches, was called the lounge. The other half, with a line, a bar, and a popcorn machine, was called the shop.

"What do you want?" Leah asked.

"Beer."

"They don't have that here."

"What?"

"They make mocktails. Like a pineapple mojito or an apple pie mule." She pointed at the colorful handwritten blackboard menu on the wall. "They're all listed."

"How do I get booze?"

"You have to know the code words."

"Tell me."

"If I tell you, I'll have to kill you." Leah pulled me in line. "Alcohol isn't listed on the menu. Coffin varnish is vodka. Mash is whiskey. Panther sweat is tequila. Horse liniment is gin." Leah paused. "That's all I know."

"It's all the good liquor, anyway," I said. "Get me a mash."

She laughed at me.

"Mash with? A mash mojito?" Leah considered the drink. "Gross."

One drink was blue with dark fruit. The other, red with bright fruit. We sat on the curb of what used to be a road surrounding the large metal boxes.

"The city only allowed five liquor licenses for the entire lot. This place didn't get one," Leah said. "The couple threw all their money, savings, and their wedding cash into this place. And they expected a bar. So, they turned the place in a speakeasy."

Now that's an American Dream.

The cocktails even tasted stubborn.

I returned to the speakeasy to throw away our empty booze cups. I left a twenty-dollar bill I couldn't afford to lose in the joint's tip jar.

Leah and I walked each other arm in arm to a brewery that was three shipping containers put together. Unlike the other businesses, this brewery didn't hide the fact you were in a shipping container. Tan wood and silver metal made up the walls, with two separate bars on opposite ends of the joint. The names of the beer on the giant chalkboard above the bar looked like blurred lines. Leah took my credit card and called the bartender for two beers. She handed me a hazy IPA. I knew from the taste. Leah sipped her dark beer.

Twenty bucks she'd hate it.

Leah spit the beer back into her glass.

What's your superpower, Wyatt?

Drunk psychic.

Leah didn't ask with her words, but I gave her my beer.

* * *

Next thing I knew, Leah and I were holding each other up outside the joint, waiting for a ride. I helped Leah into the car before crawling in on the other side.

"You two alright?" the middle-aged driver asked.

"You ever been drunk before?"

"No," he said.

"Me either," I said.

Leah nestled into my shoulder before mumbling something into my chest. I rubbed her back. The driver glared into his rearview mirror at us. He had to smell the booze. I don't know why I lied about being drunk. The guy would have been understanding if I told the truth. Sure, we drank a bit, but we weren't sick or anything.

Unless you counted mental illness.

But nobody counted that.

I leaned on the window.

Off to sleep.

"Here!"

The driver's shout shocked me awake. His slam of the brake launched Leah forward, waking her up. I pulled her blonde hair from my mouth.

"You're home," I said.

"Get out of my car," the driver said.

Leah and I fell out of the ride. Our driver didn't even let us close the door. He stomped out of the car and did it himself.

We walked around a courtyard with a pool and hot tub. Leah led me up three flights of stairs. She fidgeted with the door. Her keys clanged against the ground every time she dropped them. She refused my help. Lights flicked on in the apartments surrounding Leah's. I helped steady her hand, guiding her key into the hole.

We unlocked the apartment together.

Her place was pitch-black. I glided on the floor behind Leah. A loud bang let her know I found the kitchen table.

"Fuck!"

"Shh! My roommate is sleeping."

Leah led me by the hand to her bedroom, where we stripped to our underwear. I nearly fell over when my pant leg trapped my ankle. I slid onto the dozens of white pillows that covered her bed.

I was too drunk to for anything but sleep.

"I need music," Leah said. "Hope you don't mind."

Bob Dylan whined from her phone.

Leah climbed next to me.

My foot escaped the covers and found the floor.

The world spun a little faster.

At least for me.

California Strip Poker

January 19, 2019

The car sped across a long, gigantic bridge perched high in the sky. Fishing, cargo, and party boats filled the glistening water. I rolled down the back window to taste the salty air. As we got closer to Coronado, the bridge veered back toward San Diego, giving me a perfect view of the skyline. There was no toll in either direction of the bridge. It was a pleasant surprise because just thinking about crossing water cost five bucks in Jersey.

Coronado looked like a small town, heaven on earth, and an overpriced resort. Palm trees separated traffic on the city's main road. A beautiful landscape of mountains and palms served as the backdrop to the beach. But mansions, neighborhood homes, family-owned shops, and a giant tourist-trap hotel destroyed the natural beauty of the paradise. And if nature or price-gouging capitalism wasn't your thing, the United States Navy trained SEALs in Coronado, specifically those gunning for SEAL Team Six.

Yeah, those badass motherfuckers.

My driver parked a block away from the brewery.

My driver.

Ha.

Like I was some rich asshole who paid someone a salary to take me places. More like a broke fool who squeezed into a car with two strangers to save three dollars on a ride.

I walked straight into Coronado Mermaid Brewing like I owned the place. Servers and busboys hurried around the joint. I couldn't find the bar or the gigantic beer-list chalkboard that every brewery had. There were just booths, tables, and diners. It wasn't a good sign for a joint that called itself a brewery.

The hostess was cute but seemed annoyed I existed.

"May I help you?

"I'm meeting someone," I said. "Not sure if she's here yet."

"Not sure?"

I didn't like it here.

"Oh wait, that looks like her."

It wasn't Leah, but I jogged away from the hostess. She followed right behind me. The place was too small to escape. I found a dead end when I reached the flimsy kitchen doors. With nowhere to go, I came face-to-face with the hostess.

"Well . . . I'm . . . supposed to meet someone here. I thought that was her . . ."

She didn't hide her disgust. "Did she have a reservation?"

"I'm not sure."

"Can I ask you to find a seat at the bar or wait outside?"

"Where's the bar exactly?"

She led me to a small bar tucked away in the back corner of the joint. Six people fought with their elbows for space.

"The bar looks a little full," I said.

"You can wait outside until your party arrives."

She power walked me out of the restaurant that masqueraded as a brewery. I pulled out my phone when I got to the sidewalk, but Leah beat me to the text.

Her text said, *I'm here.*

She was not there.

I typed my response.

The place is in Coronado?

I nearly dropped my phone when it rang.

"You're at the wrong place," Leah said.

I was the one not there.

"Shit."

"It's got Coronado in the name, but it's not in Coronado."

"That's a bit confusing," I said. "What should we do?"

"Coronado is a little far."

Fuck.

"Let's meet somewhere you might recognize," Leah said. She decided on a brewery by The Palace. She figured I had less of a chance of getting lost in a neighborhood I visited often.

* * *

Leah wore a long black sundress with a loud tan hat.

"Let me buy you a beer," I said.

"Four would be a good start."

We split a flight of beers.

Then we ordered another.

Leah was an ER nurse. She enrolled in college to get her master's degree. But that's all I could get out of her regarding her career. She didn't like talking about herself.

"The hops really give it the flavor I crave," Leah said after drinking the first beer in our third flight.

I cleaned my teeth and gums with the second beer.

Then I swallowed.

"For me, it's the barley. It's what invigorates my nostrils."

"Anyone who uses the word 'invigorates' is a pretentious asshole."

"Takes one to know one," I said.

We drank the rest of our cold-brewed hops like the eloquent and cultured motherfuckers we were.

We left the brewery to find a joint with the weirdest beer names on the menu. Most bars and restaurants have menus outside their shops, so that's where Leah and I did our research.

People and dogs forced us to sliver down the crowded street. Leah took her time admiring all the new shops. A few antique stores especially caught her eyes. But she forgot all about our beer hunt when she halted in front of a little Italian restaurant.

"We have to go in here. They have this focaccia. It's the best thing I have ever put in my mouth."

It was adorable.

We went in.

Leah did the ordering.

I couldn't pronounce what I was about to eat.

We each had a glass of pinot nero, which Leah told me was the Italian name for pinot noir, before a waiter brought our dish. Leah smeared a knife's worth of honeycomb on a slice of bread and melted cheese.

"Focaccia," she said.

I used half the honey on my first piece.

"Why can't I just eat it?"

"Don't you want to be a cultured Californian?"

"Not really," I said.

"I'm not letting you eat any until you say it properly." Leah snatched the plate of honeycomb. "Fuh. Kah. Cha."

I took a slice of Italian cheesy bread off our plate.

"What's this—school? Why do I care about some Italian cheese bread?" I took a bite. "Still, plenty good."

Leah teased me by spreading a ton of the remaining honey on her next slice. "Fuh. Kah. Cha"

"Fuh. Cock. Ah."

"Wyatt! We're in public."

I laughed.

The server brought extra honeycomb to replace what Leah had eaten. It was worth the extra twenty.

After stuffing our stomachs with cheese and booze, Leah wanted to nap.

"Show me your place, yeah?" Leah said.

I'd never invite Leah over to my place.

She'd hate it.

Shit.

I lived there, and I hated it.

"Not yet," I said. "It's not ready. You know me, Mr. Fancy Apartment. Need to make it look the way I want before inviting anyone over."

"You have to show me sometime."

I wasn't ready for that.

We split the bill and took our time finishing our bottle of wine.

"This is going well for you," I said. "A second date is a real possibility."

"Who said this was a date?"

"How can I convince you otherwise?"

Leah rocked her near-empty glass.

"I know where you can try."

"Your place?"

I blurted it out.

"With Summer and Noah. They want us to come by."

"Oh. Okay. Yeah. That sounds good."

Leah put her glass on the table.

"It's a new year—I'm trying to break that habit."

"What habit?"

"Jumping right into sex," Leah said.

"Who says I'd have sex with you?"

"Your eyes."

When a woman says what a man can't admit, he can only smile.

* * *

Noah pulled out his phone and showed me pricing options for the snowboarding pass he used every winter.

The same pass he explained an hour earlier.

"It's called the IKON pass," Noah said. "Type IKON on any search engine and it'll be the first thing."

"You already told him this," Summer said.

"I'm telling Leah." He scrolled through the options on his phone. "You can do payment plans. It's cheap for what you get with it."

"He knows."

"It's only like seven hundred bucks. You should do it."

"We always gotta talk about what you want to talk about," Summer said. "Maybe they don't want to crush fresh powder with you."

Leah's face matched my unease.

We both took a drink.

Noah had ordered takeout from his favorite Thai place. The four of us sat around The Palace kitchen table, talking about nothing, drinking wine, and sharing spicy soup and yellow curry.

Summer cleaned off the table when the food was gone.

Noah walked to the kitchen and pulled a deck of cards from a drawer. "Poker anyone?"

"Can you not try to hustle my friends?" Summer asked.

"I didn't say for money."

"You will eventually."

"We can play a few hands," Noah said. "Make things more interesting if people want."

I never learned how to play poker.

"I'm no good," I said.

"He can count cards," Summer said.

Of course, Noah could.

"Let's play blackjack," Leah said.

Summer pointed a finger at Noah. "No counting."

Noah shuffled the deck.

Summer shuffled again.

We played a few hands.

Summer won most of them.

Maybe she was the one hustling us all along.

"Want to make this interesting?" Leah asked.

She reached for the bottom of her shirt and pretended to pull it over her head.

Suddenly, I was awake.

"I'm down," Noah said.

"Noah!" Summer yelled.

I liked Noah's chances of getting the girls naked.

No doubt he'd start counting cards to win.

But I'd never played strip poker with another man's woman. It never ends well. Trust me.

We played a few more clothed hands before I couldn't tell the clubs from the clovers. Shit. They're the same thing.

Noah yawned. Summer did next. Leah walked with me to the street when the couple headed to bed.

"You live close, yeah? Got any booze?" Leah asked.

I wanted to invite her to my apartment.

But I couldn't.

My place was a mess.

And embarrassing.

Especially compared to The Palace.

"I'm fresh out of booze," I lied.

"Let's grab some from Summer, then head to your place. We can reimburse her."

I was stuck living in my shithole until May 2020.

It was going to be tough to avoid taking Leah there considering I wanted to date her and all. But it wasn't the right moment. Not tonight.

"Sounds good," I said. "But when we get back there, I have to walk my dog."

"Have you bathed your animal in the last week?"

I didn't know you were supposed to bathe a dog weekly.

"No?"

"I'm tired anyway," she said. "I'll just call a ride back to my place."

"Want me to wait?"

"Nah," Leah said. "Get back to your dog."

The excuse worked, but it didn't feel good.

"When will I see you again?"

Leah gave me a kiss on the cheek.

"Don't get clingy, Jersey boy."

Super Shroom Sunday

February 3, 2019

Leah laid out a tie-dye blanket on a crowded grassy patch at Balboa Park. Tourists asked strangers to take photos with the lily pond to the right of us. Families, friends, and lovers walked or sat around, smiling and soaking up the sun on the warm winter day.

Leah pulled sandwiches from her cooler, took off the top halves, dropped some psilocybin mushrooms on the meat, and put the bread back on top.

"Shrooms help with depression," Leah said. "And they're hella fun."

The internet was littered with dozens of articles about the benefits of magic mushrooms. Celebrities supported the claims. Rich housewives admitted to taking small doses of psilocybin to help them deal with their unfulfilled lives.

I could relate.

"See you on the other side," I said.

We sunk our noses into books for a bit after we ate our drugwiches. It didn't take long before the words danced on the page. Literally.

I fell onto my back and let the sun heat my face.

The sun brightened.

The clouds were softer.

The sky?

Bluer than I'd ever seen it.

Leah nestled her head on my shoulder.

Her hair smelled like pure ecstasy.

Four ducks took an attack position around our blanket. They were after the half of Leah's sandwich she didn't finish. Leah rolled off me, ripped off some of her bread crust, and threw it toward the ducks.

One took the bait.

Leah threw a second bread crumb.

Too far left.

A different duck snacked on it.

Not our duck.

Leah tossed a bigger piece.

Perfect strike.

Our duck moved closer to our blanket.

"Let's call him Danny," Leah said, before tossing more bread.

Danny ate the fresh piece.

Leah slithered forward.

Danny waddled closer to Leah.

Leah pulled herself along the grass with an army crawl.

One inch at a time.

"Careful," I said, like I knew how to hunt duck.

Leah lunged forward and stretched her hand to pet Danny.

Too slow.

Danny flapped his wings and squawked, terrifying every animal in the vicinity. All the fucking ducks. The geese too. A frenzy of quacking and flying erupted by the lily pond. Some birds fired off shit as they flew away in a panic from Leah.

"Not even ducks like me," Leah said.

* * *

A young heavy metal guitarist who couldn't have been older than twenty-five paced around the lily pond, wearing all black, including a leather jacket.

"His band kicked him out, and now he has to tell his girlfriend," Leah said.

"How do you think she'll take it?"

"She's definitely going to end it."

"Cold-blooded," I said.

"When Paul and I used to come here, we'd do mushrooms and hang out all day. We'd people watch and make up silly background stories."

Paul was her ex-husband. Her high school sweetheart. The love of her life. But they divorced. Leah didn't tell me much more than that. She never really opened up about anything. It was something I could relate to.

"Paul and I made up an entire story about a kid who lives inside the giant organ." Leah pointed to a huge amphitheater in the distance. "We did so many mushrooms that day. And the story kept getting bigger and bigger. The organ kid was only allowed out to play the organ. His parents locked him in his room until they wanted to hear some music."

"Sounds like my childhood," I said.

"We went on for hours about the organ kid," she said. "Life was simpler then."

"What about now?"

"Things just seem to always be getting worse."

I pulled Leah into my chest.

"It's not all bad."

"I thought this would be a good distraction, but guess not," she said. "Paul always threw big Super Bowl parties. But here I am, nowhere close to anything football and thinking about him."

"I'm sorry, Leah," I said.

Leah squeezed me tighter.

"You still think I'm a cool, exotic California girl, yeah?"

"Who said I ever thought that?"

Leah lifted her face from my chest.

"Shut up."

"Divorcee or not, you're the prettiest thing I've ever seen," I said.

"I think the drugs are clouding your judgment."

"Maybe they are."

I rubbed my hand along Leah's cheek. Working my way toward the back of her neck. I pulled her in and kissed her forehead.

Leah pulled out the bag of mushrooms. Still a quarter filled. She reached into the bag, grabbed a handful, and shoved the mushrooms in my face. Most of them missed my mouth and fell into my beard. And all over my shirt. Leah picked the mushroom crumbs out of my beard and fed them to me. For each crumb she gave me, she took a couple for herself.

I shoved a handful in her face.

Some of the mushroom scraps fell between her boobs.

"Don't even think about it," she said.

Leah pinched the bits of shrooms out of her tits.

She fed me them.

"Doesn't help the flavor," I said. "But I'd love to see if there's any more down there."

Leah giggled out of control.

"I wonder what happiness is like without enhancements. Like just being happy normally," Leah said.

"You mean being happy without drugs?"

"It's not as beautiful when you put it like that," she said.

"I don't know if that exists for people like us."

We lied back down together and watched the clouds drift through the sky. Leah seemed to think every cloud resembled a Founding Father. Clearly, they were dinosaurs.

* * *

When day turned into night, Leah suggested we go to her favorite outdoor restaurant in the park.

"We can set up our blanket in there. They have an amazing jazz band that plays one Sunday a month. They're playing tonight."

"How old are you? Sixty?"

She wrapped her arm around mine.

"Let me live."

"You totally used me to get fucked up and see a jazz band."

"Duh."

We packed up our snacks, books, and blanket into Leah's bag and headed for the bar.

Prestigious gates bordered Leah's favorite joint. It was entirely outdoors with one large bar, dining tables, and sculptures inside a stone courtyard. Everything was brown, black, or white. Simple, but done beautifully. The courtyard had pillars and stone supporting a roof that wrapped around the outside of the courtyard, leaving a giant square hole in the center for a view of the sky.

Leah went to the grass section. Yeah, the joint had a giant patch of grass filled with modern art. The art was ugly, but the joint was beautiful.

I headed for drinks and saw PANAMA 66, the name, on a sign. I ordered two old-fashioneds and walked through a row of tables. A band set up their equipment in the corner. Folding chairs in front of the impromptu stage started filling in with elderly couples. Some young lovers sat down, too, but mostly everyone was wrinkled.

A few families and a couple spread out on blankets near us. Leah sat next to me with her hand on my knee. We sipped our drinks as a jazz band began performing. The old tunes echoed throughout the park. People walking by the restaurant stopped for a listen. A young couple practiced some sort of dance in a secluded part of the place. The woman taught the man a few moves. A two-step, a kick, followed by a twirl and catch. He repeated what she performed. When he got it right a few times in a row, they practiced together. They did nothing but shake and kiss.

"We should take dance lessons, yeah?" Leah said.

I agreed to dance lessons we'd never take.

Leah put on a red-and-gray hoodie she pulled from her bag. "Tell me about the girl you almost married."

"What? Why?"

"Come on," Leah said. "Tell me. I told you about Paul."

"Go out on a dinner date with me and I'll tell you."

"I'm not ready for that."

"Me either," I lied.

"Most people aren't capable of love," Leah said. "But you are. That's why I wanna know."

"That's a sad way to feel."

"I just want to know what she was like," Leah said. "I wonder what type of girl let you go."

My drink went down smooth.

"That's not how it happened."

"That's what Summer said."

"Summer doesn't know the story," I said.

Leah pushed my legs with both of her hands.

"I want to know more about you."

"I don't want to ruin a perfectly good night."

"What if we continued this conversation at my dad's place?" Leah asked. "He lives close. No one's home. And I think I know how to convince you to talk."

"Oh yeah?"

"My dad has quite the wine collection. I hear you're a talker when you're drunk," Leah said. "What did you think I meant?"

I said nothing.

I didn't have to.

We gathered our things and strolled out of the restaurant and through Balboa Park. It was dark, but the joint was filled with old architecture that reminded me of the one day I spent learning about Mexico in grade school.

Leah's phone buzzed.

Her mood changed as she read her texts.

"Fuck. My sister is there. Fuck. We can't go to my dad's."

"You have a sister?"

Leah paced around the sidewalk.

"I don't want you to meet her. Not yet. We can't."

"Why?"

"I can't invite you to stay. Is that okay?"

It seemed odd.

But I knew how fucked up families could be.

"Are you okay?" I asked.

Leah grabbed my hand.

"I will be. I just have to get there."

I didn't try and kiss Leah when we reached her father's apartment building. She was too frazzled for anything more than a hug.

"Let me know when you're okay," I said.

Leah nodded her head and went inside.

I grabbed a six pack of beer from a liquor store near Leah's father's place. When I got back to my apartment, I polished off the beers quickly, and thought about the woman I left for California.

Breaking Up for California

December 11, 2017

The most incredible woman I had ever met stood between me and the bedroom door, wearing nothing but her blonde hair and a long nightshirt. Erin grazed the stubble on my cheeks and pulled me toward her lips with both hands.

I twisted my head to avoid her kiss.

"Please. Kiss me. Just kiss me."

I walked past her, around the bed, through the kitchen, and out the door to my barely working two-door black Honda Civic. I placed another box of my things in my little back seat.

I took a deep breath before I reentered our shared condo.

Erin waited at the front door.

"We can work this out," she said.

We couldn't.

I was a monster.

"I can't do this anymore."

"Everyone gets angry," Erin said. "You did nothing wrong."

"You don't understand."

"Tell me, Wyatt."

Even with our love on the line, I couldn't find the words.

The strength to admit the truth.

About California.

What it meant to me.

And my biggest fear coming to life.

I scurried past her to the living room where a black-and-white photo of Erin and me kissing in front of the gigantic Christmas tree at the Rockefeller Center hung on the wall. Two more colorless highlights of our love taunted me before I found the bedroom.

"Please. Please, don't do this."

"Stop," I said. "This is hard enough."

I didn't want to leave.

But I had no choice.

"Wyatt."

I glared at Erin.

She left the room sobbing.

Two more trips back into our place before I crawled back home to my family. I kept my head down and carried out another box. I couldn't look at Erin.

Most of our things were hers. She was a homemaker and better at finances than me. Way better. Even if anything were mine, I wouldn't keep any of it. It would just remind me of her.

I passed Erin who cried into a pillow on our couch in the living room. I threw the box into my car. It didn't matter if things broke. Nothing mattered.

I took my time on my last trip inside.

The memories.

The love we shared.

I blew it all.

With my last box, I went to say goodbye to Erin.

"I'm leaving," I said over her muffled sobs.

Erin lifted her head, and my eyes found hers.

"That's it?"

"What do you want me to say?" I asked.

"Anything but that."

"I wish it didn't have to be like this."

Erin went from lying down to kneeling.

"No, you don't. If you did, you wouldn't be leaving."

"I'm done fighting, Erin."

"Why can't you just let it go?"

I wanted to.

I knew where I was headed if I didn't chase California.

Last night showed me who I really was.

"It's something I have to do."

"Why is California more important than me? Why?"

How could I tell her about my childhood abuse?

The neglect?

The absolute horror show that was my childhood.

Would she believe me?

I didn't even know what was true and what wasn't.

Some things were so horrible, they couldn't be real.

The only thing I knew for sure was that I spent my entire childhood living in constant fear.

"I don't know how to explain it," I said.

"We could vacation there every year. I don't care. Why isn't that enough?"

"Erin."

She slid closer to me.

"Why doesn't that work?"

"We've had this conversation a thousand times."

"Make it one more."

"It's been months of fighting in the same goddamn circles. It's fucking finished."

Tears shot out of Erin.

She buried her face in her hands.

"You promised me forever."

I wiped my face dry.

"Goodbye, Erin."

"I know you love me."

I did.

More than I ever showed her.

"I'm sorry," I said.

Erin took a deep breath.

"Just promise me one thing."

Water swelled in my eyes.

"What's that?"

"Don't stay with your family for too long."

The fuck.

"What?"

"They're not good for you," she said.

How could she know?

What did she know?

I never told her anything about my past.

"What's that even mean? What is this? I'm not falling for any of these mind games."

"I want what's best for you. Because I love you."

I backed away from Erin.

She was right.

I couldn't handle it.

"Stop. I'm over the dramatics."

"Please don't leave angry at me. I couldn't handle that."

Erin threw her arms and latched onto me. I kissed her hard when she pulled me in. The longer we held on to one another, the saltier the kisses became. Neither one of us wanted to stop, knowing this was the last one.

I forced my way out of the embrace, but not because I wanted to. Erin and I looked at each other for a moment, both tired and broken with only adrenaline keeping us awake.

She twisted off her engagement ring.

"At least let me help you get out there."

The love of my life dropped cold metal into my hand.

"Erin," I said. "I can't."

She used both hands to close my fist.

"I love you," she said.

More than anything in the world, I wanted to stay.

And tell her I loved her.

"Take care of yourself," I said.

"I don't care what you say, but I know you love me too."

I didn't bother to hold back my tears as I left our apartment for the last time.

Throw the box down, fool.

Run back into the living room.

Grab her.

Kiss her.

Make love to her.

Tell her we can fix this.

We could.

I know we could.

No.

Not after last night.

I couldn't do that to Erin.

I knew where my life was headed.

Everyone becomes their parents.

And Erin deserved more than that.

I carried out my last box filled with unfinished journals, stories, and musings. Incomplete. I never finished a fucking thing. I threw the box on my passenger's seat.

Erin's diamond ring pressed against my palm.

Only California could save me now.

Sir, We Have to Interview Your Dog
February 9, 2019

Summer handed me an old-fashioned.

"Are you going to tell me how the date went?"

"It wasn't a date," I said.

"Did you guys hook up?"

My drink burned my throat.

"We kissed."

"What do you mean? You skipped the Super Bowl for this girl! Are you dating? Who are you?"

"Everything was fantastic," I said. "But we're taking it slow."

"You're in love with her."

I was.

"I wouldn't go that far," I lied.

"Bullshit!"

"You know what was weird?" I asked. "She freaked out about her sister being at her dad's place. I didn't even know she had a sister."

"They have an interesting dynamic."

My drink tasted strong.

"What's that mean?"

"I never met her," Summer said. "I've just heard things."

"Like what?"

"It's not my story to tell." Summer tossed a familiar package of edibles onto the kitchen table. "Take these as a truce. I didn't eat them all."

"You saved them?"

"Some," Summer said. "Just in case you made it back out here. You can have them, but no more Leah's sister talk. I don't want to be in the middle of that."

I shoved one of the weed treats into my mouth.

A shriek of squeaky toy let me know Hank needed attention. I ripped some sort of stuffed animal from his mouth and tossed it across the room.

"Thanks for watching him," I said.

"You don't have to thank me every time I watch Hank."

"Yeah, I do. But I don't know what I'm going to do with him for your birthday."

Summer swished around her glass.

"You could just bring him to LA. Hide him in the hotel."

"I can't risk that," I said.

"Then there's a zillion doggie day cares in San Diego."

"That all want interviews with Hank before they'll watch him," I said. "And the dog interviews need to be in the morning. During the week. Hank needs to meet the owners and managers. They need to make sure he's a good fit. I can't show up to work late because of a fucking dog interview."

"When do I ever do anything for my birthday? I'm finally doing something a little out there, and you're not gonna show?"

I took a tiny sip of my booze.

"It's not like that."

"You better be there."

"I'll do my best."

The door knocked, and Leah entered The Palace.

"I feel like such an asshole," she said.

"Girl, you know I'm always late," Summer said.

Leah gave me a quick hug.

"Where's that handsome boyfriend of yours?" she asked.

"Big Bear," Summer said. "Another weekend snowboarding with the boys."

Summer made Leah a cocktail.

"Be careful," I told Leah. "Summer is a little heavy-handed."

"How about a thank-you for the drink?" Summer asked.

"Yeah. Jerk."

Leah pointed at the bag of edibles on the table.

"What are those?"

"My medicine." I reached in and grabbed four of the weed fruit strips and shoved them all in my mouth at once. "I'm very sick."

She laughed.

Perfect.

* * *

We all climbed into the back seat of a black compact car when it arrived. The driver watched Summer and Leah through his rearview mirror for an uncomfortable few seconds before looking ahead at the road. He jerked the wheel every time he switched lanes.

I dry-heaved as soon as I got out of the car.

I'm not sure why I shoved all that weed in my mouth.

To be funny.

Good one, Wyatt.

Mature.

We entered a fancy white lobby and took an elevator to a rooftop bar. When the elevator doors opened, we stumbled into a swanky place, way too swanky for my liking. Fire lamps and a marble bar. Everyone dressed like they were important. Even the bartenders wore bow ties.

Leah and Summer ordered red wine. I asked for a fourteen-dollar beer. The cheapest. My mouth was dry. I drank half the beer in one gulp.

The world shook.

I leaned against the bar.

Leah and Summer disappeared.

I heard them laughing behind me.

I'd fall to the ground if I let go of the bar.

A young, clean-shaven male bartender approached me.

"Need a drink?"

"Water," I said.

He rolled his eyes and handed me a four-ounce cup. I asked for more water. He ignored me and walked to another customer. The world was a blur of lights and loud noises. The skyline looked like one giant lightbulb. It twirled in the darkness.

The moon danced.

Leah grabbed my arm.

"You okay?"

"I can see your pupils dilate every time you breathe."

"You're so fucking high!"

Too many drugs.

The world knew it now.

Exposed in public.

By Leah.

Judging eyes all around me.

Shame.

"I'm going to puke," I said.

Leah rubbed my back.

"Will I see you back at Summer's?"

"If I don't die."

My stomach bubbled.

I held back an uprising of vomit.

Summer handed me a key.

I don't know where she came from.

Was she there the whole time?

"Text me when you get home," Summer said.

My arms sank.

My legs?

Rubber.

I texted for a car and hobbled to the lobby. I said a few prayers asking for a smooth, quiet ride back to The Palace.

My driver showed up as I arrived on the street. I sat in the back seat, gripping my knees.

"Where you from? California, or are you visiting?" the wrinkly man asked.

Has anyone actually ever had a prayer answered?

"Moved from Jersey," I muttered.

"Jersey?"

I swallowed some vomit.

Some escaped my mouth.

It slid down my chin.

"New Jersey," I said.

"Ah. Cool, man. Like Jersey Shore?"

Fuck off and let me die.

"Exactly."

He peered back into his rearview mirror.

"Are you okay?"

Puking was certainly in my future.

"Just a pounding headache."

"You're not going to puke, are you?"

"Not if you quiet down."

The city streets whizzed by.

I shut my eyes.

"San Diego truly is beautiful," he said after a minute of silence. This fucking guy.

When we finally made it back to The Palace, I placed one leg out of the car. Then the other. I used my hands to lift off the seat. I tripped on the curb. And fell right into a tree. The force caused me to hurl. I wrapped my arms around the tree's trunk. A red, blue, and orange mixture of some sort fell from my mouth. I looked toward the top of the tree when I finished unloading.

It was a palm.

I took a deep breath with every step toward The Palace. The walls helped me keep my balance inside. Especially on the stairs. I couldn't handle another elevator ride. Unless I wanted to puke some more.

I opened The Palace door.

The floor caught my face.

Hank licked some vomit from my beard.

The sick bastard.

I wiped the remaining puke with my sleeve.

I crawled toward my room.

My elbows helped me lift onto the bed.

Hank joined me.

I stared at the ceiling.

My left foot went to the floor to balance the world.

* * *

Hank's tail slammed against my leg and the bed. A few voices entered The Palace. I wasn't sure how long I had been lying in bed. Time is nothing but a construct made by man. At least when I'm too stoned.

"I'm gonna check on him," Leah said.

"Fucker didn't text me when he got back," Summer said.

"You think he'll want to party with us?" a booming male's voice said.

"We got plenty of coke to go around," a second man said.

He sounded nerdy.

My door creaked open.

"You alive?" Leah asked.

Leah sat on the bed beside me. She pushed Hank aside when he tried to sniff her.

"I thought it was romantic the way you shoved a whole bunch of drugs into your mouth," she said.

Say something witty.

My throat closed.

Say something.

My brain had no words.

Say anything.

Anything at all.

Make a noise.

My mouth refused to open.

I lifted my lips to smile.

My face moved, but not in a way I could control.

Whatever I did, it wasn't attractive.

I could feel that.

"You're so fucking high." She kissed me on the cheek before standing up. "If you come back to this reality, I'll be here late."

Leah closed the door behind her.

Hank whined.

They laughed in the other room.

Dishes clanked.

Cards slammed.

"Who wants to start?" Summer asked.

Someone sniffed.

"Holy fuck," Leah said. "That's some good stuff."

The snorts grew louder.

My eyes closed.

Here I was finally in California.

Blowing everything.

Go Birds

March 7, 2019

This meeting was about the last meeting, which Chuck called a pre-meeting. It took place after a team huddle, which was about the upcoming pre-meeting.

Instead of taking notes during the third discussion of the day about the same project, I wrote what was on my mind.

I feel so un-American for not enjoying Bob Dylan. I like some of his stuff, but I don't get most of it. I tried listening sober. It's trash. I tried listening with various types of booze. Still couldn't connect. I need to try listening on drugs.

Or with Leah.

If I ever saw her again.

"Is there anything else to add to the agenda?" Chuck asked.

Work was a constant interruption to my productivity.

Words came out of my mouth.

I'm not sure what they were or why I said them.

But they worked.

"You're right," Chuck said. "We didn't want to miss that. That's a great catch, Wyatt."

I doodled for another half hour, pretending to capture everything Chuck rambled about. Leah stayed on my mind.

Working sixty hours a week, and Leah doing the same, plus college classes, we could never find the time to get together.

"One more thing before we wrap up the day," Chuck said. "Give me a second to set everything up."

He went back to his office and came back with his laptop.

"One moment to boot up," he said.

We waited.

"And now for that secret project I've been teasing everyone about," Chuck said.

He fumbled on his laptop, trying to get his screen to appear on the brand-new eighty-inch mounted television. No matter which cords he pulled, he couldn't get what he was dying to reveal on the TV screen.

"You good with this stuff?" Chuck asked.

"If I was, I wouldn't be a writer," I said.

Chuck rolled his eyes.

Trish helped switch some cords, and within seconds, Chuck's laptop screen showed on one of the TVs.

"There it is!" Chuck showcased a spreadsheet to his staff. "The future of Reynolds Incorporated."

The idea sucked.

He'd provide a list of standard blog topics and content advice to targeted businesses. If someone wanted the list and content advice, they had to fill out an online form that asked for a full name, job title, email address, and business industry. Guess who got all that contact information?

Chuck Reynolds.

"Can anyone tell me what this is?" Chuck asked. "Wyatt isn't allowed to take part. He has insider information."

Chuck meant the time I spent writing his master plan. The future of his company took me two hours to create. That's why I knew it sucked.

"New business clients?" Trish asked.

"You've got it," Chuck said. "This is how we secured CJ Pharma, through this sales cycle," Chuck said. "Here's how it works . . ."

Chuck continued to talk, looking for encouragement and recognition for his stupid fucking spreadsheet idea.

I watched five o'clock come and go.

Then six came and went.

Before the meeting ended, my phone buzzed.

It was Leah with a text.

Going to a brewery by my place tonight. Come thru.

The meeting ended after seven.

I rushed home to feed and walk Hank before catching a ride to meet Leah.

* * *

I was still wearing my clown costume when I showed up at a new Hawaiian-themed brewery. Leah sat on a stool on the roof-deck in a long red sundress.

"You're late," Leah said.

I pulled her close.

"It's nice to see you again."

"Dig the outfit." Leah ducked down and peeked behind me at my ass. "That's a dad butt. Dockers confirmed."

I pulled up a stool and ordered two hazy IPAs.

"I've been too busy to enjoy anything," Leah said.

"Work has been killing me," I said. "I rarely have time to do anything. And when I do, I'm too fucking tired."

"Sounds like hell." Leah laughed. "The last time I went out was that night you got too high."

"My proudest moment. For sure."

Leah put her hand on mine.

"Are still happy you moved to California?"

"I am now," I said.

The bartender gave us cold glasses of beer.

I signed the tab.

"Meet any interesting California girls?" Leah asked.

"There's one I think I like."

"Be careful," she said. "California women are trouble."

"That's not a bad thing. It makes life interesting."

Leah and I picked up right where we left off. We talked about nothing, but it was everything. Before our second round of brew, Leah jumped out of her chair and screamed. She grabbed a redheaded woman standing next to her. The woman laughed and hugged Leah. The two talked for a bit before Leah introduced the mystery woman.

"This is my friend Paige."

Paige had long fiery hair and intense green eyes.

I stuck out my hand.

"Wyatt."

Paige looked down at my hand.

"So formal," she said. "I should have expected that from a man in khakis." She did a slight bow and shook my hand vigorously. "Paige. It's real swell to meet you."

I hate business attire.

"She's from Philly," Leah said. "I don't know why I didn't think to introduce you two before."

Philly.

Hearing the word made me smile.

"Where about?" I asked.

"South Philly, you?"

"Jersey," I said. "But go Birds."

"Go Birds," Paige said.

"What the hell was that?" Leah asked.

"It's hello," I said.

"For cool people," Paige said.

Leah flailed her credit card at the male bartender.

"Did you go home for the parade?" I asked.

"That's a touchy subject."

"What parade?" Leah asked. "Hold on. I need beer. Bartender!"

"How can the Birds winning the big one be a touchy subject?" I asked. "Did I cry? Yeah. But was it the drunkest I'd ever been? No question."

"Same, dude."

"Football. The Super Bowl. I get it," Leah said. "Hey! Three hazy IPAs, please!"

"We tried to stay in Philly for the parade, but when they delayed it, we couldn't wait any longer. We had to leave."

"We?" I asked.

"Oh. My ex."

I paid for the beers and handed one to Paige.

"Sorry for your loss."

"It was a gain if anything," she said.

The three of us drank a round of beers. Paige and Leah gossiped about work and the people they worked with. I enjoyed the view.

"I have some drugs back at the apartment, if you want to keep the night going," Leah said.

"Happy or sad drugs?" Paige asked.

Leah signed her bill.

"You know me."

"Both," Paige said.

"It's a work night," I said. "Probably a bad idea to get twisted."
Paige swallowed her beer.

"The best things rarely are."

"What?" I asked.

"Life's short," Paige said. "The best things in life are never good ideas. Let's go have some fun. Unless you have khakis to iron or something."

* * *

Paige and I found our way onto Leah's couch. Leah disappeared into her bedroom.

"Let's get drunk sometime," Paige said. "I need someone to watch the Birds with."

"I'm a nut about the Eagles," I said.

"If you weren't, we'd have a problem."

We exchanged numbers before Leah rejoined us, carrying a shoebox full of drugs.

"I have some mushrooms, Oxy, benzos, and I'm not sure what these pills are," Leah said.

She picked out one of the pills she didn't recognize and offered me a pinch of magic mushrooms. Paige grabbed a handful. Leah swallowed the pill she didn't recognize.

"The mushrooms are old," Leah said. "They might not work."

They tasted like mulch.

We threw on some Bradley Cooper movie. Leah handed out a round of canned beers. Paige was in a deep text conversation. Leah fell in and out of sleep. I drank beer. Halfway through the movie, Paige went to the bathroom. The noise jerked Leah into an upright position.

"Welcome back," I said.

"She's great, isn't she?"

"Paige?"

"I met her when she was working part-time for us. I knew she was a party girl. I could sense it in her. We hit it off immediately."

"She's great."

Leah grabbed the drug box from her end table.

"You're not feeling it, yeah?"

"Who?"

"The mushrooms are kinda old. Take some more."

"What about Paige?" I asked.

Leah poured the remaining mushrooms into my hand.

It wasn't much for me to finish.

"I don't have enough for all of us," Leah said.

The bottom bit of mushrooms somehow tasted worse. I swallowed some beer to rid the dirt flavor. I grabbed three more beers from the fridge, gave one to Leah, and sat down on the couch.

Paige shut the bathroom door and stood near the kitchen.

"I gotta go," she said.

"Why?" Leah asked.

"He wants to come over."

"Him?"

Paige looked away.

"Maybe."

"He'll never leave her," Leah said. "They never do."

Leah's eyes were the brightest ocean blue I had ever seen.

Her yellow hair glowed in the dark room.

"He just had a kid," Paige said. "He was going to leave, but he couldn't do it with her pregnant."

"She was pregnant?" Leah asked. "You little slut."

They laughed.

"He didn't know she was when we started talking," Paige said.

"Or so he says," Leah said. "Be safe, yeah?"

Paige deserved more than that.

"My ride's here," Paige said.

"You deserve more than a part-time boyfriend," I said.

Paige smiled.

"You're sweet."

It was nice to know my mouth still worked.

The mushrooms convinced me it didn't.

Paige closed the door gently when she left.

Leah rose from the couch and walked to the kitchen. She didn't bother to turn on the lights.

"I'm going to make us some food. Mac and cheese work for you, yeah?"

I paused the movie.

"Sounds great."

Leah returned to the couch while she waited for the water to boil. I turned the movie back on. Leah seemed mesmerized. She got up to check the water on the stove. Again. She came back with another beer. Leah continued to leave the couch to check the stove. She never came back with mac and cheese.

"I'll check it," I said after a half hour of Leah getting up and down.

I went to the dark kitchen.

Inside a pot on the stove was room-temperature water with noodles. Leah never turned on the stove.

I turned around to tease her, but she was curled up on the couch fast asleep. I tossed the uncooked food into the trash and scrubbed the pot clean. I covered Leah in a blanket before calling a ride back to my apartment.

Teeny-Weeny Thong Bikini
March 14, 2019

Chuck was rambling about synergy and team chemistry in one of his all-hands meetings, which caused his staff to fall behind on our client work. Another weekend in the office was quickly approaching.

My phone buzzed.

I masterfully removed it from my pocket and checked it under the table.

Leah.

Ditch work. I'm on the beach. I have wine.

How could I get out of work?

Sickness.

I pretended like I was about to vomit.

With my mouth covered, I ran out of the conference room, into the floor's shared bathroom, and into a stall.

Chuck came into the bathroom to check up on me.

"You alright?" he asked.

I shoved two fingers down my throat and yakked into the toilet. It was the first time I ever forced myself to puke.

California can change a man.

"Um ... get your stuff when you're finished," Chuck said. "Feel better."

Chuck scurried out of the bathroom.

I cleaned my face, pretended I was sick as I gathered my things in the office, and left for the beach.

* * *

Salty air and suntan lotion. Some people can't stand the smell of either, but for me the scents meant one thing. The beach. In California, it was no different.

But some things felt foreign.

Washboard abs shamed me in every direction.

Even the curvy women had flat stomachs.

I felt like a fucking whale.

But worst of all were the women's swimsuits.

They were as thick as dental floss.

Itsy-bitsy, teeny-weeny thong bikinis.

Everywhere.

The stockpile of freed California ass cheeks overwhelmed my suppressed East Coast mind.

Leah wore a black-one piece and had a cooler full of booze next to her blanket. She poured me a plastic cup of wine before I sat down.

"Meet any California girls yet?" Leah asked.

"There's one I'm kind of interested in," I said.

Leah and I cheered our drinks.

"She better not be me. I'm not ready for that."

I took off my dress shirt, loafers, and socks. It felt weird to sit on the beach in khakis.

"She might be you, Leah."

"Why didn't you ever go after Summer?" Leah asked.

"Summer?"

Leah lathered up with tanning oil.

"Never pursued her again after middle school?"

"I've seen Summer at her worst," I said. "And any fool who thinks he can change a woman deserves what he gets."

She laughed.

"That's mean."

"Summer would say the same about me."

Leah poured me more wine.

"Are you ever going to give me anything?"

"What do you mean?"

"You're feeding me bullshit," she said.

"What do you want to know?"

"About your ex. About your family. About you and Summer. Anything. You won't open up."

I took a long drink.

She wouldn't open up either.

But I guess I'd start.

"Summer sacrificed so much for her family," I said. "She was impossible to hang out with when we were kids. She was always babysitting her siblings or working multiple jobs to help with bills. Even now. Summer flies home at a moment's notice. Over a cold or something minuscule. Sends money. Talks on the phone for hours with her parents or siblings. She's the most loyal person I've ever met. She's not afraid to be herself. Crazy and all. That's something most people can't do. Shit. I can't. Hell, Summer took a leap of faith and moved across the country. It wasn't just about love, she wanted to challenge herself. That's bad ass. I've always looked up at her. She's family. And one of the few people I trust."

"That's beautiful," she said. "But intense."

This is why I kept my mouth shut.

"That's all you're getting today," I said.

"One more thing," she said.

"Yeah?"

"What do you think of Summer and Noah?"

I smirked.

"Noah is the best boyfriend Summer's ever had. It's not even close." I laughed. "But those two are damn clones of one another. Two alphas constantly battling to get their way."

"Right? It's crazy sometimes."

"It's beautiful when it's good," I said. "And a shitshow when it's bad."

"I think the best things are that," Leah said.

My birthday was a little over a week away, and Leah planned a whole birthday itinerary for me. Brunch. Beach. Boobs. She knew me all too well.

Leah checked her phone constantly.

Every time it buzzed, she grabbed it.

She smiled after reading each text.

We drank a bottle of wine and two beers.

The sunset quickly approached.

Leah looked at her phone and practically giggled.

"I've got to go," Leah said. "I have to get some schoolwork done."

Who laughs over homework?

"It's almost sunset," I said.

Leah searched for an excuse.

"Um . . . well. I can't wait. I have too much to do."

It was a lie, but I didn't press her.

She collected her things and left the beach.
I was alone, but the sunset was still perfect.

Birthday Boobs

March 23, 2019

Mike was the first person to wish me a happy birthday. It was midnight on the East Coast, so as far as he was concerned, it was my birthday. He told me it took balls to live in the Land of the Liberals. And that he was proud of me.

My mother sent a card.

Kayla and Zane called me in the morning.

My father didn't send a card.

He didn't call.

Or even send a text.

Always out of sight, out of mind with him.

My mother knew that best.

I met Summer and Noah outside of The Palace.

We walked through the city looking for a good brunch spot. That meant a restaurant without a wait. Summer and I made fun of the Californians wearing sweaters and jackets. Even Noah had pants on.

"Soft-ass Californians," Summer said. "One day in the fifties and suddenly it's winter coats."

The two of us were in shorts and T-shirts, proudly displaying our weather toughness for all of San Diego to see. We found the only joint that didn't have a wait to be seated.

Summer ordered a bottomless mimosa.

"Do you have Screwball?" Noah asked our waitress.

"Screwball?" I asked.

"It's a peanut butter whiskey," the waitress said. "It's made here in San Diego. And yes, we have it." "Can you mix it in a coffee?" Noah asked.

"I can't do that, but I can bring you coffee and a shot of the whiskey. How you choose to take your coffee is up to you. This is America, after all."

She left to fetch our booze.

"Where do you hear of this stuff?" I asked.

"Work," Noah said.

"You never fully explained what you do," I said.

"Investors hire him to look at companies, like at their expenses, profits, future projections, and all these other things I don't understand, and he basically tells the investors his recommendations on which companies are worth investing in," Summer said.

"That's a fucking job?"

"Summer is getting better at explaining it, but that's not exactly it," Noah said. "It's close enough. Closer than she's ever got it."

"I'm trying here!"

The waitress returned and stayed at our table as Noah and I poured our peanut butter whiskey shots into our black coffees. We stirred them up. Noah took a tiny sip. I blew on my coffee before trying the drink.

"Wow," I said.

"I knew it would be good," Noah said.

We ordered breakfast and drank our booze. Summer calculated that she needed to finish three and a half drinks to break even on her bottomless mimosa purchase.

But Summer wasn't looking to break even.

"How's your family handling you being out here?" Summer asked. "It always feels weird on birthdays and holidays."

"They hate it."

"I bet." Summer finished her fourth mimosa. "Do they call you all the time? My mom calls all the time."

"Not really. The time difference just makes it hard. By the time I'm home, walk Hank, and eat, they're asleep. Or headed to bed."

"It's not easy out here," Summer said. "I told you."

It made things easier for me, but I didn't say that.

"You miserable East Coasters," Noah said. "As long as everyone suffers together, it'll be okay."

I took a sip of my water through my straw. Before I could swallow, I had to spit out some pieces of paper that flaked off.

"But at least we have actual straws there."

Summer laughed.

"I still can't believe you're out here."

I used a finger and my thumb to grab a piece of paper stuck to my tongue.

"It feels like a dream."

My phone buzzed in my pocket.

Leah.

"Look at that smile," Summer said. "It's gotta be Leah."

I answered the video call.

Leah's hair fell out of her black sun hat toward her white bikini.

"Happy birthday, boo," she said.

"Wish you were here."

"Since I'm not there—"

Leah pulled down her suit top and revealed her California treasures. Round nipples that were the perfect shade. I drooled a stupid smile at the biggest tits I'd ever seen. Hopefully, I wasn't drunk enough to forget the view.

A man's voice interrupted.

"What are you doing?"

"Gotta go," Leah said.

Click.

The fuck.

Who was that guy?

Where was Leah?

Was she with a guy?

Is that why she wasn't hanging out?

"What happened?" Summer asked.

I closed my eyes.

Don't worry.

Think about Leah's boobs.

I smiled.

"Boobs," I said.

"Get the fuck out of here," Summer said.

"She flashed me."

"How were they?" Noah asked.

Summer murdered Noah with her eyes.

"I'm just glad a woman's chest still makes me this happy."

It was all rather juvenile.

But it's the little things, right?

Well, in this case, the biggest things.

"What are we going to do with you?" Summer asked.

I finished my spiked coffee.

"Order another round," I said.

The abruptness of the call bothered me.

Who was that guy with Leah?

"I told you what she did on my birthday, right?" Summer asked.

"No."

"When we met up at the hotel before going out, Leah handed me a bag of coke and said happy birthday," Summer said. "I pulled a bag with some molly and handed it to her. We both got each other our favorite drugs. We started cracking up."

"White girls," Noah said.

The whole thing seemed romantic to me.

"You missed out. The rest of us made a shit ton of memories that I don't remember. Thank god for pictures."

"Summer was hungover for a week," Noah said.

"This is thirty," Summer said.

"Thirty-one," Noah said.

"Can't you just let me have a moment?"

"I'm sorry I missed it," I said.

"Leah looked so hot," Summer said.

"I saw the pictures."

Hot wasn't a strong enough word.

We drank and ate. By the time brunch ended, Summer finished six mimosas and a whiskey coffee. It was a lot of booze, especially considering the size of Summer's mimosa glass.

"Julian wants to meet up in PB," Noah said. "Want to go?"

"If we're going to PB, I'm going to need some drugs."

"You don't need them," Noah said.

I clenched the bottom of my chair with both hands.

"I need them to keep up with you. I'm not in college anymore. All we do is snowboard or get drunk on the weekends? Or no. We could go to fucking Pacific Beach with the college babes and get drunk. I fucking can't do that without drugs. I'm too old."

My grip tightened on the wood.

Noah struggled to find his words.

"Well. No. Look—"

"If this is what the rest of your life looks like, I'm fucking out, dude," Summer said.

"It's not like that," Noah said. "You're drunk."

"It's always like this. Every fucking weekend."

Summer grabbed her purse and stormed out of the joint.

Noah called the waitress over for the check.

I pulled out my wallet.

"I got this. You get the next one."

"She's been drinking a lot," Noah said. "Way more than usual. I don't know if it's me. Her job. Or what. Has she mentioned anything?"

Marriage.

Family.

The white picket fence.

"I know she wants to start a family."

"I'm not good with this stuff," he said.

"What do you mean?"

"I want that, too."

"Tell her."

"I can't just tell her."

"Sure, you can," I said. "Just talk to her."

"Sorry about bailing on your birthday," Noah said. "But I have to go get her."

Noah ran after Summer.

I released my seat and chugged my water. The waitress brought me another shot.

"Happy birthday," she said. "This is on the house."

The walk home to my apartment was chilly.

I should have brought a jacket.

A Fine Piece of Art

April 11, 2019

Expensive leather furniture, fancy gadgets, and priceless art that I could never afford decorated Leah's father's penthouse. Giant paintings with gold frames. Weapons from World War II. Everything in the joint belonged in a museum. It made sense. Leah's father was a board member at some prestigious San Diego arts and culture agency. Or something. Some organization that worked to continue to cultivate arts to ensure San Diego remained an international tourist destination. Whatever the hell that meant. For me, it meant I didn't want to touch a thing in the place.

The best part of the five-bedroom, three-bathroom luxury suite was the balcony. It had a folding sliding glass door that opened up the kitchen and living room. Fresh air engulfed the apartment. I stepped onto the stone balcony, which overlooked Balboa Park on the left and the city's skyline on the right. Imagine sitting there every morning, coffee in hand, writing. Every sunset sprawled out with whiskey, music, and a good woman. What else could a man want?

"Grab whatever from the fridge," Leah said. "There's a wine cooler in the island. Just don't take anything aged over twenty-five years. And grab me a beer."

She disappeared into her bedroom at her father's luxury suite. When would I have a shot at getting wine this expensive again? For free? Wines I could never afford.

No.

I avoided the wine cooler.

The kitchen fridge was the most perfectly organized thing I had ever seen. The vegetables were labeled and grouped together by color. There were ten types of alcohol. I grabbed two hazy IPAs.

Shit.

Did I move the ketchup to get them?

I walked back into Leah's bedroom as she took off her shirt. She smiled at me when she took off her pants.

"See something you like?"

In nothing but tiny, lacy black lingerie, she took one of the beers from my hand before she slid past me to the bathroom. My head followed her matching bra and panty set. Leah's cheeks were more than a handful. And tanner than any part of my body.

"I'm just a man," I said.

"That's why I'm wearing a bra and panties," she said. "If you weren't here, I'd be nude."

I cracked open my beer.

"It's hard to concentrate . . . on my words."

Leah bent over the bathroom sink, using the mirror to put the finishing touches on her eyeliner. Her ass exploded out of her thong, perked up in perfect position.

"Is it . . . hard, Wyatt?"

Leah stopped doing her makeup and gave me a seductive stare through the mirror. A sound was all I could muster.

"Oh my god! Stop. I'm cute, but I'm not hot."

"Says the California bombshell."

Leah returned to her mirror.

"You're crazy."

My eyes were glued to Leah's body.

"That'll never change."

Leah finally put on a revealing dress.

She looked like she was about to walk the red carpet of a movie premiere.

"There's going to be a lot of rich men there." Leah hiked the bottom of her skirt up a bit and pushed up her breasts. "Want to split some wine before we go, yeah?"

Leah opened the wine fridge and pulled a bottle of red out.

"You didn't check the age," I said.

"Dad said I couldn't have wine over twenty-five years, but he didn't say I couldn't have twenty-five-year-aged wine."

Semantics.

The best way to justify anything.

She poured us each a glass.

And then another.

"We have to finish it," she said.

"We have to get rid of all the evidence," I said.

After we did, Leah threw on a pair of black heels. I swung on my black velvet jacket over my black tee. As we walked toward the museum inside Balboa Park, Leah handed me three poker chips.

"Those are free-drink tickets. You're only supposed to get one per event, but my dad never uses them."

* * *

Suits, tuxedos, evening gowns, and expensive jewelry surrounded us at the museum. Talks of yachts, day-trading, and the best nonprofits to create to cheat taxes polluted my ears.

"Let's find the bar," I said.

Leah and I squeezed our way through the crowd until we found it, where we exchanged our drink tokens for complimentary cocktails. We explored the "refurbished" museum, as Leah described it, full of old European and American art and paintings. There were a ton of old artifacts too. Stuff like dioramas, religious statues, and recovered outdated caveman technology. Despite the rare collection, I couldn't take my eyes off Leah. She glided through the exhibits, getting excited at funny-looking paintings and the religious relics.

"That's my third favorite overall, but probably my favorite Victorian piece," she told one of the collection's curators.

She chatted with museum staff about certain pieces that she liked. Each painting had a plaque next to it describing details of the work. Leah read every single one. I secretly snapped photos of a rare piece she liked when the male guard whose only job was to prevent such a crime from occurring, turned away from the painting.

In the next room, there was a giant painting with four large naked women showing off their bodies.

"You can see vintage titties in this one," I yelled from across the crowded gallery room.

Dammit.

Booze will make a man forget social rules.

Leah shook her head in disgust as she approached the painting that featured a large naked woman. She examined the art. She stepped over the strategically placed line of duct tape, which prevented civilized people from getting too close to the art. Leah searched around to see if any guard saw her before she threw out her tongue, pretending to lick a nipple from the Napoleonic era.

"Take the pic," Leah said. "Hurry."

I fumbled with my phone.

"Step behind the line, ma'am," a security guard said.

I snapped a few pictures before Leah and I ran to another room.

"Another drink?" Leah asked.

And downstairs we went.

An elementary school chorus sang to the crowd in the entrance room, but everyone was talking over the kids. Except for the asshole standing in front of Leah and me.

The middle-aged man turned his head. "You want to shut up?"

Leah grabbed my hand.

"Can we get out of here?"

"All bark and no bite," I said.

He snarled at me.

The alcohol gave me stupidity.

I snarled back.

Leah whispered in my ear. "Please?"

I led Leah into a plain white room with boring art stamped on the walls. Modern art, so they say, but I've seen toddlers make more creative things. We walked around for a bit, but Leah walked around with her arms folded, not looking at anything or anyone in particular.

"Are you okay?" I asked.

"Let's . . . just get out of here."

She tossed her drink into the nearest trash can and walked ahead of me. I chased her out of the museum. Outside, an Italian singer serenaded as many people as he could with his powerfully loud ballads. I caught up to Leah as he hit his climax.

"He proposed to me today."

Leah dove into my chest and started sobbing.

"Paul?" I asked.

She didn't lift her head, but confirmed it was Paul.

I rubbed her back and held her.

"It's okay to be sad."

When Leah finally reemerged from my chest, I used my pocket square to wipe the smeared makeup from her face.

"Three years ago," she said. "Today."

"Want to talk about it?"

"No."

"What should we talk about, then?"

"We can't go back into the museum." She cleared the makeup running down her face. "Tell me about the girl you almost married."

"You're still on this?"

Leah gave me the look that got me to take molly.

"Please."

"Only if you walk with me," I said.

Gardens, a giant fountain, shops, half a dozen museums, castle-like church buildings, a massive organ, an outdoor theater, and restaurants filled the park. Leah held my hand and pointed out some of her favorite things about the place.

"Why didn't we take a stroll when we came here for the Super Bowl?" I asked.

"Because we were too fucking stoned," Leah said.

We laughed.

"I still want to know about the girl," Leah said. "I don't even know her name."

"Erin."

"Keep going."

"I'd make her coffee in the morning while she showered. I'd drop it off in the bathroom right before she was done. I tried to time it perfectly. That way I could try and convince her to have sex before work. Worst case scenario, got to see my lady naked to start my day."

"Why does that not surprise me?" Leah asked. "But that's not what I want to know."

"I just wanted to remember what she looked like naked."

Leah pulled her hand away from me.

"Wyatt."

"California," I said.

"Stop talking in riddles."

I grabbed Leah's hand.

"California ended my relationship."

"How?"

"Her parents bought her and me round-trip flights to San Diego as a birthday present," I said. "Her family knew I wanted to move to California. Or at least experience it before I died. That trip was the first time I ever went."

"What happened on the trip?"

"We stayed with Summer and Noah for a night. Erin couldn't stand Summer. The whole day and night in San Diego was a complete disaster. We rented a car and drove up to LA to visit one of Erin's friends from college for the rest of the vacation. Her friend had this little LA apartment, and Erin and I slept on the couch together. I'm sure the place cost a fortune. We did a tour of one of the movie studios. I took surfing lessons in Venice Beach. Ate at fancy restaurants and drank at the bars celebrities visited."

Leah and I made our way to a large fountain.

We sat on its edge.

"On the last night we were there, we had dinner at some fancy outdoor restaurant. Right on the beach in Malibu. The place was well known for its shrimps and scallops. Erin was highly allergic to both. Her friend's boyfriend booked the reservation, and he had no idea Erin couldn't eat that stuff." I shook my head. "You should have seen those bacon-wrapped scallops. But I couldn't have any.

"It had already been a long trip. I was mad about bailing on Summer. Tired. Hungover. Sunburned. Of course, I blamed Erin for everything. But everything changed when the sun started to set. I'm sure this sunset lit up the sky in every color imaginable. They always do in California. But my eyes weren't looking at the horizon. I watched the fading rays light up Erin's smile as the sun fell into the ocean. I'd sneak peeks back to the sun every so often, but my attention was on Erin. I tried to be sly about my staring at her, but she caught me. And when she did, she didn't say anything. She just smiled."

Leah put her head on my shoulder.

"What happened?"

I was no different than Leah's ex.

Just another ignorant and reckless man that had no idea what he had, when he had it.

"She would have made a hell of a California woman," I said.

"Why didn't she?"

"She was practical. Smart. And she loved her family. She didn't want to be far away from them. She needed them. It was actually sickening how good they were to each other."

"Then what?" Leah asked.

"I needed California," I said. "She didn't."

It wasn't a lie.

"Are you happy you moved here?"

"Life feels like a vacation," I lied.

Leah stood up.

"I'm glad you're here."

We walked past the lily pond into the House of Hospitality. That's what Leah called it. A two-story building surrounded the stone courtyard. It had an old-Spanish feel to the design. There were offices and a restaurant called Prado. In the center of the courtyard sat a fountain with just a few pennies inside.

"If we're forty and single, I'll marry you here," I said.

"I already got married here," she said. "And I already have one of those agreements, but if you're willing to compare bank statements with him, we can talk."

"You've seen my apartment."

"No, I haven't! What do you have in there that you don't want me to see?"

I didn't even know where to begin answering that question.

* * *

When we left the park, Leah took off her heels.

"Enough of that," she said.

I offered to give her my socks to protect her naked feet. She refused. She wouldn't let me carry her either.

"You heard about my heartbreak," I said. "Tell me about yours."

"Paul?"

"Yeah."

"He was angry," Leah said. "And had no impulse control."

"I know what you mean," I said.

"You?" Leah asked. "No. Paul was a monster. He didn't talk to me for a week because a beer I poured him was too warm."

"That's horrible," I said. "But child's play."

"Child's play?"

"My father thought I was an idiot. He might be right. When I was a kid, he printed out a cartoon of a man with a head shoved up his own ass. My father taped it to my bedroom door. He was sick of telling me to get my head out of my ass, which he told me at least twice a day. Now he didn't have to. Our fucking bedroom door did it for him. He'd tell me to go to my room, look at the door and come back and tell him what I learned."

"Sounds like your father didn't do any work," Leah said.

"He'd force me to say that I had my head shoved up my ass. Then he'd hit me for saying ass."

"Did you do this often?"

"I can't remember," I said. "But I know it happened more than once."

"Does it really count if you can't remember?"

I laughed.

"That's dark," I said. "Even for me."

We walked along an overpass across a major highway.

"First anniversary," Leah said. "Paul forgot to get me a gift. But whatever. I still wanted to get fucked. I mean, it was my anniversary, too. But he couldn't get it up. For hours we tried. He got so frustrated, he spat in my face and screamed, 'You stupid fucking whore.' I spent the rest of the anniversary locked in the bathtub, comforting myself with a few bottles of wine. He sat outside the door crying for forgiveness."

"Fuck. That's awful," I said. "Did you at least come?"

"Of course not," she said.

"That's the worst anniversary story I ever heard," I said. "But I think I can top it."

Leah pulled her hand away from mine.

"Really now?"

"It's no anniversary story, but it's a good one."

"Let's hear it," she said.

"After cereal and Saturday morning cartoons, my father would ask my sister and I who wanted to help him on projects around the house. Mike always enthusiastically replied in the affirmative. He loved that shit. Cars, tools, and work. Mike was my father's favorite," I said. "I never wanted to help. Who wants to help someone do work? It's Saturday. I want to have fun and play. I was a kid. I wanted to write, draw and make up stories with my action figures. My father hated that I did these things. 'Gonna go play with your dolls?' He tried to emasculate me by calling my action figures, dolls. But the worst part was that he'd call me a fag for playing with dolls."

"What the actual fuck?" Leah asked.

"That's just the tip of the iceberg," I said.

Leah grabbed my hand.

"I can't beat that."

"That's a lie," I said.

She smiled because she had more stories to tell.

"That was pretty fucked up," Leah said. "Enough reminiscing tonight. I don't know how you got that out of me."

"That's what makes now so beautiful," I said. "It's not that."

It didn't take long to get back to her father's penthouse. We stripped out of our clothes and went to her bed. I moved closer to Leah. When I went to kiss her, Leah turned her head.

"Just hold me."

Something told me this had to do with that guy from the birthday call. Not asking Leah about him may have been a mistake. I didn't want to ask now. I was afraid of the answer.

Leah turned on some music.

It was Bob Dylan.

And I hated him.

Tiki Speakeasy
April 19, 2019

The bar sat on the corner of one of the busiest roads in the Little Italy neighborhood. Summer and I ran into Noah's best friend, Julian, there. Julian wore a thin mustache and a business executive's haircut. He talked of day-trading and the best ways to get rich. And quick. It was all very smart. But mostly it was boring.

After a round of old-fashioneds, Summer, Julian, and I headed to the back corner of the joint, where a server led us through an unmarked door. We walked a few steps through a black hallway, before we arrived at the secret bar.

Wood carvings, vibrant colors, and even island music transformed the room into a tiki paradise. The ceiling was covered with huge, bright, colorful bulbs held in place by rope netting.

"San Diego was well known for its tiki scene back in the day," Julian said. "There're drinks on this menu from some of the old tiki bars that closed. It's the place's homage to the fallen bars of the past. To the history of the city."

"Wow," I said.

The information was interesting.

But useless.

"Did you know they also import some of the rarest rums in the world to this bar?" Julian asked.

He started listing them and their prices.

How did he know this?

Why did he know this?

Rum gave me the same result.

No matter where it came from.

Or how much it cost.

Taste was a luxury I couldn't afford.

I ordered the cheapest drink on the menu.

Twenty-two bucks.

Gone.

The cocktails came in brown tiki mugs that had an old tribalistic god's face carved into it. Fruits and fancy umbrellas decorated the tops of the colorful booze.

"Everything seems so perfect out here. Minus the price gouging," I said.

"Taxes suck. Rent is a little out of control, but you know what they say," Julian said.

"What's that?"

"The sunshine tax is always worth it."

"I don't know about that," Summer said.

"The biggest issue is that there's way too many beautiful women," Julian said.

Julian and I hit our expensive drinks together.

"We're not doing this here," Summer said.

"What do you think of the scooters?" Julian asked.

"They're a gift from God," I said. "I save so much money."

"Well, I know how to profit off them," Julian said.

Summer shook her head in disgust.

"How?" I asked.

"My buddy, he rents a moving truck. He drives through the city, and we load up on these scooters. Plug them into outlets at his house and charge them. The scooter companies pay per scooter charged. Five of us split the scooter money after paying for gas, a portion of the head guy's electric bill, and the moving truck rental."

It sounded shady.

"Oh," I said.

"It's been good money so far, man," he said. "You won't want to miss out on this."

"He tried charging some scooters at my place," Summer said. "I wasn't having that."

We bullshitted a bit more.

Julian finished his cocktail.

"We should go out some time," he said. "Meet some ladies."

With things with Leah going nowhere, I took Julian's number. He left to meet up with a coworker.

"I can't stand that guy," Summer said.

"He seemed nice."

"Because you have a dick. I don't know why Noah even hangs out with him," she said. "Fuck. Let's move on. What's going on with you and Leah?"

"Not tonight," I said.

Summer didn't force the issue.

She just drank with me.

It was well over a hundred-dollar night.

Too wasted to drive, Summer made sure to stay under the speed limit as she drove home. She didn't want to risk dropping me off. More of a risk of getting caught driving tipsy, as she put it.

It was a twelve-block drive.

Twelve blocks too far, if you ask me.

But we made it.

Good Vibes Singles
April 28, 2019

J ulian told me there were over two dozen women attending a
singles mixer in Pacific Beach.

"Every day for the last two weeks, Quinn posted photos of total
baddies on the Good Vibes Singles social media pages," Julian said.
"It's all women attending the event tonight. The women are gonna
be top notch, bro."

"Quinn?" I asked.

"She's a friend of a friend," he said. "She founded Good Vibes
Singles. They're hosting the event. It's going to be a gold mine. I'm
considering investing in the company. Depending on how tonight
goes."

After a pre-event beer, Julian and I stumbled through a
CrossFit gym to an outdoor patio space. There were two corn hole
games set up next to one another. Two tents, one with a table
holding a cake and some giveaways, and the other protected a pop-
up tiki bar. There was a long table filled with pizza, a roll of red
tickets, and bowls of candy. There were a few outdoor couches and
standing tables scattered throughout the artificial grass.

Quinn handed me and Julian drink tickets for the six-hour
event. She called herself a strong, independent woman who
overcame a terrible marriage and started her own career helping
others find the love she so desperately craved.

I counted my tickets.

I'd be out of them with hours left to mingle.

Julian and I got a beer and played a game of corn hole with two
nerdy transplants from Arizona. The guys were lame, but only
because what they loved bored me.

Julian wasn't a fan, either.

"Californians hate Arizonans," Julian whispered to me.

"Why?"

We grabbed another beer.

"They drive like assholes and clog up the roadways when they invade during vacation season," Julian said.

There were beautiful women everywhere at the event. I didn't care where they were from. Some dressed California casual, jeans and a top that showed a lot of skin, while others debuted nightlife dresses and heels.

Two single California casual mothers, one with dyed red hair and the other dyed black, were looking for a drunken night out while their kids stayed home with babysitters. We politely flirted before Julian and I went to talk with another group of women. These people shot daggers at us every time we opened our mouths.

We strolled to a cluster of four women.

They weren't interested in talking to us.

Either was the next circle of women.

Or the next.

We fired down another beer.

Julian and I split up to do more damage.

I sat on a bench and chatted with a woman in a baby blue dress. It highlighted her brown eyes, dark skin, and colorless tattoos. She had two kids. Toddlers.

"Bullshit," I said. "No way you have two kids looking like you do."

Savannah scrolled through her photos showing me her son and daughter, born two years a part. We exchanged numbers. But I wasn't going to call her. She was a young mother, not even twenty-five, with two toddlers.

But that didn't bother me.

Her living an hour away from San Diego did.

I was too lazy for that.

And I wasn't ready to give up on Leah.

I headed for a slice of pizza.

"Any luck?" I asked Julian when I found him scarfing down a slice of pizza.

"They don't seem interested," he said.

"Wonder if they smell the asshole on you."

"Probably."

Julian and I used our last drink tickets. He pulled me aside before we went to approach more women.

"Where you working again?" Julian asked.

"It's called Reynolds Incorporated."

Julian didn't hide his disgust, but he didn't say anything.

"You've heard of the joint?" I asked.

"Yeah," he said. "One of my good friends owns an advertising firm in the city. She's mentioned that place. They hire a lot of good workers who leave there. She said the owner has quite the reputation."

Shit.

Maybe that's why Chuck paid to fly me to San Diego.

His reputation was tarnished in SoCal.

He needed an outsider.

I finished my beer.

Near the bar, Julian and I stood around a large group, with two women and triple the number of men. The two nerdy guys we played corn hole with were among the dejected and lonely.

"What's the deal with this?" I asked. "Anybody meeting anyone?"

"They all have boyfriends," a guy with glasses in a baggy polo and brown khaki shorts said.

He pointed out the scene.

All the women had men on their arms. Men who I hadn't seen all night. Savannah, too, had her arms wrapped around the bulging neck of a body builder.

"Quinn gets her sexiest friends to pose as singles online," a woman in our group said. "She posts their photos on Instagram. Dudes pay to meet those girls. Except those girls already have boyfriends. She makes a bunch of cash, and parties with her friends."

"For free," Julian said.

Money comes and goes.

Time just goes.

This mixer was a giant waste of both.

"This isn't the first time this has happened either," another guy said.

"Same thing happened at the last event I went to," an athletic man with an unkempt beard said.

"What a bitch," Julian said. "I can't vouch for her. Seems like a total bitch."

I shook my head.

Such a California move.

I wasn't sure why these fools would come to another event after being duped, but I was too pissed off to ask. The beautiful couples started disappearing. According to Julian, within an hour of their boyfriends arriving, most of the women Quinn highlighted online as singles cleared out of the joint. It's one thing to want to make money and party with your friends. It's an entirely different thing to lie and take advantage of people desperate for love.

With still two hours left in the singles mixer, Quinn and her friends started packing up. I looked around for something to smash. Throw some leftover pizza all over the place. I could break her expensive corn hole set.

But that wasn't enough.

And it wouldn't work.

"You're not thinking about doing something stupid, are you?" Julian asked.

The drink tickets were sitting on a table in a corner.

No one was in sight of them.

Quinn, her few remaining friends and their boyfriends drank in a corner away from the rest of us.

Laughing.

Enjoying their free party on my dime.

"Grab us another beer," I told Julian.

"I don't have any more tickets," he said.

"I'll have some soon."

I tilted my head, threw my palms face up and gave Julian my 'you don't want to know' look.

He nodded and didn't ask any more questions.

I walked to the roll of tickets sitting next to the two remaining pizza boxes. I opened one of the pizza boxes with one hand, reached my other hand to the ticket roll, and yanked as hard as I could. I ripped dozens of tickets off the roll and stuffed them in my back pocket.

I met Julian at the bar and ripped two tickets from my ass. I ordered an extra beer for each of us. I kept a handful of tickets for Julian and me and gave the rest to the group. Julian, me, and the remaining loners drank. And drank. The plan was to drink all of her booze before the mixer ended. Hit her where it hurt. Bankrupt the bitch.

With an hour left, the few of us who weren't in on the scam had tickets for drinks, but there was no booze left. We all stood around the bar waving what we pretended were our last tickets.

"We paid for four drinks. I've only gotten two!" I shouted.

"I'll run out and get more," Quinn said.

She sent one of the fit, tall, tatted and tan boyfriends to the liquor store across the street for a thirty pack of light beer. He gave them to the bartender when he returned.

Quinn apologized and offered everyone' a ticket to a future Good Vibes Single event.

No one accepted.

"How about a drink ticket instead?" Julian asked.

I knew I liked the guy.

I used my last two tickets and shoved two beers in my back pockets. Julian did the same. We walked a few blocks to the beach. It was dark, but we sat in the sand and enjoyed our brew. It was a small victory. But I had to take what I could get in California.

The Pregnant Homeless Runaway
May 5, 2019

I pretended not to hear Hank. He crawled to my face. I squeezed my eyes shut. He nudged me with his nose. I'd throw up if I moved. Hank slathered me with his tongue in an attempt to drown me. I scratched Hank's back and got out of bed.

I sparked a half-smoked bowl and chugged a water bottle. I waited a minute. I packed more weed into the bowl and took a rather large hit. My throat burst into a fit. Coughing meant I'd be really high. Which could only help me forget about my debilitating headache. And the fact that the woman I chased to California was probably fucking someone else.

I took another hit.

I threw a leash on Hank and left my place in what I wore last night. Jimmy, one of the recovering crack addicts who lived next door, struck up a chat with me on my way to the dog park. He wore one of his standard dirty white T-shirts, torn jeans, and beat-to-hell boots. He smoked a pack of cancer sticks a day, which was obvious when he spoke.

"And that's when I says, 'I'm not clocking in. You can't violate my rights like that.' I never went back. I got paid for the day, though."

Hank loved the way Jimmy scratched him.

I endured his rants in exchange.

Hank and I walked towards the rich neighborhood that had luxury apartments, fancy restaurants, and a dog park. But as we passed a horrid-smelling trash can a block from the dog park. I folded in half, clutched my stomach, and threw up all over the side of the street. A decent pile of yellow vomit and colorful chunks lay on next to the curb.

What did I eat last night?

What were those chunks?

I'd be damned.

I couldn't figure out what the fuck it was.

"Ugh. What's wrong with you?"

"Ewww!"

The Sunday dinner crowd made aggressive sounds of disgust as they hurried by me.

I imagined some rich housewife would peek down from her penthouse window, speed-dialing 9-1-1: "Someone puked outside my home! We don't tolerate that type of behavior on Front Street. He's a hooligan. Oh my God! He's getting closer to it. Arrest him!"

If I were in Jersey, I could have paid a homeless guy five bucks for each correct thing he named in my puke. But these fuckin' California snobs. Here I was, staring at my own puke and damning the Californians like a self-righteous ass. If I didn't move soon, someone would call the cops. I was high and possibly still drunk. Not ideal for a conversation with an officer of the law.

* * *

By the time I made it to the dog park, sweat leaked down my back. I slouched on a bench away from the world. It was getting dark out, which meant that civilized people weren't out. I couldn't handle engaging in California dog park small talk, anyway. I sagged down, avoiding eye contact with dogs and their animals.

Someone approached me.

Dammit.

I didn't feel like playing nice.

I snuck a peek at her without moving my head.

Her.

She had smooth, toned legs that led right up to a short white sundress. I followed her dress up past her chest to the diamond stud that protruded from her nose.

Never mind.

I could deal with humans today.

At least this one.

"Which dog is yours?" she asked.

The recent dad-bod craze helped my cause, but she was too sexy to be sitting next to someone in my condition. Case in point, I wasn't entirely sure I cleaned the puke remains from my beard. I snuck a smell of my armpit.

Yikes.

Hannah introduced herself and sat down next to me. Her dog's name was Sir Dunk-A-Lot. It was an awesome name for a bulldog. I told her how I rescued Hank from Alabama after breaking up with my fiancée. Hannah told me how she got Sir Dunk-A-Lot from a friend's accidental litter. She was from Chicago. Hannah had more issues with the cold than me, and rightfully so. She was a big Kurt Vonnegut fan. She pretended to get mad at me when she found out I didn't read all of his works.

Hannah didn't mind my stink or didn't smell me. I forgot about my hangover, mostly. Every so often, a shooting pain would fire through my brain. I also caught a few whiffs of dog shit, which caused me to gag.

Twice.

"What brought you out here?" I asked Hannah.

"Drove from Chicago straight to California a week ago," she said. "But you don't want to hear my sob story."

"Sure I do."

I did not.

Hannah paused before she spoke.

"I don't want to kill the mood."

"You want a sob story? Met the love of my life. Blew it. Because I'm a piece of shit. Got a terrible job out here. Left the East Coast. Fell for a California girl. Haven't seen her in weeks. And that job I told you about? That's somehow worse than my love life."

Brutal honesty scares most people off.

But not Hannah.

She pointed at our dogs a few feet away from our bench.

"At least our dogs are friends."

Oh shit.

Hank.

Right.

I was at the dog park.

Forgot about the little guy for a second there.

"Now you have to tell me your sob story," I said.

"Are you sure?"

"I'm too hungover to beg."

Hannah put her hair behind her ears. "Well, my boyfriend broke up with me before I could tell him I was pregnant."

Everyone always had better stories than me.

But I wasn't sure I wanted to hear this one.

"Well, that's brutal."

"He was cheating on me. The whole time we were together. Got the other girl pregnant. Bought her a ring. They're getting married in September. He never told her about me. He told me to take care of our problem. That's what he called her. Our problem. I asked my parents what to do. They told me to get an abortion. They even offered to pay. I thought about . . . you know . . . taking care of it. But it felt wrong."

This was not how I thought this was going to go.

"What did you do?" I asked.

"I packed my things and headed west. I didn't know what was right. You know? My first night driving, I tried to make it to a rest stop, but I pushed too far. I didn't want to double back, but I couldn't go any further. I found a perfect spot to sleep. It was on a quiet road in the middle of nowhere. You should have seen the stars. I'd never seen so many in my life. I fell asleep smiling. I can still see them still when I close my eyes. And that night, I saw God in my dreams. He told me to keep the baby."

"Jesus Christ," I said.

"I told my family. They told me not to come home."

"What? Why?"

"Their child having a child out of wedlock would make them look bad."

"Aren't they the Jesus types?" Hannah glared at me. "I mean, the religious types. Catholics."

"Devout."

"I haven't read the good book in a bit, but I'd argue that killing an unborn child would piss off Jesus even more than having a child out of wedlock."

"Getting away from them is what's best for me. And my family."

She rubbed her flat stomach.

The world hit differently when I was hungover. I could treat everyone as shitty as I felt, or I could show some compassion and hope the world would do the same.

"Your baby is lucky to have you."

"My little princess, Hope."

It was too cliché not to be beautiful.

And too outrageous to be fake.

"Are you alone out here?" I asked.

"A couple people I grew up with moved out here. Anyone who escapes Ford Heights moves to San Diego. It's like a tradition."

"You have a place to stay?"

"Some nights. I sleep in my car sometimes. Don't want to be a mooch."

I hated it.

"What about work?" I asked.

"I've been doing Postmates for cash. I had a few waitressing interviews too," she said. "I should hear back from one today or tomorrow."

Hank flopped down in front of me, panting like a maniac. Between the blazing sun beating down on me and Hannah's story making me feel worse. I needed an excuse to leave.

"Listen, Hank is dying here. I have to get him home. Is there anything I can do to help?"

"I could use a place to stay," she said. "Kidding. I appreciate you talking to me. It can get a little lonely out here."

"Don't I know it."

Hannah rose to her feet.

"I guess I'll be going too."

"I can walk you home," I said.

"I can manage."

"I insist. I could use a few more minutes to sweat out my hangover."

Guilt and curiosity led me to Hannah's beat-up, silver four-door hunk of shit from the late nineties. Two hubcaps were missing. It had its fair share of dents and scratches. The trunk wasn't closed properly. A struggling rope barely held it shut. The back seat was stuffed with boxes. The front seat was empty, but the floor held two plastic containers with baby clothes and toys bursting out of them.

I pulled out my wallet and gathered what cash I had.

"I have, like, sixty bucks," I said.

"I'm fine," she said.

"I can send you some more."

"You don't have to," she said.

Hannah took the cash.

"Are you living in your car?" I asked.

"Not every night," she said. "Tonight, yeah. A car night."

I should have "sucker" tattooed on my forehead. I didn't like the idea of a stranger, no matter how homeless, desperate, pregnant, or beautiful, being at my place without me there.

But I couldn't just leave a homeless, desperate, pregnant beautiful woman on the streets, either.

Curse my fucking luck.

"I have to get to bed early for work tomorrow. But maybe we can hang out this week. You could stay over," I said.

"I'll clean the place. Cook. Walk the dogs. Take care of them." She paused. "Take care of you."

Hannah could help cure my loneliness.

I had nothing valuable she could steal.

Besides Hank.

"Uh," I muttered.

"You won't even notice I'm there," Hannah said.

What if she was a con artist?

What if she was really alone?

Or tried to kill me in my sleep?

What if she texts her accomplices, gets them into my place, robs me? What if I smoked too much weed and now I'm paranoid?

Stop watching serial killer documentaries.

Smoke less weed.

Idiot.

"It's a small place," I said. "A studio. I don't know if we'd all fit."

"I'll sleep on the couch, if you want." Hannah rubbed my arm. "But I'd rather sleep with you."

This seemed like a great idea.

Wait.

Was I really considering letting someone I knew for less than two hours stay at my new apartment solely because she was attractive and insinuated sex? If it were a guy that approached me at the park, I would have ignored him from the get-go.

Stop.

She was pregnant and alone.

I imagined she'd do anything to keep her and her baby safe. Allegedly.

"Let's hang out tomorrow," I said. "If things go well, you can stay over."

I was too hungover to think.

"Okay. I'd like that."

I sent her a hundred dollars from my phone when we exchanged numbers. It was enough to quell my guilt.

"I have to take this." Hannah pulled her phone from her purse. "It's a friend. Might be a job. I'll call you sometime."

I didn't hear the phone ring.

We waved a silent goodbye.

The whole thing left a bad taste in my mouth.

Just like California did.

Five Days of Drunken Debauchery Before a Business Trip

May 13, 2019

Chuck called me into his office.

"Great news," Chuck said. "We're going to Boston."

He didn't ask.

"When?"

"Monday."

One week's notice for a business trip.

Great.

"I'll have to see if I can get someone to watch my dog," I said.

"You have to be there. Jessica doesn't have the hours. Gary can't leave his kids. Trish is too junior." Chuck paused. "And between us, she's not well versed in the new venture."

I knew Summer and Noah would watch Hank. They minded, but they were good to me. Chuck wasn't.

"I'll make arrangements," I said. "What's the date of the trip?"

"Next Monday and Tuesday," he said. "The twentieth and twenty-first."

The business trip was the day after Radek's San Diego vacation ended. The timing wasn't ideal. In fact, it was horrible. A long weekend with a guy we called "The Hammer" in college, meant I needed more than a night's rest to recover. I factored in a week of sitting at my desk to repair my organs. Potentially a sick day. Or four.

I promised myself to show Radek a good time, but I wouldn't get too crazy.

May 15, 2019

I picked up Radek from the airport a little after dinnertime. I took him to where everyone should go after arriving on the West Coast. I told him to forget the Double-Double and order the 3x3 from In-N-Out's secret menu. After a twenty-minute wait, Radek ate everything in four bites. He got back in line and ordered another combo meal. I held our table for his return.

"How's Cali treating you?" Radek asked between chomps.

"California. The locals know you're a tourist when you call it Cali."

"You're really turning into one of them."

"Maybe I always was."

Radek slathered his fries in ketchup.

Murdering the fry flavor.

"How's work?" he asked.

"My boss is such a prick."

Radek shook his head.

"Do you cause trouble everywhere you go?"

"This one isn't even my fault."

Radek dipped his dripping red fries in burger sauce.

"You don't want to be jobless out here."

"It's not a bad place to be homeless," I said.

"You apply for other jobs?"

"Nope," I said. "I get a nine-thousand-dollar bonus after ten months. Once I get that, I'll quit."

Radek devoured his second burger, and we headed to my apartment. Radek wrestled with Hank for a bit. The tour of my shithole took only a minute.

"At least it's in California," Radek said.

We spent the night drinking too many beers at a bar a few blocks from my place. It was exactly what I needed.

May 16, 2019

I had six cups of coffee at work. The entire day was a haze of pointless meetings prepping for our Boston trip. Chuck was nervous. He screamed at me to relieve his pressure. Today, it was my fault that there was a paper jam in the office printer. The office printer that I never touched.

After the longest day of work, Radek and I walked downtown to check out a Major League Baseball game. We spent most of the night exploring the stadium. There were shops, bars, restaurants, craft brewery pop-ups . . . fuck. Just about anything and everything one could buy had its own store. It was a baseball field surrounded by a giant outdoor mall. The capitalists called it an experience, but it was really a tourist trap.

Radek and I found a local rave club on our walk home from the game. The buzz we drank ourselves into to make baseball watchable influenced this poor decision.

The two of us stood at the bar to talk to women ordering drinks. Why be anywhere else? Everyone has to visit the bar. Even if we didn't meet anyone, at least we'd get drunk. And fast. The thing was club drinks were expensive.

No one was interested in me or Radek. Well, most women were interested in us buying them a drink, but nothing more than that. Women didn't even try to treat us like human beings. No "hello" or "how are you." No compliment. No generic questions to pass enough time to ask for a drink.

"I'm Kendall," one attractive woman in a slim black dress said. "You should buy me a drink."

"Does that line work for you?" I asked.

Kendall turned away from Radek and me.

We shimmied our way around the overcrowded, sweaty dance floor after we each dropped eighty bucks on drinks. It seemed like we drank a lot of booze, but we didn't come close to drinking what we paid for.

We did a couple of laps around the joint. Neither Radek nor I made a move on the women shaking their asses to the beat. The thought of going up to a sweaty stranger and rubbing my growing crotch rhythmically on her ass without saying a word kinda repulsed me.

We took one last round of shots before we left.

Twenty-seven bucks each.

Clubs were the fucking worst.

A majority of my morning at work was spent on the shitter. The stench of other men's feces as they groaned in pleasure seemed like a better alternative than sitting through a Reynolds Incorporated meeting.

At lunchtime, Radek met me at a restaurant with an ocean view. The staff made Radek put on his tank top before he entered. We walked through the joint to the outdoor seating section.

"San Diego is beautiful, but confusing," Radek said.

"Confusing?" I asked.

"All these people keep coming up to me and asking if I serve in the military."

"It's a military town. Well, city. A pretty patriotic one too."

"But why ask a stranger that?" Radek asked.

"They probably wanted to thank a service member."

"It's nice to see that sort of stuff go coast-to-coast."

"Do you know the only way to tell the difference between a military member and a cop?" I asked.

"You better watch yourself, broski."

"The beer belly."

Radek lifted his tank top to reveal nearly perfect abs.

"Get outta here with your bullshit."

"And that's why no one confused you with a cop," I said.

Radek laughed.

"Not all of us cops just eat doughnuts."

The waiter dropped off two beers at our table.

"You're not going to get in trouble for this?" Radek asked.

"Only if I get caught."

We had another beer before I forced myself back to the office. The beer helped my hangover, but it certainly didn't help inspire me to work.

To pass the time at work, I wrote some words of my own and read *Game of Thrones* series finale spoilers. People were outraged. I felt betrayed. Which was weird considering it was a TV show and not a living thing. But that's what American culture is these days. Sitting on our asses, watching TV.

After barely surviving nine meetings, Radek and I drank vodka ginger ales, his favorite, while playing my old Super Nintendo at my apartment. We ran out of vodka before we left to explore San Diego's weekend night life.

We landed at a country-themed bar in the city. The joint had a riding bull, American beer, neon signs on the wood-log walls, and a giant dance floor with a stage for a band. The bartenders and waitresses dressed as sexy cowgirls. There wasn't a male on the entire staff. Or maybe I just didn't notice.

"I got the drinks tonight," Radek said. "For letting me stay at your place for the weekend."

"Yippie ki-yay, motherfucker," I said.

The rum tasted hostile, but I still drank it.

We hit the dance floor when the sound of a country guitar came from the stage. It was a country cover band. Apparently, those exist. We sang country songs and kept drinking the funny-tasting rum. We tried to talk with a few women, but like at the club, Radek and I struck out.

We did a few shots at the bar. A short beauty in overalls with frizzy black hair stood next to me. She called herself Shelby. Radek and I followed her to the dance floor where she introduced us to her friends.

Shelby and I pulled away from the group and grinded on our own for a few songs. None of the women accepted Radek's advances, and before long, I lost track of him.

"It's too hot," Shelby said. "I'm going to get a drink."

"Want me to get it?" I asked.

"No, but you're sweet."

She left for the bar.

Radek was nowhere to be found.

I headed to the bathroom, and when I returned to the dance floor, I found Radek moving side to side with a tall strawberry blonde. I leaned against the closest bar and let him do his thing.

The band came back on for their last set.

I searched for Shelby in the sea of ass shakers.

She was gone.

Where did she go?

What happened?

How did I blow this one?

I ordered a rum and coke from the bartender.

"Bacardi work?" she asked.

"Yeah," I said. "That's fine."

That must have been why the drinks Radek bought didn't taste right. It was clear rum. The worst kind. The night got worse when the crowd cheered for the band's next song.

My wedding song.

Me and Erin's first dance at our wedding.

I remembered why I avoided this bar.

Everyone in the crowd found someone to slow dance with.

Those who knew the words belted them.

It appeared everyone knew the fucking words.

Leaving Erin was a mistake.

I finished my drink.

I ordered a beer with two shots of whiskey.

California was an utter failure.

Two shots went down quick.

Things weren't getting better, either.

But at least I was drunk.

The band played a few more songs.

I had another beer.

Radek found me leaning against the bar. He must have struck out, because he was alone.

"You good, broski?"

"Don't worry about me," I said. "Where's that girl?"

"Nothing but a tease."

Radek and I left the joint, bought two slices of cheap pizza, and walked the streets.

"What happened with that girl you were dancing with?" Radek asked.

"She disappeared."

He took a bite of his pepperoni pizza.

"It's not our night."

"It's not been my year, man. I keep fucking up."

"It's one night, broski."

I tossed some crust into a trash can on the street.

"No, it's not."

"What do you mean?" Radek asked.

My fist clenched in rage.

"I'm not good enough."

"Not good enough? What the fuck are you talking about?"

"Everything, man. I fucked up."

"What are you talking about?" Radek asked.

173

I launched my second slice of pizza into the empty street.

"My job blows. Summer is going to move to the suburbs. It's only a matter of time before she lives far away from the city. The California girl I always talked about? She's not interested in me. At least not in the way I want. I fucked up bad, dude. What the actual fuck was I thinking when I came out here?"

Radek swallowed his second slice in three bites.

"You always get yourself in and out of this shit. Why's this any different?"

"I shouldn't have ended things with Erin."

I regretted the words as soon as they slipped out.

"Did you just say Erin?" Radek asked.

"I don't know what the fuck I'm saying. I'm just so frustrated."

Radek patted my back.

"It's a rough night and too much booze."

"I shouldn't have come out here. I shouldn't have dumped her."

"Erin?"

I kicked an empty fast-food cup that was littered on the sidewalk as hard as I could. It moved an inch.

"Fuck! I never dealt with this shit. I fucked up. Really bad. You have no idea."

Radek threw an arm around my shoulder.

"You can't be yelling in the street this late."

I pushed him off.

"Not like things can get much fucking worse for me."

"You need to relax."

"Fuck that!" I yelled.

Radek grabbed me by my collar, pulling me toward his face and pressing his nose against mine.

"Don't let a few girls ruin your night, broski. I had a good time. You had a good time. Not every girl has to be the fucking one. You build this shit up in your mind. Always telling yourself a story. This perfect moment. Sometimes it's a fleeting thing. You live in fucking Cali. Enjoy this shit while you can."

He let me go and walked ahead of me.

I didn't bother to correct his use of the word Cali.

"We're talking about Erin when your ass is sober," Radek said.

Fuck.

Why couldn't I catch a break?

Why couldn't one thing go my way in California?

I tried not to think about Erin, Shelby, Leah, or how horribly wrong things were going. Nothing helped me clear my head. That's the thing about booze. Sometimes it brings out the worst in us. Maybe it was just one of those nights. Even if it wasn't, I couldn't let Radek have a bad trip.

After a few blocks of self-loathing, I jogged to Radek.

I took a deep breath.

"You smell that?" I asked.

"You fart?"

"Nah, man. You don't smell that?"

Radek sniffed the air.

"I smell nothing."

"I smell bacon."

"Fuck you, broski."

"Like a pig," I said.

He put me in a headlock until we made it back to my apartment. Thankfully, it was only two more blocks.

May 18, 2019

I t took an hour before I got out of bed to face Radek.

"Sorry about last night," I said. "I don't know what got into me."

I stared at the living room floor.

Radek sat up on the couch.

"Broski, we got to have a talk about some shit, but it's not all your fault."

"What do you mean?" I asked.

"I ordered Jack Daniel's last night. It's all they had. I didn't want that Bacardi shit."

Jack Daniel's was poison.

It turned me into a rage monster.

Always.

"You know what Jack does to me," I said.

"I forgot how you get," he said. "I was a lotta drunk."

Hank whined at the apartment door.

It was a late start to the day, and he had to pee.

"You going to make me ask or you going to tell me?" Radek asked.

"What do you mean?"

"You know what I mean."

Erin.

Right.

I connected Hank's chain to his collar.

"Just a bad night," I said.

"You smoking too much pot?"

"No more than usual," I lied.

I locked the apartment door behind me. Hank bounced excitedly down the hallway with Radek behind us.

"Why you bringing up Erin?" Radek asked.

"I don't know if I did the right thing."

It was the truth.

"You're out here now. She's moved on. You moved on."

"I never dealt with it."

"There's nothing to deal with, broski. It's over," Radek said. "Now let's forget about it and meet some Cali girls."

"California. They're California girls."

"When am I going to meet your California girl?"

"I don't have one," I said. "We're friends."

"Sounds like more of a reason to expand your horizons."

How could I say no when Radek put it like that?

* * *

The young and free of San Diego poured into the restaurant turned club. They weren't spending their Saturday night debating climate change at some lame-ass dinner party. None of them were resting from a grueling work week or conserving their energy to prepare themselves for forty-eight straight hours with their kids. They all came here to get fucked up. So did I.

The waitstaff and bouncers moved tables around the restaurant to create a makeshift dance floor. I stood on the side and leaned against an empty table, waiting for Radek, who had the bladder of a small child.

"Mind if we sit down?" a man asked before pulling a chair out for himself. He had a scraggly beard, black New York Yankees hat, and baggy white T-shirt. His name was Rich, and his wife and his wife's sister took the remaining seats at the table. The four of us made awkward small talk until Radek returned with two rum and cokes. After introductions, Radek's eyes wandered to the dance floor.

"You guys aren't like cops, right?" Rich asked.

"He must have noticed my figure," I whispered to Radek.

"Can you watch our drinks while we do some?" Rich sniffed his index finger from tip to base. "Want some? I'll save you some. We've got some good stuff."

Radek declined the offer on our behalf.

They had no idea Radek was actually a cop.

Not sure they would have cared either.

Rich and his wife's sister left to do coke while Radek and I attempted to entertain Rich's wife. She gave barely audible one-word answers to everything we asked.

After a few awkward minutes, Rich returned.

Radek talked long enough to him to be polite.

We left the table.

"Are people always so open about drugs?" Radek asked.

"Everyone does drugs," I said. "In California, nobody has any shame."

We flirted with some women. We took some shots. We danced with fewer women than we flirted with. We took some more shots. We stopped even trying to dance with women. Because all the women in the joint disappeared.

West Coast or East Coast, the Cinderella phenomenon always happened. Women vanished as the clock was about to strike midnight. Where did they go? Sleep? Mozzarella sticks? Survival instinct? A magical women-only bar? Or did Cinderella hypnotize all women who read or watched it to skedaddle from bars at midnight?

Either way, all the horny drunk men were about to realize they were in a joint full of dudes. That's usually when the fights started. And it was my cue to exit.

Radek and I walked along the beach, looking for a singles bar. We had only an hour before everything closed. The sky started spitting down on us, but we didn't think about calling it a night. We heard loud rap music and spotted a few women dancing on the bamboo roof-deck a block away.

This must be where all the women disappeared to.

Inside, the place was dead. A few stragglers. Mostly men. We climbed a flight of stairs and made our way outside to the deck. A dozen men and women moved around on dance floor. Surrounding them was double the amount of people watching the dancers.

I got shot down by two groups of women in record time.

Then it rained a little bit harder.

Almost everyone scattered.

There was only a little room under the roof overhanging the bar, so most people fled inside.

"Want to head back?" Radek asked.

"Follow me."

It wasn't a light rain.

It wasn't a downpour.

But it was enough to ruin a night outside.

For anyone.

Except the two women who danced in the rain.

"Care if we join?" I asked.

They inspected Radek and me from head to toe.

"I think this will work," the tall brunette said before reaching her hand out.

She had dark brown eyes and curly hair. My moves didn't match the music, but she danced with me. It was her last night of vacation. She and her best friend turned thirty that year and planned a trip to California. They drove down Route 66 and crossed thirty things off a trip checklist. Some rain wasn't going to ruin their last-night celebration.

Radek and I spun, twirled, and swayed with the best friends from Kansas. We were the only ones on that rain-soaked dance floor. The girls requested "Girls Just Want to Have Fun" for the last song. Radek and I watched the two dance with each other from the empty bar. Before the song ended, they pulled us back on the dance floor.

May 19, 2019

My liver shriveled up like a raisin.
I could sleep the rest of the day and still need more.
Radek wouldn't let me.
He opened my door and forced me out of bed.

I didn't bother to shower.

We got beer and a sandwich from one of the liquor stores by my place. Afterwards, I took Radek to an old warehouse that was converted into a brewery. It was on the outskirts of the city, where new high-rise apartments were being built. The joint had a giant shuffleboard table, an impressive, long oak bar that wrapped around half the place, and six silver vats brewing beer.

My phone vibrated.

Leah.

A text.

Did you find a blonde to get him to do molly and move to California? I know a girl.

I hadn't heard from her in weeks.

Radek motioned me to the bar and pulled up a stool.

"Is that the Cali chick? I see the way you're looking at your phone. She coming out?"

I texted back.

We're doing a brewery tour.

Leah responded.

Can't. Too much homework. Lots of love. Miss you.

"It doesn't look like she's going to make it," I said.

I struggled, but I added another beer to my belly.

Radek ordered us each a strong, dark brew.

My liver hated me.

Good thing I hated myself more.

"All I'm saying is that one of your best friends came out to visit and she didn't make it out once. That should tell you all you need to know," he said. "I bet you text her every day."

My silence convinced Radek he was right.

He was.

Obviously.

"Give her up, bro," he said. "I know you're still into her."

He wasn't wrong.

We drank a few more beers. I couldn't remember how many we had or how late it was, but the sunlight burned my eyes when we left the brewery.

Radek called a ride.

* * *

Our driver slammed his brakes. That's what woke me up. Radek yanked me out of the back seat. Next thing I knew, a hostess seated Radek and me in the back corner of a little restaurant. I downed two glasses of water.

"You got HBO, right?" Radek asked. "If not, I got to set up the app."

"Prepare for disappointment."

"Don't say anything, broski."

I drifted in and out of consciousness during dinner. Surprising myself with a cold sip of water every so often was the only thing keeping me awake. My body ached in places I didn't know could hurt. Why did getting drunk hurt my lower back? It made no sense. The bread and oil helped sop up the poison in my body. Radek chatted away, grinning between bites of red pasta and drinking a dark brew. I took three bites before giving up on dinner. I rushed Radek through his meal.

Back at my apartment, I showed Radek how to work the TV so he could be pissed at the *Game of Thrones* finale.

"Godspeed," I said.

"You're not going to watch?"

"I'm about to die."

Radek laughed.

"California has made you soft."

"At least you finally got the name right," I said.

"You're just a bitch-boy. It's okay."

"It's crazy how Jon Snow—"

"No spoilers, broski. I'll kill you."

I gave Radek a hug.

"I'll be back for Doug's wedding."

"Take care of yourself."

I drifted off when I found my bed.

But I didn't stay asleep long.

Somewhere between sleep and awake, Radek cried in agony.

"That's how it ends? Are you fucking kidding me!"

I let out a laugh.

That's exactly how I felt when I read the spoilers.

"Are you serious!" Radek yelled.

The sound of Radek's silent screams lulled me to sleep.

I was going to miss that guy.

Business Class

May 20, 2019

I showed up hungover to the airport. Somehow, I was just twenty minutes late. Chuck arrived forty-five minutes after me.

"Don't buy the Wi-Fi on the plane," Chuck said. "I have it, so I'll handle anything that comes in over the internet."

Good morning, Chuck.

Thanks for making me show up an hour early to the airport for no reason. I didn't need that extra hour of sleep.

"I need you to finish the presentation for our meeting tomorrow," he continued.

"You got it, boss."

I was one to procrastinate, but to ask an employee to put together an entire presentation on a plane less than twenty-four hours before meeting with a client seemed not smart, considering fifty thousand dollars a month was on the line.

"I'm going to get some breakfast," he said. "Want anything?"

Chuck walked away before I could respond.

He came back to the gate with an extra-large coffee and a bagel smothered in cream cheese. He sat a few rows away from me. I knew I looked bad, but I couldn't have looked as disheveled as Chuck. He had cream cheese all over his tie with a coffee stain to match. Hard to believe he owned a business.

Anyone could make it in America.

On the plane, Chuck sat in first class. I found my row—six seats from the very back of the plane.

At least it was a window seat. I spent the flight revising and proofreading the presentation for the meeting. It wasn't my best work, but whatever. Chuck didn't care about his company. Why should I?

We waited for our luggage and caught a ride to our hotel. Being stuck in a car with Chuck was miserable. Something on his phone excited him. He wanted me to ask him about it.

I refused.

"I can't believe Trump thinks he can avoid impeachment," he said. "I don't like to talk politics at work, but today's news affects our industry. Have you heard what happened with the president?"

I had no idea.

I'm not sure I gave a shit either.

"Nope."

"Come on, Wyatt. This is what I'm talking about. You need to be dialed into this stuff. You should be telling me this story."

"Sorry boss."

"A federal judge won't let Trump block his financial records from Congress," Chuck said.

"Didn't see that coming," I said.

"Trump called the move crazy. He's the one who's nuts."

"Unreal," I said.

"The guy constantly lies."

A politician who lies. Alert the press.

I nodded my head in agreement at Chuck's remarks.

"Pelosi thinks he'll cry election fraud next November," Chuck said.

Seemed like a stretch to me.

Or a bold strategy.

Chuck scrolled through his phone.

He spat out propaganda.

Chuck called it news.

I made a few grunts.

One or two "wows."

Couldn't believe Chuck was still going.

"Did you see the drunk Nancy Pelosi video?" I asked.

"Those were doctored," Chuck said. "You don't believe that's real, do you?"

"Fake or real, shit . . . I mean, it . . . it was hilarious."

Chuck didn't think so.

We checked in and sat in the lobby, waiting with our luggage. Chuck scheduled a last-minute conference call with the team. He wanted to do our first run-through of the presentation. Twenty-two hours before we were scheduled to give it.

We spent two hours rehearsing in the hotel lobby.

I needed food.

And a bed.

After the meeting I ran and grabbed some fish-and-chips from a joint across the street from our hotel, then dropped an order off for Chuck at his room. I took a long hot shower. It was the first decent shower I took since moving to California. The water at my place dripped out of the shower. And was barely warm. It felt like paradise in the hotel shower.

After forty minutes, I dried off and put on a casual clown suit and tie to meet Chuck and the head of the marketing department for some biotech company, Debbie, and her assistant, Corey, at a tapas restaurant in the city.

I hate tapas.

I didn't know what anything was on the menu at tapas joints, but that wasn't the worst part. You could take only one item off each small plate. When I taste something small and delicious, I want it all. Give me a plateful. Who wants a sampling for dinner?

I barely talked at the restaurant.

Shit.

I barely ate.

As the dinner meeting winded down, only one plate remained. Debbie and I locked onto the last spicy beef tapa. It was by far the best dish. We had asked for two orders, and now there was one bite left.

The check was on the table.

I eyed up the beef.

Chuck reached for his card.

"We got this," he boasted.

I studied the table.

Chuck didn't care.

Corey was too polite to take the last piece of food.

Debbie licked her stupid lips.

Her eyes glued to the nearly extinct meat.

"Want the last one?" she asked.

Cheap move.

"All yours, Debbie."

I couldn't take something the client wanted.

Especially one with an expiring contract.

Debbie knew that.

She enjoyed the last bite.

I hate tapas.

But people more.

* * *

I called my father when I got back to my hotel room.

"Not going out in the city?" my father asked.

I was too hungover for a late night in Boston.

No matter how tempting.

"Radek was visiting. We got pretty banged up yesterday."

"You ever going to grow up?"

"When it kills me."

My father grunted. "Did you talk to your boss about more money?"

"Well, no," I said. "Not yet."

"You need that."

I paced toward the window. Chuck was a few rooms away, and I didn't want him to hear. "We nail this meeting, I have more ammunition to get paid."

"You shouldn't need ammo. He's working you like a dog."

"There's not much I can do."

"Contact a lawyer."

"I'm not going to do that."

"You need that money," my father said. "Have you talked to Kayla? She was asking me about some letter. I didn't know what she was talking about."

Shit.

"Yeah, I did," I lied. "I'll have to text her."

"Don't lie to me, Wyatt."

After I got off the phone with my father, I headed down to the hotel floor's ice and vending machines. I paid five bucks for a chocolate bar and a soda. As I walked down the hallway, a slim, twenty-something blonde in tiny jean shorts jumped into Chuck's room. Chuck slammed the door closed when his eyes met mine. It was a little late for visitors.

And that wasn't his wife.

May 21, 2019

C huck was waiting for me in the hotel's lobby with a coffee. He called Gary and Trish to practice our presentation once more. After our last practice presentation, we caught a ride to the meeting. I guess we weren't going to talk about Chuck cheating on his wife. That wasn't really on brand for Reynolds Incorporated.

Chuck's legs shook the entire ride.

He kept sipping his empty coffee cup.

When we arrived at Skylar Pharmaceuticals, Debbie led us into an empty conference room.

"We'll give you five to set up," Debbie said. "Let me know if you need anything."

She left.

What if I needed something?

I plugged my new Reynolds Incorporated laptop into the HDMI cable that stuck out of the center of the white marble conference table. My screen projected onto the giant wall the chairs of the table faced.

"Everything is connected and ready to go," I said.

"Can you hide the screen?"

"I'd have to disconnect it."

Chuck shuffled papers in and out of his briefcase.

"I don't want it up until after they're all in here."

"It might mess it up," I said.

"Hide the screen."

I unplugged the HDMI cord. The screen disappeared from the wall. Debbie and eight expensive suits entered the room.

We made our introductions.

"My marketing director, Wyatt, will begin our presentation."

Didn't realize I was promoted.

When I plugged the cord back in, my screen didn't appear on the wall.

I took the HDMI cord out and plugged it back in.

Nothing.

"This is why we set up our equipment before the meeting," a bald guy in a suit said.

A suit with more jokes than hair.

Cool.

I fidgeted with my laptop and the sixteen cords sticking out of the table. Unplugged all the cords. Plugged them back in. Tried sticking cords in different ports. Nothing worked.

"What are you doing?" Chuck said under his breath. "Show your screen."

I fidgeted with cords.

Stabbing them in and out of my computer.

"This is unprofessional," Chuck whispered.

My laptop was working fine until Chuck demanded I unplugged it. Couldn't ruin Chuck's grand reveal of his presentation. What a tool.

He connected his laptop to one of the cords that didn't work with my computer. His screen showed on the giant wall.

"How was that so difficult?" Chuck whispered.

The mishap threw Chuck off. Still, he did most of the talking. Trish and Gary called in but stayed quiet. I helped Chuck where I could, but he would talk over me when I tried to speak. I stopped interjecting my ideas.

The meeting dragged on.

No one should care this much about the efficiency of an email campaign. Who really wants to stress about clicks, reads, and opens? The people who high-five at meetings and say words like "synergy." That's who. Bragging how they worked eighty hours a week. Like that's somehow an enjoyable existence. Suits chasing the next promotion. Selling their souls for a paycheck.

Just like me.

Right before a working lunch, President Suit asked, "How do you handle bad reviews?"

Chuck shuffled the papers in front of him.

"Well . . . what . . . what do you mean?" Chuck asked. "With that."

"Online. We have a ton of negative reviews from some of our customers. And those . . . PETA people. Glassdoor. Facebook. The things we do aren't always viewed in a positive light. How would your organization handle that? Is that included in your proposal?"

Chuck muttered something no one understood.

Trish and Gary remained silent on the conference line.

I hated that I needed money.

"That's something we can handle," I said. "But what specifically are the reviews complaining about? Is it the same problem over and over or different issues?"

"People spewing hate about the company. How we test our products. How we're inhumane. There's no way to just erase these people from our sites?" President Suit asked.

I wanted to ask him if he ever read the First Amendment.

"You can't silence people for saying how they feel, unless we can prove it's a lie," I said. "Here's the bad news. People are more likely to write a negative review than a positive. You know how when you get mad, you need to vent? That's what happens most of the time with businesses online. People are all pissed off and rage out on their keyboard. There's nothing we can do about that. We'd recommend a campaign that will email customers an hour after meeting with your team or making a purchase from your company. It'll ask them to rate their experience. If they say it sucked, we can ask why and try to correct the issue."

"Or just ignore them," President Suit said.

"You can do that. With the positive reviews we receive in this campaign, we will send a follow-up email requesting they copy and paste their review on your social media sites. We can send them emails with links, and all they have to do is hit copy and paste. We can't get rid of people's comments, especially over your organization's practices, but we can flood your sites with positive reviews."

Chuck scribbled notes.

President Suit seemed impressed. I took a couple of questions from him and other members of the executive board. Chuck tried to jump in, but the board members brushed him off and waited for my response. I bullshitted every single answer, acting like I believed each syllable as gospel.

We paused the presentation for a working lunch. The suits deemed it a social hour. Debbie ordered New England clam chowder for everyone. A lunch tradition at Skylar Pharmaceuticals. Executives slung their ties behind their backs. A few even removed them. Men and women slurped the boiling seafood from their spoons. But not me.

"You going to dig in?" Debbie asked.

Eating soup was messy and sounded gross. Doing it in a civilized setting? Impossible to enjoy. Plus, Chuck instructed me to "mingle" while he ate. He'd take over when he was done with his soup.

"I'm waiting for it to cool down," I lied.

Chuck ate his soup.

I did all the talking.

By the time I got a spoonful of soup, it was cold.

I hate business meals.

Chuck presented for another hour.

Followed by another question-and-answer session.

Debbie let us know that she would be in touch in two weeks with the company's decision. Chuck called a ride when we got outside. He didn't say a word.

"I thought it went well," I said.

"You were totally unprepared. That whole cord thing—that might cost the company a lot of money."

Chuck and I didn't speak for the rest of the trip.

Cocaine Blues

June 1, 2019

Summer and Noah were a half hour late to the downtown concert venue. I knew Leah would show up even later. Summer wore a ponytail positioned on the side of her head, with a jean vest and a bright pink shirt. Noah wore a rocker's headband, with jeans and a T-shirt. He didn't particularly care for costumes.

"Nice pants," Noah said.

"Don't be mean," Summer said.

I had a red bandanna around my long-haired rock-star wig. A light-blue denim jacket covered my Queen T-shirt. High black boots with skintight zebra pants that left nothing to the imagination.

"If I had any balls, I'd dress like this every day," I said.

"When's Leah getting here?" Noah asked.

"Soon," I said.

"Don't get crazy," Summer said.

"Or be nervous," Noah said.

"I'm good. Relax."

I was nervous.

It had been almost two months since I'd seen her.

"Let's get a beer," Summer said.

We each had a glass of hops before we went to meet Leah at the lower level of the joint. More than half the crowd dressed in eighties fashion to celebrate what Leah called the best eighties cover band on the West Coast.

I hated myself for thinking it, but I forgot how beautiful Leah was in person. She wore a long-sleeve crop top, blue neon leggings, a green headband, and leg warmers. Leah gave me a hug without making eye contact.

Next to her was a tall, rugged, and handsome man who somehow pulled off a better eighties outfit than me.

"This is Tony," Leah said.

"What's going on?" Tony said.

Fuck his awesome whitewashed jean vest.

Fuck his biker gloves.

Fuck his bandanna.

Fuck his eyeliner.

"Great outfit, bro," I said.

"You look like Tommy Lee, man," Tony said.

Fuck this awesome human.

"That's what I was going for," I said.

Leah kissed Tony on the cheek before she and Summer scurried to the bathroom together. I guess that was the man from the phone on my birthday. The guy Leah was fucking. And why I hadn't seen her in two months.

I wish she would have told me.

Because this sucked.

"Have you ever seen this band before?" Noah asked.

"Yeah, man," Tony said. "They're huge in LA. I was surprised we were able to get tickets at the last minute. It's only because I'm basically an honorary roadie."

Noah and I made more awkward small talk with Tony. I concentrated on my beer. It was gone quicker than usual.

Summer pulled me toward the other side of the venue when she returned from the bathroom. At the bar she finally spoke.

"That's her boyfriend."

"I figured," I said.

"Don't get mad."

I closed my eyes and took a deep, angry breath.

"I . . . don't . . . What happened?"

"I don't know," Summer said. "It's not going to last with this guy."

"You don't know that."

Summer ordered three light beers.

"She wouldn't shut up about you on my birthday."

The sound of guitars ripped through the crowd.

Summer handed me a beer from the bartender.

"Let's have fun tonight," she said. "Don't start shit."

I didn't have a choice.

We made our way toward the stage. There were no seats, just a giant mosh pit in front of the band. The joint crawled with assholes attempting to record a marginally talented eighties cover band with their phones. I could imagine the people in the crowd posting the grainy footage with unbearable sound quality that no one watches on social media:

Look how fucking cool I am. I do stuff. I go to concerts. Look at me! Look how awesome I am! My life is the best. Right? Like to confirm. Please. Follow for follow. #blessed.

Assholes.
Digitally keeping up with the Joneses.
Fuck this joint.
I caught Leah gazing at me a few times. She'd quickly look away when I'd catch her. Eye tag. Summer kept an eye on me keeping an eye on Leah. Summer glared with death and mouthed "no" whenever she caught me. It always took Leah and her boyfriend forever to get back to the group when they went to the bar. Probably peeing after every beer.
"They have some weak bladders," I told Summer.
Summer pretended to snort a line of cocaine off her finger.
That made more sense.
The band played all the classics.
I forgot the band's name.
Some pun on an eighties pop culture reference.
The couples sang and danced.
I watched Leah make out with Tony.
It was a great.
I fired down another beer.
After the band's last set, Leah and Summer posed with their boyfriends in front of the empty stage. Guess who they asked to take their photos?
Fuck love.

* * *

The five of us walked in our eighties gear through the city to the Palace. People in cars hooted and hollered at us. I couldn't tell the jeers from the cheers. Not sure I cared. The night blew. Boring small talk. Cocktails. Two couples in love. Me with booze.

Noah made us a second round of old-fashioneds before he headed to bed.

"Don't stay up too late," Noah said. "We have to get up early to look at houses."

Summer kissed him good night.

Tony pulled a small bag of cocaine from his jacket.

The degenerates sat around the kitchen table, drinking and snorting cocaine off a dinner plate.

"You should try some," Tony said.

He was a pushy druggie.

"Nah. Thanks."

"He's never done it," Leah said.

"Really, man?" Tony swallowed his drink. "That's a shame. It's a lot of fun."

"He doesn't need coke to be fun," Leah said.

"Actually, it looks like I do," I said.

I shoved my nose into Summer's best dinner plate.

The drugs shot up my nose.

A direct hit to my brain.

"Wow," I said.

"I've been telling you that for how long?" Summer asked.

I took another, bigger bump.

"This stuff ain't bad," I said.

We cleared a plate of cocaine.

Leah threw on eighties music.

We sang the songs we knew.

My heart broke a little more each time Leah kissed Tony.

Tony filled our plate with more cocaine.

I wanted another line.

Cocaine addiction probably started just like this.

I took another long sniff.

June Gloom

June 2, 2019

I don't know why I agreed to visit open houses in the suburbs with Summer and Noah. We were all pretty hungover. My muscles hurt. Everywhere. My sinuses were clogged. Summer told me it was the cocaine comedown.

I swore to never shove another drug up my nose.

They picked me up in Noah's expensive sports car, which forced me to cram into the tight back seat. Noah figured the car would help him with real estate agents.

As soon as we walked into a two-story house in suburbia, a blonde-haired woman who could have passed for a model rushed to Noah.

"She definitely noticed the car," Noah said.

"It's close to a major road," Summer said. "That's a minus. Subtract five."

Summer kept announcing plus or minus points as we walked through the open house. She wasn't keeping track of the overall house score, though.

The house was fine. Nothing special. The inside was mostly painted blue, white, and gray. The place was boring except for a long skinny support beam covered in zebra and cheetah prints that shot up to the ceiling. It was in the middle of the living room.

"You can't take the pole out, but you can paint it," the real estate agent said.

"Minus a hundred."

Noah wandered off upstairs, leaving me and Summer in the kitchen.

"Have you heard from Leah?" I asked.

"It was last night we saw her."

"I don't get it," I said. "You see the way she looks at me."

Summer looked around the room for Noah.

"There's definitely something there."

"What's the deal with this guy?" I asked.

"She told me all they do is snort coke and fuck."

Noah and the attractive real estate agent talked in front of the TV in the living room. They both laughed.

Summer turned red.

"Bitches. All the models who can't make it out here become real estate agents. Hacks. These assholes better back off my man."

"She's trying to make a sale," I said.

"You know nothing about California."

Summer stomped her way to Noah. She grabbed his hand and kissed his cheek. Summer pulled him to another room.

"This could be our baby's room."

I walked over to the real estate agent.

"What did you do before this?" I asked.

She didn't even pretend to smile before she left to chase another potential buyer.

* * *

The next house was twenty minutes away from the first one. The place was two stories tall and looked massive, but I learned to never judge a house by its exterior. The hallways were smashed together, making them feel like one of those enclosed waterslides. But way worse. Noah ducked as he walked from bedroom to bedroom on the second floor.

I snuck to the backyard for air. I knew there was no way they were going to buy the house when I saw the yard. The grass was flat for a few feet before it shot up on a tight angle into a forest. The hill was bigger than the house.

Summer walked outside.

"Nope! Minus a billion. Nope. No way!"

"It would be perfect for sledding," I said.

"We're in California," Noah said.

Sometimes a man can forget these things.

* * *

The third and final house seemed to be just right for the couple. The hallway walls didn't cause anyone to suffocate. There was a large grassy backyard with a deck, pool, and hot tub. There were no decorative poles in the middle of the living room or slanting yards.

Summer and Noah went upstairs to explore the bedrooms. I toured the first floor and found a pool table inside what looked like a library. An oak bookshelf towered in the room, filled with hundreds of books.

I wanted to smoke a pipeful of weed in a silky robe with whiskey in hand while acting like I knew an actual thing about life. It was the perfect room for writing.

Summer and Noah emerged from the upstairs into an open loft that overlooked the writing quarters. Noah walked down floating wood stairs that led from the loft to the library.

"The steps are too dangerous for children," Summer said. "Our babies could fall right through! Minus a million and a trillion. Oh god. Noah. What would we do?"

"We'd get a different house," he said.

And the just-right house turned into another dud. Summer and Noah would call The Palace home for a little longer.

June 7, 2019

Chuck was in the office from eleven to three. That was his schedule. He claimed he worked all morning and night, but it was nearly impossible to get a hold of him before or after eight o'clock, whether in the evening or morning. But the worst thing Chuck did was organize a weekly four o'clock end-of-week recap meeting. Friday afternoon meetings. Chuck was always in the office for those.

The man was a monster.

He rambled on about urgency during his most recent demonstration of his inflated ego. I hunted the internet for employment-law articles on my laptop while Chuck talked about a "three-pronged approach" to his new venture. He thought I was taking vigorous notes. I used an incognito browser for my research because, according to Trish, Chuck monitored everyone's internet history.

Chuck was in the middle of discussing social media advertisements when I found what I was looking for online.

The biggest scam in our country was the forty-hour workweek, and now I had the internet evidence to prove it.

The Fair Labor Standards Act.

According to the Fair Labor Standards Act, employers can force employees to work ninety hours a week but pay employees for only forty. All the employer has to do to avoid paying employees overtime wages? Tell the government the job requires a college degree. How can businesses do this? Class the employees as exempt.

Being paid for forty hours a week while working close to seventy saved Chuck a lot of money. It cost me a small fortune. I guess that's what happens when one-hundred-year labor laws aren't updated.

"We can provide a resource in exchange for their contact information," Chuck said. "The reciprocity principle says this will help build a relationship we can leverage in the future. That's what we have to tap into. Any questions?"

"That makes sense to me," I said.

I should have asked his thoughts on hiring more staff, exempt employees, or overtime pay, but it was close to six, and I needed the weekend.

June 9, 2019

Paige called it Sunday Funday.

We stopped at a pool bar on top of a hotel first. Music blared. Dudes raged out. Shot girls poured vodka down eager twentysomething throats.

"I'm not ready for that type of day," Paige said. "I do have to go to my friend's play tonight."

We then went to a rooftop bar across the street. They didn't serve light beers, but they had three different types of fruit beers. I got a whiskey neat, and Paige did the same.

"What's the deal with you and Leah?" Paige asked.

"Nothing," I said. "At least not anymore."

"Why not?"

"She's got a man."

Paige took a drink.

"So, you're not into her?"

"You could say that," I said.

"Don't give me too much here."

I swallowed my drink.

"Ask me something else," I said.

"Give me anything."

"I know a place where we can get the best old-fashioneds."

"Show me."

* * *

I took Paige to Half-Door Brewing.

Noah recommended it.

It didn't take us long to get to our third round.

"It's late," Paige said. "I have to shower and go to this fucking play."

"You don't have to do anything."

"Are you trying to get me to get another drink with you?"

"I was going to even offer to pay."

We walked three blocks to another rooftop bar. It surprised us both when the bartender served us. We looked around and found a couch to hide on

"Let's chill on one of those couches," I said.

"They're called daybeds."

Everything wanted a label.

"I was so young when I started drinking," Paige said. "And doing drugs. I've been doing this since I was twelve."

"Philly tough," I said.

"I don't want to do it forever, but what else is there?"

"Cute redheads."

"Don't even."

I leaned to kiss Paige, but she turned away.

"I'm seeing someone."

"He's married," I said.

"Doesn't mean I won't be faithful."

"I can respect that."

Paige downed her drink.

"You don't have a choice."

"I'm sorry I tried to kiss you," I said.

Paige leaned in and kissed my lips.

"That's it," she said.

She called a ride and left for her friend's play.

Trish screamed when the automatic doors slammed shut. Our computers flickered down. The power zapped. The office went dark. The lights flashed when the building's emergency generator fired on.

Trish, Gary, Jessica, and I fled to the conference room.

I shut the door.

Worst case?

We're in a room with one way in or out.

"Is it a lockdown?" Gary asked.

Trish paced around the room. "What should we do?"

"We're fine," I said. "There's only one door."

The power goes out and I'm thinking about an active shooter. Humanity was fucked. And I was terrified.

"Why did the door slam shut?" Gary asked.

I needed to think but couldn't with all the damn questions.

"It could be anything," Jessica said.

Trish screamed when the fire alarm shrieked.

The siren continued to ring and flash.

Gary peered out the window.

"The building's on fire."

I saw the smoke rising outside. We crowded around the window. Flames engulfed a portion of the roof a few floors down. It looked like some type of ventilation shaft caught on fire. Thank God. Just a fire.

We walked fifteen flights of stairs to the street. We stood on the other side of the street with the rest of the building's inhabitants. Four fire trucks blared in front of the building.

Chuck walked over to us, sitting on the curb with a bagel and a large, iced coffee in his hands. Most bosses brought breakfast to their jobs, but it was well after noon.

"What happened?" Chuck asked.

"Buildings on fire," Gary said.

He pointed to the fifth-story roof. Black smoke rose toward the sky with the tips of the flames visible. Chuck examined the scene for a few moments. He hummed a few things to himself.

"Let's work from here," Chuck said. "Nothing can stop the team at Reynolds Incorporated. Right?"

We sat on the curb with our laptops.

I pretended to work.

Who knows what everyone else did.

Chuck called a meeting while firefighters battled the blaze. The sun beat down on us. Business attire isn't good for the California heat.

The fire trucks left at three.

The building didn't burn down.

Chuck went inside to assess the damage.

"So much for an early day," I said.

"It's too hot," Trish said. "I can't take this."

The suffocating humidity soaked Trish. Her face was red, with drips of sweat falling from her forehead.

"I was hoping we could go home," Gary said.

Chuck reappeared.

"Building is clear. Let's get back to work in the office."

What a bullshit blaze.

The power was still out inside. It meant no air-conditioning. Chuck assured us the building's power would be fully on in a few minutes. Ten minutes felt like a hundred. My armpits were drenched. After an hour, I heard swishing sounds every time I typed.

"I can't work like this," Trish said.

Gary walked into Chuck's office.

Trish and I pretended to work while we tried to listen.

We couldn't hear anything.

Chuck may have had his office soundproofed.

After a few minutes of not working, Gary emerged.

"Get out of here."

"But finish your work!" Chuck yelled from his open office door as Trish and I ran out of the office.

June 14, 2019

I called my father. In case I was too hungover to remember to call him on Father's Day. I blamed the time difference for the early holiday wishes.

"What are you doing Sunday?" I asked knowing Kayla would be making him dinner.

"Kayla wants to do all that stuff she usually does, but I'm busy," my father said.

I gripped my phone harder. "Doing what?"

"I have other plans."

What could be more important than spending Father's Day with his daughter?

"Other plans?" I asked.

"Candace wants to spend the weekend in the city."

"Come on, man."

"I told Kayla I'd spend the day with her, but I didn't know about this. It was a surprise. You're the writer—what should I say?"

"The truth," I said.

"That's not advice."

"It's the only writing advice worth a damn."

There was a pause.

"I can tell Kayla I need to reschedule," my father said. "I need a reason."

"I will not help you lie to your daughter."

"It's not a lie," my father said. "It's rescheduling."

I put my phone on speaker so I could free my hands to roll a blunt. "Tell her you'd rather spend the day with your girlfriend."

"That's really helpful."

"I've got to eat some dinner. It's getting late."

"Yeah. Thanks. Helpful as always."

With my perfectly rolled joint in hand, I walked to my bedroom and screamed into my pillow.

When my throat began to hurt, I gave up yelling.

I pulled my journal from my top dresser drawer.

It's always good to write while in pain.

An envelope fell out of the journal.

I pulled out three handwritten pages.

Wyatt,

I must admit, you moving to Cali has me feeling very conflicted. On one hand, I am so proud of you for following your dreams. But selfishly, I am going to miss you so very much. Our life has not been easy, but I like to think we survived together. My favorite memories from childhood are the ones we share. I remember laughing with you so much, even when everything else was falling apart. I remember we used to pretend we were from the WWF (before it got lame and changed their name to WWE). I always had to be the villain. It made me so mad. But I realized it wasn't about me being the villain. You always wanted to be the hero, saving the world and making it right again. That's one of my favorite things about you. You have saved countless of my days just by setting aside time to talk to me. I remember our movie nights; we were so young when we started that. We stayed up all night, ate tons of snacks, but most importantly, we laughed. Because of you, my first crush was Harrison Ford. I remember you making out with my Hilary Duff poster on my wall when you were mad at me. I remember you letting me hang with your friends, no matter how annoying I was. I remember you waking me up at night sometimes because you were sad. Sometimes it was after a midnight nerd movie, which you would spoil for me, or it was to tell me I was your best friend.

I remember you saving me from my first out-of-control party. The cops were coming, and you picked me up. But then you made me stay up and watch The Dark Knight with Mom. The punishment fit the crime, considering I made you have to leave your friend's graduation party.

I remember when I hated myself. And didn't want to live. The only reason I didn't end it all was because of you. I couldn't burden you with that. Or abandon you in this world.

But you already knew that.

I remember dropping you off at college.

I bawled my eyes out on the whole way home.

I remember you taking me and Zane out for my 21st birthday.

I remember you jumping in the way of dad whenever he'd try to hit me. Usually, he'd end up beating us both, but it never stopped you from trying to defend me.

You were my first best friend and I'm so thankful for everything I have with you. I know I lose myself sometimes, especially in the last few years. I am not always the version of myself that I want to be. I am sorry for not always being kind and welcoming to you. I regret moments I was stuck on myself when I should have given my attention to you. I thank you for being one of the few people in my life who don't write me off as crazy or give up on me. You never make me feel judged. Or like an outsider. You listen to me. You don't make me feel like my pain isn't real. You have always made me feel so important. You are the best big brother I could have asked for, and I mean that from the bottom of my heart. No matter our fights or differences, I will always be here for you. Even on your worst days.

I'll never give up on you. I hope I've been there for you the way you have for me.

I wish you could see yourself from my eyes. I like to think I know you better than most, and I know you can do anything you put your mind to. You are so creative, passionate, and emotional. Those are your greatest strengths. Don't ever give up. You are so hard on yourself. I wish you weren't. People don't understand you, it's why they're so cruel. You just have to find the right people who truly appreciate who you are. You are a fantastic person, so much kinder than you realize, so much better than you give yourself credit for.

I know you're going to do amazing things out there. Don't forget about me while you chase your dreams. I'll make time to talk to you whenever and however we can. If you lose hope or want to quit, you let me know and I'll tell you why you shouldn't. Just because you're away doesn't mean you aren't a huge part of my life. When I get a home, there will always be a room for you. You can text or call me about anything, even stupid sports.

I'm sorry this is long. I just wanted you to know how much of a difference you've made in my life. As much as I'll miss you, I'm so excited to see this next chapter for you. I hope it is everything you dreamed of and more. Thank you for being there for me, always. I love you very much.

Love,
Kayla

Tears exploded down my face.

I should have read the letter earlier.

It was late on the East Coast, but I texted Kayla anyway.

I just read your letter. Sorry it took so long. I knew I wouldn't be able to handle it. I love you. Always. You were always there to pick me up from the bruises. You always listened. And didn't make me feel crazy. I guess we did that for each other. I couldn't have survived without you. You never gave up on me. And I'll never give up on you. I feel like the luckiest guy in the world to call you my sister. I love you more than I can ever put into words.

It took me a while to stop crying. I lit my blunt and cracked open a beer. I didn't bother to write. Nothing would be as beautiful as Kayla's words.

California Girls

June 22, 2019

Usually after a breakup, I'd find myself in a weed, whiskey, and women bender for a few weeks. Or a few months. Once, a whole year. That woman put a real humble on me. I wasn't completely over Leah, but it was summer in SoCal. There was no point in sulking.

I downloaded all thirty-nine dating apps. Uploaded some unflattering photos of myself, wrote cringey bios, and started shallowly swiping.

Melanie and I met at a brewery. She had started her own daycare three years earlier. She said the worst part was dealing with the snobby asshole parents. Melanie grew up in Alabama, where she shot guns and learned to hunt with her father. We joked about *Seinfeld*. We grabbed dinner. We hit two more breweries before she invited me back to her place.

"It's messy," she said. "I'm so embarrassed."

"You should see my place."

Melanie made me sit outside her apartment while she cleaned up inside. She took a long time to make her place presentable. I sat down on the ground and put my head against the door. My eyes drifted closed.

Stay awake.

Sex is on the horizon.

My head grew heavy.

I needed to store some energy.

Just a little rest.

Close your eyes for a minute.

I fell into the apartment when Melanie swung open the door. My head slammed onto the floor.

"That's a real comfortable door," I said.

June 29, 2020

I met Rachel at a hookah bar downtown. A fresh phoenix tattoo covered her forearm as a permanent reminder of her escape from an abusive marriage. We smoked from a hookah, which she told me the natives called a shishya when she lived in South America. Rachel loved tequila, but I couldn't stomach it. She ordered a smoked tequila that didn't have as rough a kick. It wasn't bad after a few shots.

We drunkenly made out in the lobby of her hotel in front of a horrified old couple. Rachel buried herself in my chest embarrassed until they left. She kissed me one more time. I asked her to her room. She told me she wasn't that type of woman.

July 4, 2019

Despite the federal holiday, Chuck made his staff come into the office. No one did any work. Corporate America was shut down across the country. Chuck let us leave at three. He expected everyone to acknowledge his kindness on their way out. I mumbled a hurried thanks when I passed his office.

A man has bills to pay.

I met Summer and Noah at an Irish pub. Leslie, a college athlete, caught my eyes. I bought her a beer. Leslie was doing a pub crawl for the holiday. Noah, Summer, and I joined her and her friends on their booze journey across the city. At the last bar we visited, Leslie and I made out to the terrible sounds of Bon Jovi. Noah gave me a high five. Summer scolded me for Leslie "being too young."

The four of us watched fireworks over Mission Bay. When they finished, Summer told me she and Noah bought a place. Closing was in a month.

"Congratulations," Leslie slurred.

I never saw her again.

July 14, 2019

Nora was exactly my type. Cute, funny, and her online dating profile read "insert slutty undertones here." Surprised I actually read a bio. We went to a rooftop bar for Sunday Funday. We noticed an extremely giggly gay couple staring at us from the bar. They came over to say hi. After pleasantries, Dennis and Brad pulled out their wallets and revealed the reason for their happiness. Magic mushrooms were stuffed in their wallets. No bag protecting the drugs. No nothing. Just mushrooms where money should have been. They gave Nora and me a healthy pinch when she told them it was our first date. In exchange, Nora and I played a game of corn hole with them.

We had another drink before we left the bar.

The date was just to ensure neither one of us were nuts.

Both of us were lonely.

Back at my place, we fucked.

It wasn't my best work.

Not because of anything Nora did.

I blamed the drugs.

But still, I found a way to enjoy myself.

July 20, 2019

The Gaslamp Quarter was known for its bars, restaurants, and stores. The historians will tell you a different story.

Superheroes, comic book characters, and other adults dressed in lavish costumes flocked to the streets. No cars, traffic jams, or scooters allowed. Some joints turned into specialty pop culture bars for the week.

Comic-Con.

Just another excuse to drink.

The joint I met Paige and some of her friends at served six specialty cocktails, each named for an Infinity Stone from the Marvel Comics movies. In the films, collecting all six Infinity Stones allowed a person, creature, or alien to wield unlimited power.

"I'm gonna drink them all," I said.

"That's stupid," Paige said.

"The best things rarely are," I mocked.

Paige hit my arm.

"You can't use my motto."

"I believe I just did."

I ordered my first of the six Marvel-themed drinks.

We sat on the patio of the bar and watched the cosplayers for a bit. Because that's what Californians did during Comic-Con. Got drunk and watched all the creative people show off. Two of the six drinks went into my stomach while we watched the nerds.

Paige's friends Lauren, Wendy, and Jamie grew bored of people and decided we should play corn hole. Their interest in the game didn't last long. I crushed two more drinks.

Wendy wanted to play one of those card games where whoever says the most fucked-up shit wins. We played for a dozen hands before everyone got sick of it. I crossed off another Infinity Stone–inspired drink during the game.

Paige's friends left when I had only one cocktail left to complete my boozy Infinity Gauntlet.

"They always do this," Paige said.

"What do you mean?"

"They invite me out, get drunk, and then go meet up with dudes."

I pointed to the last drink I needed on the menu.

The Time Stone.

A green mojito cocktail.

"Then the glory is all ours," I said.

The bartenders on the first floor refused to serve me. We knew they wouldn't serve Paige either. They told me I'd be too drunk. Joke was on them. I already was.

Paige snuck to the second story of the joint and bought my last drink. Paige passed me the Time Stone cocktail behind her back. She stood in front of me to block anyone from seeing what we were doing.

"Hurry," she said.

One of the downstairs bartenders caught me. He alerted the large bouncer standing at the entrance of the joint. The giant man marched toward me. I kept chugging.

"You got this!" Paige yelled.

The bouncer grabbed me and spun me around.

I slammed my empty glass onto the table.

"I am Iron Man!"

The bouncer dragged me out of the bar by my arm.

Paige couldn't stop laughing.

"With great power comes great responsibility," I told the strongman.

"Whatever you say, Yoda."

July 24, 2019

Alania ended a sexless three-year relationship and left Mexico for California. She traveled all over the country, chasing high salaries and executives in suits. I was an in-between fuck. But I didn't mind.

July 27, 2019

Emily was a single mom who recently got out of a long-term relationship. She didn't want anything serious, but I was glad to help her with her oral fixation.

August 7, 2019

After pregaming at my apartment, Paige and I caught a ride to an outdoor concert venue to see a punk rock concert.

A pop-up shop sold band shirts for forty dollars. The hoodies were eighty. A shitty throw blanket would set me back two hundred big ones.

Paige stared off into the distance.

"I want one of those."

I followed her eyes and saw a yellow stand that sold giant red alcohol slushies in guitar shapes.

"You're pretty high-maintenance, huh?" I asked.

"What?" she asked.

We stood at the back of the line for the booze slushies.

"You picked the place with the longest line," I said.

"There are a ton of attractive men over there."

"But how many of them are going to buy you a slushy full of booze?"

"I imagine quite a few," she said.

"It's like that?"

Paige laughed.

The second act began their set before we finally made it to the counter.

"Two guitar slushies and a giant water." I looked at Paige. "Or do you need your own water?"

"We can share."

The server made our drinks and returned with them and the bill.

"Fifty bucks."

Of course, it was.

We took our drinks and headed to the lawn section of the venue.

"These are really good," Paige said.

She had drunk almost a quarter of her drink in a long sip. I took a drink. There was a lot of alcohol in it.

* * *

The crowd erupted when the headliner hit the stage.

We screamed.

We danced.

We sang.

We drank our slushies.

We didn't sit down.

Before the set finished, Paige handed me her drink.

"I can't," she said. "I need to go."

I took the straw in my mouth and sucked as much alcohol as I could. Instant brain freeze. I closed one eye and followed behind Paige. She hurried through the crowd. She put a hand on her stomach and pointed to a secluded section at the back of the venue.

We stumbled toward the remote spot. Paige covered her mouth. She leaned over. I heard the splash of puke hitting the ground. I ran to her and held her hair until she was empty.

I handed her what was left of our water bottle.

She chugged it.

"I've never gotten a date so drunk she threw up," I said.

"This isn't a date."

"I can throw up if you want."

"You're not going to puke from all that drinking?" she asked.

"I certainly can't drive or walk too well."

We started walking back to our spot on the lawn. As we did, a bright light flashed us. We used our arms to shield our eyes.

"What are you two doing back there?"

It was a deep voice. I put my arm around Paige, and we walked toward the security guard.

"Trust me on this," I whispered to Paige as we came face-to-face with the large man. "Trying to get a little privacy." I leaned into him and pretended to whisper but spoke loudly. "I'm trying to make a move. Any suggestions?"

"You can kiss her anywhere but there. But only kiss. No hanky-panky." The security guard started walking toward Paige's vomit. Paige and I hurried our way to the exit of the joint. In a matter of seconds, the security guard would find her puke. When he did, he'd call for an ambulance. Or arrest us. I grabbed her hand, and we jogged out of the venue.

August 17, 2019

Catrina and I met at a bar that was also an arcade. Her online pictures were dated, to put it nicely.

"We have to play the Zoltar machine if they have it," she said.

"Zoltar?" I asked.

"You'll see."

We played a basketball game where you shoot the ball as many times as possible in thirty seconds. Then we played a few different games after that, but Catrina didn't talk much. She laughed little. I'd say things, and she'd smile. That was it. It wasn't a smile that made me feel good about myself either.

I ordered myself a whiskey.

Booze helps in these situations.

Right by the exit of the joint, Catrina found what she had been hunting for all night.

"There he is," she said. "My sexy man."

Catrina fired tokens into the fortune-teller machine. This robot had a long beard and red eyes of terror. She mimicked the creepy thing's stiff motions. It was kind of cute.

The first time.

Catrina played the damn game over and over. She danced with each fortune the machine spit out on a little card.

Over and over.

"That fortune is lame," Catrina said. "One more time."

A line formed behind us.

I'm not sure who was worse, Catrina or the six people waiting for this waste of tokens. Why would anyone blow money on a fake fortune-teller? I guess it was cheaper than therapy.

"You should play," Catrina said. "Let's see if our stars align."

I reached my hands into my pockets.

I didn't grab the coins I felt.

"I'm out."

"Fine." She grabbed my hand. "Let's go dance."

I wasn't sure what her twelve fortunes told her, but suddenly Catrina came to life. We wandered a few blocks to a little place that was nothing but a dance floor and a wood bar. Loud music blared and strobe lights flickered. Fog hissed out from underneath the DJ table. Yeah, it was a folding table holding a laptop, but the guy had a fog machine.

I ordered two shots from the only bartender.

Thirty bucks gone.

Fucking clubs.

Catrina dragged me out onto the center of the dance floor. She shoved her ass into my denim crotch. Hard. Pounding my balls into my stomach. It wasn't even that type of beat playing. She turned around, grabbed my face, and shoved her tongue down my throat.

"I need to piss," I said after peeling her teeth off my lips.

Catrina grabbed my fuckstick a little too hard. "Don't get started without me. I have something special planned for you." She squeezed.

Catrina laughed and went to the women's room.

I never went to piss.

My credit card stayed at the bar that night.

And I left without saying goodbye.

August 24, 2019

Jane was a cougar in her forties who moved to San Diego from LA after her divorce. She used her settlement money to enhance her chest. Jane loved to prey on younger men. She invited me over to her apartment to fuck her until I couldn't get it up anymore. Jane bragged about fucking the last guy she hooked up with nine times in a row. That seemed like a ton of work, so I never showed up at her place.

August 31, 2019

The sun baked Noah, Summer, and me on the day the couple moved out of The Palace. Summer and Noah found their dream home, put in an offer on the house, and just like that it was theirs. Noah never liked to wait for anything. Either did, Summer.

Leah was too busy to help with the move. Julian was on call for work at his new job. He was now some sort of important manager with a suit at a recruiting firm. Or something. Julian explained it to me a few times, but I was usually too drunk to understand. Or care.

Noah and I loaded most of The Palace into a moving truck while Summer held doors and steered us. Summer did some heavy lifting, but she mostly just barked orders.

The new place was forty minutes from the city. It had five bedrooms, two massive living rooms, three bathrooms, three showers, a pool, a hot tub, and tons of palm trees shading their property from nosy neighbors.

With the couple in suburbia, I knew they'd settle down. Everyone always did. No matter what they said. Their joining me on wild nights would dwindle. But it's what Summer always wanted. She deserved it.

Summer flashed her empty ring finger to Noah.

"All I need now is one more thing."

Corporate California: Such a Dreadful Place

September 4, 2019

When Chuck was in the office, I worked on Reynolds Incorporated projects. When Chuck wasn't in the office, I wrote short stories, funny lines, or things I thought about. Since Chuck only worked from eleven to three, I wrote a lot of words.

"This is how we've secured new business," Chuck said. "My idea works. We need to execute it better."

Another bullshit meeting.

Chuck is awesome.

We suck.

Chuck received a ton of cash from two businesses he swindled. Rather than investing the money into new hires to lighten his staff's workload, Chuck upgraded his computer, bought four standing desks, bid on a ping-pong table for the office, and purchased Reynolds Incorporated–branded polo shirts. The shirts were barf green, with the Reynolds Incorporated logo in white on the left chest. Chuck thought they looked great with khakis. Before team meetings, Chuck would put one of his branded polos over his shirt and tie.

Every single meeting, he did this.

"Here's the new approach," Chuck said. "We're going to develop an interactive landing page. The web page will do all the work for us."

Interactive?

Web page?

Was it 2002?

The only reason I still tolerated his self-indulgent bullshit was for the money. Once the first of November came, Chuck would owe me eight thousand big ones. Then I could quit this shithole. And be done with the bastard.

"I need more effort from the team," Chuck said. "We need to live and breathe this."

It was well after six when Chuck dismissed the staff.

Well, everyone but me.

"Hang back a second, Wyatt," he said. "There's some things I want to go over."

This wasn't good.

I knew that.

"I'm concerned with your effort lately," Chuck said. "It seems like you're always somewhere else. I can't have that. It's our highest grossing quarter. Here's what we're going to do temporarily. Until we get you back on track."

What Chuck did was force me to send him a daily list of the tasks I completed before I was allowed to leave the office. I'd have to link or attach my work to the emails. Every single day. He wanted to make sure I was getting things done. But that wasn't the truth.

Chuck didn't want to cough up ten thousand dollars.

But he knew he couldn't fire me without cause.

I'd be able to sue him for the bonus money and more.

I did my research while Chuck did whatever he did at home. Probably building a case to fire me. I guess his strategy was to overload me with work and hope I'd quit.

That's what I imagined he did to Danielle.

I nodded along as Chuck berated my work.

In two months, I'd be free from this asshole.

And ten thousand dollars richer.

Stuck in Vegas

September 13, 2019

R eynolds Incorporated didn't exactly offer a comprehensive
vacation plan. It's why I had to go straight from work to the
airport.

San Diego to Las Vegas. An hour layover in Vegas. Vegas to
Denver. Two-hour layover in Denver. Then a straight shot to the
City of Brotherly Love. I'd land early Saturday morning. Spend
some time with Kayla and Zane. Head to Doug's wedding. Spend
some time with the guys post-wedding. Fly home. Land in Denver
at eleven on Sunday night. Land at five in the morning in San
Diego. Be at work at 8:00 a.m. on Monday.

My schedule was tight, but I could make it work.

I had to.

My first flight went smoothly.

I landed in Vegas with time to spare, but not too much. No
more than five people sat in the terminal with me waiting for the
flight to Denver.

There was no plane pulled up to the terminal, either.

I checked my phone.

The flight was leaving in less than an hour.

It didn't make sense.

I walked to the closest digital flight board. My flight to Denver
was nowhere to be found. My phone didn't alert me of any delays
or changes. No emails or messages from the airline either. I
approached the customer service desk in the terminal.

"Where is the ten fifty to Denver?" I asked.

I didn't like the look the young man gave me.

"That flight got canceled. Here's a two-hundred-dollar travel
voucher or a . . ."

I clenched my fist. "What did you say?"

"Here's a two-hundred-dollar travel voucher," he said.

"No. The flight. What about the flight to Denver?"

"We had to cancel that flight."

"I have one of my best friend's weddings tomorrow. What do you mean it was canceled? I never got an alert, a message, an email, or a call. What the fuck?"

"We made an announcement an hour ago."

I might have missed that.

"I wasn't here then," I lied.

"Sir, I'm sorry. There's not much we can do. We can look up flights for you. But I don't know if we have many more to Philadelphia."

It was too much for me to handle.

"Get me to Philly. Now. If you can't, get me someone who can."

The young man looked around.

"Cassie, can you come help?"

A supervisor came to greet me after the young man waved her frantically over.

"How can I help you, sir?" she said.

I didn't have time for this.

"You canceled my flight. I need to get to Philly by tomorrow morning."

The attendant pointed across the hall to a flight that was completing boarding.

"That's the last flight to Philadelphia."

The doors to the plane shut.

"Are you fucking kidding me? You can't just not contact your customers. You would think an airline would tell you if your flight got fucking canceled. I'm fucked now. Are there any flights in this airport to Philly tonight?"

"Well, sir. You can go to the—"

"I'm not going anywhere." I paced around in front of the customer service desk. "You're going to get me to Philly. This isn't on me."

"We can only look up flights for our airline from this kiosk," she said.

The word "kiosk" always pissed me off.

"Find me a goddamn flight."

"If it's not a Boundary flight, we can't buy you a ticket. We can make only Boundary purchases from this kiosk. I can look up other airline flights, but you can't buy tickets here."

Fuck this kiosk.

"Well, look up flights. And give me my damn voucher."

I snagged the paper from the terrified man. I searched for flights on my phone while the Boundary employees did the same.

"There's a flight that lands Saturday night," Cassie said.

"I have a wedding tomorrow afternoon."

The two employees were on their computers, and I scrolled on my phone, searching for flights to Philly.

I found nothing.

"There's a flight leaving in one hour. You'll land tomorrow at ten a.m.," Cassie said.

"Book it."

"We can't."

"Why?"

"It's a different airline."

"Which?"

"Omega."

I jogged toward the Omega terminal.

But I was missing something.

"Where's my luggage?" I yelled back at the Boundary employees.

"You need to go down the end here, sir, and take the train to the terminal . . ."

There was no way I was going to make this flight.

I sprinted through the airport to the train that drove passengers to baggage claim. The train arrived just as I did. I jumped on, and the train sped toward everyone's luggage.

I was the first one off the train.

People huffed as I pushed by.

I was going to make it.

My luggage wasn't spinning around the baggage carousel.

In fact, no bags were there.

Did those Boundary bastards tell me the wrong one?

My suitcase wasn't anywhere.

I headed for a customer service office behind the baggage claim. There it was. A falling apart green suitcase sitting outside the office. I snagged my luggage. And waved at the worker inside.

"It's mine," I yelled as I ran. "I have to catch a flight."

I was going to make it.

Back on the train.

I bought an eight-hundred-dollar first-class ticket to fly to Philly. While in an airport. On my phone. With a credit card.

The American Dream.

I carried my suitcase with both arms wrapped around it and ran as fast as I could to the Omega Airlines front desk. Pulling the thing would make running harder.

At least that was my logic.

The woman at the Omega Airlines front desk wore a grim look. I asked her about the flight to Philly.

"Boarding closed ten minutes ago."

I launched my suitcase into the empty airport.

"Fuck!"

I walked over to my luggage, picked it up, and screamed into it. I placed it on the ground, pulled up the handle, and rolled it back to the counter.

Deep breath.

Speak.

"I didn't make my flight," I said. "May I have a refund, please?"

Ashley refunded my ticket and asked about my outburst. I told her about Doug's wedding and the Boundary mishaps. She told me she'd look up flights while I called the Boundary customer service line.

Most people were better humans than I'd ever be.

The clown on the Boundary customer service line wasn't.

"If I don't arrive by tomorrow, I'll miss my best friend's wedding," I said.

"We can offer you a two-hundred-dollar flight voucher," the customer service rep said.

"Are you listening? How does a two-hundred-dollar flight voucher get me to Philadelphia? At least pretend to listen while you read from your damn customer cheat sheet that's probably hanging right next to you. Goddamn. I want your manager. I know that's twelve steps too early, according to protocol, but I promise I'll make your goddamn life hell if you don't get me a manager."

The phone got disconnected.

The bastard.

I called my father.

"Hello?" he said.

"I'm stuck in Vegas. I don't know if I'm making it back."

"Wyatt? What? What happened?"

"Nothing has gone right," I said. "Nothing. Nothing since I moved out here. Just one. One goddamn break. That's all I need."

"What are you doing?"

"My flight got canceled. There's nothing to Philly."

"It'll be alright. Call the airline."

"What do you think I did before calling you?"

"If you're gonna be an asshole, I'll go back to bed."

My father talked me down.

It took fifteen minutes.

I yelled most of the time.

Mostly about how awful California treated me.

I called the Boundary Airlines customer service line when I was calm. Spoke to a manager. After forty minutes, he found me a flight to Philly. The manager booked it over the phone and didn't charge me a penny. I'd fly out at 6:00 a.m. to Detroit. Layover in Detroit for three hours. Then land in Philly at three thirty.

With the flight booked, I had a few hours to kill.

Here I was alone in Las Vegas.

No.

I'd never make my 6:00 a.m. flight. A man like me on a time limit in Vegas would lead to a missed flight cliché.

I called for a ride.

* * *

Boundary Airlines promised to reimburse me for my hotel stay on the phone, but I had a feeling their word was just as good as Chuck's. I stayed at a cheap motel next to the biggest Hooters I'd ever seen. When my driver stopped in front of the entrance, he turned and looked back at me.

"You sure you want to stay here?"

I grabbed my luggage from the trunk.

Four people waited ahead of me.

It took an hour to get checked in.

I walked into the room.

The place reeked of a strip club.

Cockroaches fucked on the floor.

The bathroom was nothing but a sink, toilet, and tile floor.

No shower curtain.

Just a drain and a nozzle in the corner of the room.

I called the front desk and asked for a courtesy call in three hours. I also set my phone alarm for three hours. It seemed like a place that would forget to call.

Three-hour power nap.

Shower.

Change into my suit.

Get to the airport.

Fly around the country catching flights.

I slept on top of the covers.

No way I'd let my skin touch the sheets.

September 14, 2019

RING!

"Hello, Mr. Lewis, this is your courtesy call."

She didn't have to sound so fucking cheery.

Showered in socks. Put on my suit and a pair of dry socks. Caught a ride to the airport. Chugged coffee. Flight check-in. Luggage check. Security search. Sitting. Waiting. Boarding. Sitting. Flying. Vegas to Detroit. Landing. Food. Rushing to a connecting flight. Standing. Waiting. Sitting. Waiting. Detroit to Philly. I landed twenty minutes after three.

My father waited for me by the curb of the airport.

I threw my luggage in the front seat.

We sped down the highway as I combed my hair, sprayed cologne, and tied my tie. Or at least tried to.

"You think the Birds will make the playoffs this year?"

His icebreaker was always Eagles related.

"I can't think about that right now," I said.

Another failed knot.

"You'll make it," he said.

I still couldn't get my tie right.

"The ceremony is happening right now," I said. "I'm already missing it."

"We'll get there when we get there. No point in worrying about it now."

My tie refused to knot properly.

"How's California?" my father asked.

"Feels like a vacation," I lied.

"That's not how it sounded last night."

I tried tying my tie for the fourth time.

Unsuccessful.

"It was the stress of missing Doug's wedding. That's all."

"Your mother is worried."

"Why?"

My father looked into his rearview mirror.

"You're coming back for good after the holidays?"

The tie didn't want to cooperate.

"Doubtful."

"Do you really think it's a good idea to stay out there?"

"The best things rarely are," I said.

My father rolled his eyes.

"You're struggling, Wyatt. It's obvious."

"We'll see what happens."

"I think it's about time you give up on this California fantasy. It's no good for anyone."

"Except me."

* * *

I missed the entire wedding ceremony. My father parked in front of the reception hall.

"You're acting like an idiot."

I got out of the car.

"I'll see you."

"Yeah, real soon," he said.

The smug jackass.

I grabbed my luggage and slammed the car door shut.

My father chuckled.

"You're so sensitive."

I ditched the tie and opened up the top two buttons of my shirt. I'd call it California style.

Inside, a hostess held my luggage at the front desk.

Doug, Radek, and Todd broke away from wedding party pictures to greet me. We high-fived and hugged. It was great to see familiar faces. They all asked about California.

"Feels like a vacation" was what I told them.

I didn't want them to worry.

Not on Doug's wedding day.

* * *

I found my way into the reception hall after cocktail hour. The DJ introduced the bridal party. And finally, the couple, who strolled out on the dance floor. I heard a familiar voice. It was a slow Bob Dylan song I had never heard.

Doug wore a deep blue tux with a black tie.

Nancy, a black wedding dress.

They were horror fanatics.

The only reason they didn't get married on Halloween was because Nancy wanted to get married as soon as possible. When she didn't drink at the reception, we all knew why.

I sat down at a table with Todd's parents. I enjoyed talking to them, they'd been around a long time. There's a lot of knowledge in that. But I wanted to strangle Todd's father when he started whistling along to Dion's "Runaround Sue."

I hated whistling.

It was one of my worst triggers.

My father would whistle for me. My brother and sister, too. We had to drop whatever we were doing and run to him. In the middle of homework? Playing a game? Watching TV? Reading? Out in the neighborhood with friends? Didn't matter. Drop it. Run to your father. He needed something. If we didn't arrive quick enough, we got a beating.

Like dogs.

Whenever I heard whistling, I'd become furious. Uncontrolled rage. I couldn't figure out how to stop the trigger. Another drink at the bar calmed me down.

Doug, Radek, Todd and I flexed for the photo booth. I grabbed huge sunglasses. Doug wrapped himself in a boa. Nancy wore a large crown. Radek and Todd hid behind masks. We made stupid poses with each flash. All the pictures came out horribly. It was my favorite part of the wedding.

"Staying out there in California?" Todd asked me on my way to the bar. "Maybe I was wrong."

"You better believe it," I lied.

I told the bartender to keep the drinks coming.

Nancy and Doug cut the cake in secret. No cake smashing. No sharing a first bite. It was the first time Nancy had her makeup done professionally. No way she'd risk ruining that. Her friends threatened to shove cake in her face. But they didn't have the guts.

No one did.

I danced a bit with the wedding party in a giant circle on the dance floor. One of Nancy's bridesmaids ran out to the dancefloor to grind on me. It wasn't even that type of a party. She was drunk. And nuts. The crazies are just broken people. And we're like magnets to our own. Her boyfriend pulled her away from the rest of the party.

Poor bastard.

I grabbed another drink.

Someone caught one of Doug's aunts rummaging through the wedding gift envelopes. Families got pissed. Assuming she was trying to steal money. But Aunt Nina was looking for her envelope. She couldn't remember if she put it in the stack of cards. Turned out she forgot it in the car.

Aunt Nina was crazy.

No doubt.

But not evil.

I ran into my Doug's father right before the last song of the night. He was a hard man to pin down. Everyone wanted to talk with him. He was funny. And don't give a fuck what anyone thought about him.

"Congrats," I said. "Hell of a night."

"You look more and more like your father every day," he said.

"Only when I look in the mirror."

We all become our parents.

It's why I didn't want to have kids.

I wasn't arrogant enough to think I'd be any different than my father.

The DJ played the final song of the night.

It was "Last Dance" by Donna Summer.

The reception ended.

The guests left.

Besides me, only the bridal party remained.

Doug and Nancy bought most of the decorations and wanted to keep them. A ton of Halloween stuff. I couldn't blame them. We loaded them in boxes and carried them to their SUV. Doug, Nancy,

Todd, Radek and I crowded into Todd's hotel room. A few bridesmaids joined us with their husbands. I tried to convince Nancy to name her child after me. Radek did the same.

After two rounds of beers, Doug and Nancy went to their suite. Todd kicked Radek and me out when he wanted to go to sleep. The bridesmaids went to their rooms.

Radek and I hung out in his room. I had a few hours to kill before I had to fly back to California.

"You seem worse than the last time I saw you," he said.

"Thanks."

"How are you doing out there?"

"Fine."

Radek stared at me.

"Would I lie?" I asked.

"No," Radek said. "You'd call it bullshitting."

"Work is tough. I'm adjusting. It's nothing I can't handle."

It was myself I was trying to convince.

"Don't hesitate to call me, broski," he said. "You got me, if you need anything."

"I know."

"I noticed you avoided me at the wedding," Radek said. "You knew I'd call you out."

"I didn't want anyone to worry."

"Don't give us a reason to," he said.

We polished off a six pack.

There was a big part of me that didn't want to leave.

But I had to.

Drunk and still in my suit, I grabbed my suitcase and headed back to California.

The Dreaded Four P.M. Firing Meeting
September 27, 2019

Wake up. Hit the snooze button. Fall back asleep. Battle with the alarm until staying in bed any longer will cause me to be late. Curse every God I can remember. Climb out of bed. Walk Hank. Contemplate showering. Skip it. Put on my clown suit. Drive to work. Hope I get into a car wreck. Arrive at Reynolds Incorporated alive. And disappointed. Attend pointless meetings. Convince myself that this terrible existence was worth the paycheck. Eat my sorrow for lunch. Get the silent treatment from my colleagues. Avoid work. Watch the entire staff conduct interviews for my job. Apparently, no one wanted to work at Reynolds Incorporated. I didn't. Surf the internet. Leave work at five on the dot. Drive home through California rush hour. Get high. Walk Hank to the dog park. Sit in a corner away from animals and their dogs. Scowl at anyone who came near me. Walk home. Smoke more weed. Shower. Some days. Watch TV. Get more high. Skip dinner. Sleep.

Every day was the same.

Except the day Chuck forgot about his longest-tenured employee's one-year work anniversary. Trish didn't care that he didn't give her a yearly raise. Or meet with her to discuss her future at Reynolds Incorporated. No. She was mad that Chuck didn't acknowledge her for one year of service with his company. Trish started looking for new employment from her work computer.

October 4, 2019

It was Friday morning when Chuck canceled the weekly end-of-week recap meeting. He did it because he wanted to meet with Gary and me. A four o'clock meeting with management meant only one thing.

I was a few hours away from the unemployment line.

The entire staff ignored me that day. No one wanted to be seen talking to the walking dead man. I stared at the clock. It didn't move. I reviewed my defense on why Chuck shouldn't fire me. The Boston trip had led to a new client signing a year-long contract with Reynolds Incorporated. And my bullshit speech had gotten them to agree to an extra two thousand dollars a month. Two more clients signed a contract through Chuck's plan, which I developed. He took the credit, though. I printed out emails from clients and colleagues praising my work.

The hours dragged on.

I had nothing to put on my daily task email.

Except anxiety.

I hated the job, but I needed the money. Especially the bonus. The clock stood still. I couldn't concentrate on my computer screen. I grabbed another cup of coffee. My sixth of the day.

I texted my father while I waited for the cup to brew. *I'm going to get fired today. My boss scheduled a meeting for 4.*

My father called me seconds after I hit send on the text.

"What do you mean, you're getting fired? What the fuck did you do now?"

"I'm not sure, to be honest."

"What's wrong with you?"

I jumped into one of the many empty offices at Reynolds Incorporated and shut the door behind me. "There's a lot going on. It's not—"

"Why can't you keep your mouth shut and do your fucking job like everyone else?"

"Listen—"

"No. You listen. Keep your mouth shut. Do whatever you need to do to keep your job."

"I need—"

"I need to get back to work. Keep your job. Call me after your meeting."

* * *

Four finally came.

Chuck and Gary were already waiting for me in the conference room.

"It pains me to have this conversation a second time," Chuck said. "I want you to succeed here, but you haven't been working up to our Reynolds Incorporated standards."

He was one to talk about standards.

"We've noticed your attention to detail has been lacking," Gary said.

"You have become very disorganized," Chuck said. "And inconsistent with your daily emails. The expectation is you send them every day. And you haven't."

"I'm trying my best," I said.

It was a lie.

"You're not," Chuck said. "I've seen your best."

"You have incredible talent, but the focus isn't there anymore," Gary said.

It was a fucking tag team.

They piled on me.

Telling me where I was weak.

And where they expected improvement.

I gripped my leather seat tight.

Neither said a thing about my job being on the line, but I knew this was the prefiring meeting before the meeting to discuss firing me, which was right before the firing-me meeting. That's how Chuck ran his business. And his process would have me fired right before November came. Chuck would have plenty of documentation to prove he did everything he could to work with me. But I was just an inadequate employee.

"We know you can improve," Gary said. "The talent is there. We just need that drive back."

"Your attitude has been really hurting the office," Chuck said.

"My attitude?"

"You're not excited to be a part of the team," Chuck said. "There's no enthusiasm in your work. I brought you in here to inspire company culture."

Hire a fucking cheerleader.

"The office energy has been dragging," Gary said.

"Do you want to work here?" Chuck asked.

"What?" I asked.

Chuck slammed his fist on the table.

"Do you want to work here!"

Gary jumped from his seat.

It brought me back to my childhood.

"Well," Chuck said. "Do you?"

"Yeah," I lied.

"That doesn't sound inspired to me," Chuck said. He took a breath to compose himself. "Listen, if you don't want to work here, I can arrange another job for you. We can have an agreement and work toward us both moving on. I don't want to put you out on the streets. I know you just moved out here."

Yeah.

Let me tell you I hate my job and want to quit. I'm sure that'll have zero consequences. Like forfeiting my bonus check.

"I'd be happy to get back to my job now where I am happy," I said. "I want to keep our clients satisfied, but I can't do that in this meeting."

"We're not finished here yet," Chuck said.

"We've developed a plan of action," Gary said.

Another one?

Chuck and Gary explained a new way of reporting the work I did on a daily basis. Weekly check-in meetings. Daily one-on-one meetings. More supervision. Less freedom. The plan was to make my life at work even more hellish. It was going to work.

"Any questions?" Chuck asked.

"When should I expect my bonus? It's almost been ten months."

"Your bonus?" Chuck asked. "Seems like an inappropriate time to ask about that. Here you are, asking about a bonus when for the last four months your work has been below average."

"It was in our contract."

"I expected better work."

I took a deep breath.

"It feels like you're picking on me for no good reason."

Chuck scoffed.

"You're too sensitive."

My father's words coming out of my boss's mouth.

That's who the bastard reminded me of.

"Chuck, we can't say that," Gary said.

"It hasn't been a full ten months. You'll be paid the first day of November." Chuck smiled. "Any other questions?"

He looked too content for my liking.

And I knew I'd never get that bonus.

I didn't say anything until Chuck stood up from his seat.

"One more question." I paused. "Who was that woman that came to your room on our business trip? Was she a client? It was a little late for a meeting. And she didn't look like your wife. Who was she?"

Chuck lunged across the table. "You're fired! Get out!"

Gary pulled him back with all his might.

"I'll go get my things," I said.

"Not without a fucking escort!" Chuck yelled. "Call security. I don't want him stealing anything. The fucking liar."

Gary walked Chuck down to his office, pulling his arm.

"Stay in here," Gary directed to me.

I sat and waited patiently for the building's security. It probably was a mistake to blow ten-thousand dollars like that, but there was no way Chuck would ever pay me.

A husky man showed me to my desk.

He watched me gather my things.

I didn't even get to say goodbye to Trish.

But I waved at Chuck and smiled when I left.

California Freedom

October 18, 2019

A	s soon as I released Hank from his leash, he sprinted in the sand toward the ocean. Every so often, he'd stop and turn around to make sure I was still following him.

The beach was filled with surfers, dogs, and people just trying to escape the world for a while. My California beach days were numbered.

Hank bolted around the beachgoers and kicked up sand in excitement. He licked awake a young woman in a teeny yellow bikini as she tanned on a towel. Natalie thought Hank was cute, and threw his ball for him. She told me she had no time for anything but work, law school, and the occasional beach nap. She kept tossing Hank's ball into the ocean. Her arm didn't appear to get tired.

The afternoon faded away.

Natalie asked if Hank and I wanted to come by her place. I told her I was usually agreeable to that sort of adventure, but I had work to do.

"What kind of work?"

"I write," I said.

"For who?"

"Myself."

Natalie crossed her arms.

"You don't have a job?"

"I write every day. It's honest work."

She pulled down her sunglasses.

"How long have you been doing that?"

"Two weeks."

"Are you looking for work?"

"Not yet," I said.

Unemployed writer.

Two words that dried up every vagina on the planet.

Natalie excused herself from the conversation.

I made my way back to my towel, just beyond the ocean's touch. Hank splashed in the water, taunting other dogs to chase him. The sun sank into the ocean. I pulled my notebook and pen from my book bag.

She was exactly how I imagined. A perfect smile formed on her plump lips. Even her teeth were orthodontist approved. Her blue eyes lit up her platinum blonde hair, which fell past her teasing chest and rested on the biggest fake tits I'd ever seen.

I hadn't planned to take molly for the first time that day, but things change quickly in California. In my hand, a napkin holding a semi crushed pill. I looked up from the drugs to find the first California girl to ever speak to me. I tossed it in my mouth and washed it down with the last of my giant-size margarita. There's just something about a California girl that makes a man say fuck it.

It wasn't perfect.
But it wasn't bad for a first draft.

* * *

I didn't tell anyone about being fired.
After two weeks of pure bliss, I told my family and friends about losing my job. Everyone offered condolences like I lost a loved one. I didn't understand it. My family each had their own thoughts on the matter, but the same conclusion.

"Maybe you should come home," my mother said. "California isn't working."

"California isn't meant to be," Kayla said.

"It doesn't seem worth it," my father said. "You're unhappy and broke."

Broke?

Yes.

Unhappy?

Things were trending up.

But the government didn't help my situation.

The California Employment Development Department withheld my unemployment payments. The Department of Labor sent me a letter demanding I appear for a telephone hearing to determine if I was eligible for unemployment benefits. The government said there was no reason given on my termination form, therefore I needed to explain to the government why I was fired from Reynolds Incorporated.

Chuck really didn't do any fucking work.

With no unemployment checks, I couldn't afford to eat.

Breath even.

California was on life support.

Leah's Halloween Birthday Disco at the Roller Rink

October 19, 2019

Leah greeted me at her sister's front door in tiny cheetah shorts and knee-high socks. She wore pigtails, and her tits popped out of her low-cut black shirt and leopard-print vest.

"Happy birthday, beautiful," I said.

She gave me a long hug.

"I'm glad you came," Leah said. "I missed you."

"I missed you too."

"You're going to skate right? You have to when we get there."

For her birthday, Leah wanted to dress up and go drunk roller skating.

"I haven't since I was a kid," I said.

"It's my party, and that's what I want," Leah said.

She pulled me into the kitchen which was filled with smoke from a fog machine. Cobwebs, spiders dangling from the ceilings, and orange lights decorated the rest of the house.

I knew which friends were Leah's work friends because they dressed as sexy nurses. Stockings, bright red lipstick, zombie eyes, slit throats, and escaping ass cheeks. Even one tall, ogre-looking bearded guy played nurse. Hairy ass hanging out and all.

More people showed up at the party, and Leah had to play host. I didn't see Leah's younger sister anywhere—not that I would know what she looked like—but I figured she looked like Leah.

A coked-out doctor named Bernard kept trying to unhinge his jaw as he talked to me about some video game series. He wore a superhero's logo and a cape and was awfully boring. Paige, in a sexy nurse outfit and red lipstick, brought him a beer.

Bernard was the married douche Paige dated.

She could do better.

Way better.

"You nailed it," Paige said.

I posed in my skintight zebra pants and opened my jean jacket revealing a tight Motley Crue T-shirt. It was the same outfit I had worn on my eighties night with Leah. I couldn't afford a Halloween costume.

"I wish I could wear this out every weekend," I said.

"Maybe you should tomorrow."

I crushed my beer can.

"Pub and Pool?"

"Duh. We need a fucking win."

I grabbed someone else's beer from the fridge. "I'm not sure I should watch them in public."

"Come to the bar," Paige said.

Paige poured vodka into three shot glasses. She, Bernard, and I threw them back.

"Go Birds."

Before Paige could pour another, a woman who oozed confidence walked into the house with Tony and four more cases of beer. I hated seeing Tony.

"Place was fucking packed," the woman said.

She and Tony filled the fridge with the fresh beer. Leah kissed Tony hello before she dragged the new woman over to me.

"This is my sister, Nicole," Leah said.

She looked nothing like Leah.

Leah's sister had dyed, short jet-black hair, dozens of piercings, and tattoos covering her body.

"The infamous Wyatt," she said. "It's nice to finally meet you."

"Nicole. The pleasure is all mine."

And it was.

"Call me Nikki," she said.

Nikki, Leah, and I did a shot of whiskey together. Then we did another round when Summer and Noah showed up. He wore a tie-dye T-shirt and jeans. Summer wore an entire flower child costume, hippie glasses and all. When Leah introduced Summer to Nikki, Summer lost her mind.

"Oh my god," Summer said. "So beautiful. Wow! How old are you?"

Nikki put her eyes down and kicked her feet on the floor.

Before she could answer, Summer spoke again. "Wait. Let me guess."

"Twenty-five," Nikki said.

"What I wouldn't give to be twenty-five," Summer said. "You're so young. Ugh. Look at your face. A baby!"

Nikki turned her head away from Summer.

"Where have the years gone?" Summer asked. "Look at her skin. I haven't had skin like that in years!"

Noah and I hung out for a beer while Leah and the rest of the party did blow. I walked outside with a new beer when the party resumed. Nikki was in her driveway setting up a folding table for people to play beer pong.

"What do you do for work?" Nikki asked.

"Telemarketer," I said.

"Shut up."

"There are worse ways to make a living."

"You're quite tan for a guy who works in an office."

I laughed. "It's amazing what being unemployed does for your skin."

"You got a lady? Any kids?"

"None that I know of," I said.

Leah poked her head outside. "Let's get some pictures and go. I'm ready to skate!"

"Fucking Leah," Nikki muttered.

She didn't bother to continue to set up the folding table. Nikki turned around to go back inside. She walked right by me. Don't do it.

No.

Nikki's ass bounced as she walked through the door.

Dammit.

I couldn't help myself.

In the kitchen, Noah wasn't feeling drunk enough, so he found a bottle of Jack Daniel's.

"Shots before we go?"

A curvy woman with a face full of Botox told Noah she wanted one.

"I'm in," I said.

Jack Daniel's was bad news.

But if Noah did a shot with just this beautiful woman, Summer would blow a gasket.

"Are you going to ask me if I want a shot?" Summer demanded.

That's when I knew the night was fucked.

"Who's that?" the woman, Rita, asked.

"It's his fucking girlfriend," Summer said. "That's who."

Noah poured the shots. Rita, Noah, Summer, and I took them. Summer never took her eyes off Rita, even as she threw back the booze. Rita rubbed Noah's arm before leaving with her friends to catch a ride.

The rest of the party cleared out, and I followed Noah and Summer along the sidewalk to his car.

"Are you fucking kidding me?" Summer yelled.

"What?" Noah said.

"You need to be better," Summer said.

"You knew what she was doing," Summer said.

"She came out of nowhere," Noah said.

Poor Summer.

There were beautiful women everywhere in San Diego. And there were always younger women ready to pounce on someone else's man. Because in California everyone went after what they wanted with no regard for anyone else.

Summer and Noah bickered the entire two-block walk to the car. They didn't stop as we drove to the roller rink.

"Are we just not going to talk about that?" Summer asked.

"I didn't do anything."

"Don't even play fucking dumb with me right now."

Noah hit the gas. "We just did this."

"And did we finish? No. We didn't."

I squeezed my leather seat with both hands.

"I don't want to do this now," Noah said.

Summer crossed her arms and sat back in her seat.

"You know you're wrong."

"I don't want to fight in front of Wyatt."

My toes curled inside my boots.

I didn't know how much more I could handle.

"He's seen me at my worst," Summer said. "He's an adult. He can handle it."

I couldn't.

"Enough," Noah said.

Summer flailed her arms in the air. "You were wrong. You know you're wrong. You checked that chick out and poured her a fucking shot. I saw you. That's why you don't want to talk about it."

My feet pushed down onto the floor.

"I was offering anyone a shot. Then she asked for one. It's a friend of Leah's. What was I supposed to do?"

"Ignore the bitch."

"Help me out, man," Noah said.

My mouth stayed shut.

As a kid, my parents would get into late-night arguments. My father would pull my brother and me from bed and demand we weigh in on his martial issues. School in the morning be damned.

"Tell me he wasn't all over that girl," Summer said.

Noah whipped the car around a corner and gunned the engine.

"You're overreacting."

"What did you say?" she asked.

Noah didn't take the bait.

He drove faster.

"You want to see me overreact?" Summer said. "Do you want to see who can get more numbers tonight?"

"Me," Noah said.

"Do you really want to do this?"

I didn't want them to.

"You're going to embarrass yourself," Noah said.

"You have no idea," Summer said. "I ain't got no ring. I'm a free fucking woman."

"I guess a million-dollar house and fake tits isn't enough." Noah said.

"You wanted these! And I deserve a fucking ring for dealing with your wandering fucking eyes."

She folded her arms and faced the car window.

I let out a sigh of relief.

* * *

Summer and Noah argued by the roller rink's snack bar. It was kind of funny from a distance. Two hippies in a heated argument. A bunch of coked-out people in Halloween costumes skated around children on the rink. In the arcade, Bernard refused to stop playing Mortal Kombat. He beat child after child who challenged him to the game. Paige yanked on his arms, but he'd pull them away from her to keep smashing buttons.

The world was fucked-up.

I did a few solo laps around the rink on skates. I never learned how to rollerblade. Tony and Leah flew by me a few times.

It sucked.

I stayed on the rink until Leah decided she wanted booze and drugs. A child's roller rink didn't offer those benefits.

We all left.

* * *

Summer and Noah never made it to the after-party. I caught a ride with Paige and Bernard. He played jazz music the entire way back.

What a douche.

Leah played Bob Dylan over Nikki's speakers. Pills were taken. Drugs snorted. Shots thrown back. Bottles uncorked. Despite all the creative potions and narcotics, the conversations were terribly boring.

Who gets high and compares 401(k)s?

These drug-addicted wannabe capitalists.

The conversation grew dull when the drugs were all consumed. Leah led Tony by the hand into Nikki's spare bedroom. Instead of leaving, I stole a six-pack from the fridge and sat on the porch. It was a quiet night in San Diego. Nothing like the summer, when rented cars and ride shares polluted the air. The beer tasted crisp. It was a hazy IPA, definitely a beer bought for Leah.

Paige walked by me when she left with Bernard.

He said nothing.

She said a quick goodbye.

Fuck that guy.

After my second beer, a creak caused me to turn around. Two more people left the party. Nikki came outside and shut the front door behind her. "It's boring as shit in there."

"I hear it's worse out here," I said.

"Thanks for not making a big deal about my age," she said. "I hate that."

I handed her a beer.

"Sorry about my friends. They have this complex. They can't handle the years."

Nikki laughed.

"I don't think anyone can."

"That's why you gotta enjoy it," I said.

A tall and attractive guy powered outside and sat next to Nikki. His biceps couldn't be contained by his extra tight black T-shirt. His name was Dom, and he wouldn't shut his mouth.

It was ten minutes before Nikki, or I, could get a word in.

"Man, I hate when people just take over a conversation," Nikki said.

"Dude," Dom said. "Me too. Some people have, like, no social skills."

"It's rude," I said. "Makes someone look like a real asshole."

Dom pulled Nikki onto his lap.

She jumped off and sat back down on the stoop.

"I'll have my own seat," she said.

He rubbed her leg.

She slapped his hand.

Dom pulled back his arm.

We talked some more about the party, and how awesome Dom was. He was on the verge of being a tech billionaire. He just needed a little extra funding to get where he wanted to be.

Yeah.

Okay.

He returned his hand to Nikki's leg.

Nikki grabbed his index finger and threw his hand off.

We talked a bit more.

Well, Dom did.

He learned how to hack his body for optimal gains. He explained his process. It made no fucking sense.

Dom slid his fingers down Nikki's inner thigh.

She stood up.

"I'm going to start cleaning up now," Nikki said.

She headed into the house.

Dom followed right behind her.

Dammit.

I couldn't leave.

Not with Dom still here.

I didn't know if the guy was capable of rape, but I didn't trust him alone with Nikki.

I finished the six-pack before I went inside.
Being drunk would help me in a fight.
If it came to that.
In the kitchen, Dom had Nikki by the hips.
He grinded behind her.
Holding her tight as she wrapped a dish with plastic wrap.
Somehow Nikki ignored the prick.
I couldn't.
"Need any help?" I asked.
The creep jumped back.
"We're good," Dom said. "We got this."
"I could use some help, actually," Nikki said.
Nikki pushed Dom and handed each of us a trash bag. We threw out plates, half-filled beer cups, and left-out food from the table in the kitchen. Dom started making more small talk with me. Asking me what I did, how I knew Nikki, if I were single. It wasn't asked in a kind way, either.
When Nikki bent down to move a cooler, Dom ran behind her, grabbed her, spun her, and forced his lips onto hers.
Nikki shoved him off.
"Everyone out!" she yelled. "I'm going to bed."
"I can finish this," Dom said.
"I'll do the rest in the morning," Nikki said. "Out!"
Dom and I found ourselves on the porch.
Nikki slammed the door behind us.
"You need a ride, bro?" Dom asked.
"I just called one. Thanks."
"All good. Hope to see you around, man."
Dom walked to his silver Jeep. I sat down on Nikki's stoop. I pretended to call for a ride. He sat with the engine running for ten minutes before he peeled off down the street.
The asshole did three laps around the block.
I waited another fifteen minutes before I called a ride.

California Blondes and Molly: the Remix

October 27, 2019

If Summer arrived at the bar any later, we wouldn't have gotten a table. Paige and I ordered a cheesesteak for breakfast. With an Irish coffee.

Leah showed up midway through the second quarter of the game with the tags on her new Eagles hat. She tried to learn the words to the Eagles fight song, but she was too fucked-up from the painkillers the doctor prescribed.

"How's your back?" Summer asked.

Leah fired down another shot.

"I'll let you know in ten minutes."

"How did you do that?" Paige asked.

"Tried to lift up some fat guy that passed out at work," Leah said. "I got him up. But it cost me."

Paige didn't believe Leah.

Summer and Leah went to the bathroom to snort some coke. Paige and I polished off two pitchers of light beer. We were well on our way to being twisted for the day.

Paige left after the game to meet up with Bernard.

Leah couldn't keep her eyes open.

At least the Birds stomped the Bills, 31–13.

Leah suggested we meet up with her sister, who was only a few blocks away.

Nikki was with her old roommate, Sarah, and a tall, stubble-bearded, handsome guy with long dirty-blond hair and tattoos, named Tim. Leah went to the bar and rested her head on the polished wood. The rest of us drank fancy yellow-and-pink cocktails that Tim ordered.

"They look fruity, but they're damn delicious," Tim said. "And get you real fucked-up."

Another round went down.

Leah slept at the bar. Alone. The bartenders didn't say anything. Tim slipped them a twenty. But when the manager came outside, he asked Leah to leave.

I sat down next to her and rubbed her back.

"We gotta go."

She lifted her head.

"No."

It was the first coherent sentence she'd said in an hour.

Leah buried her head back into her arms.

Summer sat down on the other side of Leah.

"I'll handle this," she said. "You enjoy Sunday Funday."

"You sure?" I asked.

"I think it's drugs," Summer said. "Painkillers and booze aren't a good mix. I'll meet up with you once she goes to bed."

"Bed?" Leah slurred. "We're going all day! I have molly! Remember Wyatt? When we met?"

She tried to step off the barstool but stumbled. Summer caught Leah before she wiped out. They waited outside the bar for a ride.

Tim suggested we go to his house to finish the afternoon. Nikki still had a ton of booze left in her glass. Expensive alcohol that we didn't want to waste. Sarah had a water thermos with her. Californians always carried these, like there was always about to be a drought. I dumped the water from it into one of the nearby decorative plants. Nikki flirted with the bartender while I poured the rest of her booze into the thermos.

Tim, Sarah, Nikki, and I took turns sipping from it on the sidewalk outside the bar as we waited for a ride. A white minivan pulled up to the curb.

I took another swig.

The driver gave me a death stare as I climbed into the car.

"There's not alcohol in there, right?" the old man asked.

"No, sir," I said.

I sat in the very back with Nikki. As soon as the driver put his eyes on the road, I took a long swig from the thermos.

"Gotta hydrate."

"You need some water?" I asked Nikki. "It's hot out there."

I handed Nikki the thermos, and she took a long chug.

"Just what I needed," she said.

The rest of the ride, the driver paid more attention to me in the back seat than to the road.

He assumed I'd lied.

He was right.

Nikki and I emptied the thermos before we got to Tim's.

Tim, Nikki, Sarah, and I smoked a joint on Tim's backyard deck. We drank some beers and talked. No one got angry or screamed, just four people bullshitting about life and drinking. It was nothing like life with my father. Everything was always a fight. And my father was never wrong.

"Did I tell you about Dom?" Nikki asked Sarah.

"Dom?" I asked.

"He was there with you at the end of the night," Nikki said.

The touchy douche.

Him.

"That guy," I said. "How do you know him? Doesn't seem like someone you'd hang out with."

"He was just really drunk. He's never like that," Nikki said.

"Wait," Sarah said. "Who? Dom? I was there. How did I not see this?"

"It was nothing," Nikki said. "He was drunk. Gotta little handsy. But the next day I woke up to flowers and a letter at my door. They were from Dom. Apologizing for his actions. Asking me out. Confessing his love to me. A love he's always desired."

I rolled my eyes.

"As if the mouth rape wasn't enough," I said.

"He asked about you," Nikki said. "If we were dating. What our deal was."

"You haven't told him about us?" I asked.

Nikki smiled.

"I told him we shouldn't chill for a bit. Shit was weird. Then he told me he's always loved me."

"Fucking creep," Sarah said.

Nikki moved the conversation to the Women's March, sexist men, and abortions. A topic Nikki wasn't shy to discuss. It was a part of her charm. Her edge. She and Sarah were pro-choice, and I couldn't blame them. I couldn't imagine what I'd do if someone with no accountability for my life told me how to live it.

"I don't care," Sarah said. "Rip that baby out of me. My body, my choice. Fuck it."

I hoped I was never in a situation where abortion was on the table. Not because I didn't believe in it, but the whole thing was so damn complicated. And to generalize as either yes or no on something none of us really understand, and only half of us can experience, seems tacky.

"Have you ever had one?" Tim asked.

"Shit," I said. "That's blunt."

Nikki shook her head.

"Five," Sarah said.

It felt wrong.

Sarah had enough abortions to start a basketball team.

But it wasn't my body.

I didn't say a word.

"Damn girl," Tim said.

"Watch it," Nikki said. "She can do whatever she wants. If men carried babies, there would be an abortion clinic on every corner."

"No there wouldn't," I said.

Nikki and Sarah glared at me.

"Men would never have the patience to carry a childhood for nine months," I said. "If men were responsible for procreation, humans would have gone extinct centuries ago."

Everyone laughed.

I was serious.

"Enough of the serious shit," Nikki said. "It's Sunday Funday!"

"Woo! Woo!" Sarah yelled.

"What's next?" Nikki asked.

There was a dive bar a few blocks from Tim's place that played old-school hip-hop on Sunday nights. Tim figured we could get there early and enjoy the music for a bit before the crowds.

"Once it gets late, you can't move," Tim said. "They have no air in there either. It gets really gross."

"I could go for some molly," Nikki said. "It would make the club fun. And tolerable. I'll text Leah. You text Summer. I know Leah has some."

"Because she dates a drug dealer," Sarah said.

"Oh, Leah," Tim said.

I knew that Summer had scored some pills from Leah before Leah had passed out, but I told Nikki that Summer couldn't get the drugs. I thought it would be fun to mess with Nikki. She seemed to be the type of person that always got her way. Those people are the best to fuck with.

Nikki didn't hear back from Leah.

"Fuck," she said. "I don't know about this club without molly."

Tim and Sarah hopped onto the hammock on the other side of the deck. Nikki and I watched, giving a play-by-play of the action. Cuddling first. Then kissing. Rotating the hammock to hide their romance, like we didn't know they were making out. By the time Summer arrived, Tim was inside fucking Sarah.

"Leah wanted me to give you something," Summer said to Nikki. "She said you'd appreciate it."

She dropped five blue pills on the patio table.

Nikki grinned.

"Wyatt! You're such a liar!"

Sarah and Tim decided to wait, but the rest of us took our drugs. But then Nikki insisted we put food in our bellies before drinking more. So she, Summer, and I walked a few blocks to some upscale Italian restaurant that I'd never visit again. The place had the lights turned down and candles on every table. There was a saxophone player in the corner playing smooth jazz with all the patrons wearing fancy dinner attire.

I hated it.

Summer sat next to me with Nikki across from me.

Nikki's half smile lifted as my eyes found hers.

She giggled.

The way she smiled with her eyes.

It was the way Leah looked at me.

Maybe it was the drugs.

I was rolling.

"And for you?" a server with a pixie cut asked.

I hadn't looked at the menu.

Or realized there was a waitress at the table.

"You got any chicken tenders?" I asked.

Mature thought, Wyatt.

Nikki looked at me like I committed a crime. I didn't even want chicken tenders. It was just the first edible thing that popped into my head. And I needed to say something.

"Alright, but it's from our kid's menu."

She walked away before I could give a rebuttal.

* * *

There were about twenty people in line for the club. When we got in, Nikki took off her flannel shirt and tied it around her waist, revealing a white tank top.

We squeezed our way to the bar.

A beat dropped that sounded like Ginuwine.

"I love this song!" Nikki shouted when "Pony" erupted over the club speakers.

"I'll get us beers," Summer said. "Get out there."

Nikki grabbed my hand and forced her way onto the dance floor. She spun around and pushed her ass against my hips. Moving side to side in perfect rhythm. Nikki pressed harder against my jeans. Rolled her ass around. She dipped it down. Brought it up. Nice and slow. I grabbed her hips. And held the fuck on.

Summer mouthed an exaggerated "Whoa" when she saw me and Nikki. I threw my hands up to let her know it was my bad, but I wasn't going to stop. Summer walked away with Nikki's and my beers, disappearing into the sea of people.

The DJ should have played "Too Close" next.

Even though he didn't, Nikki and I stayed on the dance floor until we were drenched.

"I need some water," Nikki said.

She led me to the side of the bar where a clear, giant ice-water jug sat. We waited in line behind a few people. Sweating a puddle as we did.

"There's no fucking air in this place," Nikki said.

I wiped my head with my arm.

"I don't think the drugs are helping."

Nikki moved up in line, one person closer to the ice-cold water.

"I think they are."

She gave me a seductive smile.

We drank three restaurant cups' worth of ice water when we made it to the jug.

It didn't help.

"It's still hot as fuck in here," she said.

My shirt was glued to my skin.

But I didn't want to leave.

"It's not too bad," I said. "Minus all the people."

We couldn't even move to get back to the dance floor.

"I'm over it," Nikki said.

Nikki walked out of the joint.

I wanted to chase her.

But I couldn't leave Summer.

I squirmed through sweaty people swinging their hips, trying to avoid hitting their drinks while looking for Summer. I couldn't help but dance when "Return of the Mack" came on.

I left the dance floor after the song.

Summer was drinking beers with Tim and Sarah, who I was surprised to see. She handed me her beer to chug. After the booze was gone, Sarah handed me hers. I looked at Tim. He shook his head and patted his belly. I downed the beer.

With no booze or patience for the heat and crowd, we left. Sarah went back to Tim's place. Nikki was sitting on the joint's giant windowsill, fanning herself with her hands. I sat down next to her.

"You shouldn't do it," Nikki said.

I put my hand on her knee.

She didn't move it.

"Do what?"

"Don't date Leah."

I moved my hand.

"I'm not. I—"

"I see how you look at her," she said.

"It's not like that," I said. "She's got a boyfriend."

"It won't last." Nikki swiveled her body to face me. "Just keep an eye on her for me, okay?"

"For what?"

She looked at me, dumbfounded as her ride arrived.

"Have a good night."

Nikki gave me a kiss on the cheek and left.

Wait.

What?

But then the molly wave went up.

The drug intensifies throughout the trip.

The happiness comes and goes.

I was rolling.

Again.

Can't kill my buzz.

Not when I'm feeling this good.

"Let me take you home," Summer said.

"Are you okay to drive?"

"I drive his car better a little fucked-up."

"Didn't realize you were allowed to drive it," I said.

Summer stopped walking and faced me.

"I break them all."

She laughed.

We continued our walk.

Noah's sports car was parked outside a house.

Along the street.

Noah always put his car in a garage.

Never out in public.

But there it was.

Next to a curb.

I didn't even want to ask.

"That was a crazy Sunday," I said. "Can you believe—"

"Don't even."

"What?"

"Don't," she said.

"I didn't."

"Don't even think it."

"I'm not thinking anything."

"Don't say it," Summer said.

I smiled.

"Nikki."

Summer unlocked the car.

"Dammit."

"She's cute."

"Why?"

"She's fun," I said.

"I'm always dragged into your shit."

I slid into the front seat.

"You started it."

"Me? Me. How did I start this?"

"You told me to stay with Nikki," I said. "I was gonna go back with Leah."

Summer started the engine.

"I would not let you waste a Sunday dealing with that."

"Still."

"Leah didn't want you to see her like that."

"But Nikki's cute, right?" I asked.

"Obviously."

"Leah would kill me."

"She'd kill me too," Summer said. "Be careful. Nikki's a flirt."

"So . . . she *was* flirting."

Summer's voice rose. "Why do you always drag me into this shit?"

"When was the last time?"

"Every day since I've known you."

"You know, you haven't always been supportive in my endeavors," I said.

Summer slammed her hands on the steering wheel.

"Like when?"

"Remember that party at my house when Kristen asked if I cheated on her?"

"What was I supposed to do!"

Summer went around the highway bend at full speed.

"You know, help me out," I said.

"Say it. Say it, Mr. Self-Righteous."

I stayed quiet.

"You wanted me to lie for you!" Summer yelled. "Admit it."

"How many times have I lied for you?"

"I never asked you to lie."

"Bullshit," I said.

"Misremembering is different."

"How is that different?"

"It was college, for Christ's sake," Summer said. "I was so young and stupid."

"Some of us still are."

Summer parked in front of my apartment.

"You and your bullshit. I swear to Christ, you're the first person I'm calling if I murder Noah. God forbid. But maybe. Who knows? You men drive me fucking nuts. You're bringing shovels and bleach. You better get your ass there too. Or I'm digging another grave."

I laughed, but I also knew she wasn't kidding.

One Last Letter

November 10, 2019

I didn't know how much molly I had taken. I tore off my clothes, slammed the sliding glass bedroom door shut, and cranked up the air conditioner. It didn't help. I couldn't cool down. I chugged three waters, but I was still thirsty. And so hot.

I stumbled into the shower and sat. The cold water poured down on my body. Freezing. It felt terrible. And great.

I'm not sure how long I lasted in the shower.

I went to bed without toweling off.

Naked and soaked.

Wrapped in my blanket.

Thump. Thump. Thump. Thump. Thump.

My heart tried to pound its way out of my chest.

Come on buddy.

You're gonna kill us all.

The heart-to-heart failed.

In fact, my heart worked harder.

I found a half-drunk water in my bed.

Down my throat the liquid went.

Hank went to sleep on the couch.

Abandoning me.

I'd die alone in bed.

"God, if you can hear me, it's Wyatt. Yeah, I only ask for things when I think I'm about to die or in deep shit, but have you thought of me in a while? I promise I'll pray every day, if you let me live." I rose from my bed, got on my hands and knees, and spread my arms wide, waiting for an imaginary hug from God. "I'll stop doing drugs. Well, I'll stop doing molly. I mean, I'll do less. Once a year if that. Maybe not at all. But maybe a few times. You never know." My heart punched my rib cage. "Actually, you know, fuck it, I'll lay off it. Please just don't let me die."

I recited what I remembered of the Hail Mary and Our Father prayers before making the sign of the cross and jumping back into bed. I used to be such a good Catholic boy.

My heart continued to beat at a rapid pace.

God must have been working slowly.

Or he wanted to kill his demon spawn.

I needed something—aspirin?

No.

Food?

No.

Weed.

I threw off my covers and ran toward the living room. The ruckus caused Hank to wake up. I took some hits off my weed pen. Drug science. Weed would help me not die. Obviously. Hard to believe I once scored a thirty-eight during an entire semester of chemistry in high school.

My heart sped up.

This was it.

The weed didn't work.

I pulled out my phone and started typing.

If I'm dead, don't feel sad.

I lived a great life. Not everyone gets to live for thirty-two years. I'm a lucky one. Sure, I'll never get married, which is a total bummer, but I had a lot of love in my life.

I want to leave the world with something. Well, besides funny, embarrassing shit that I'm sure my family will discover about me by going through my things. Just the thought of that makes me cringe. Fuck. Can I die already? I'm ready.

Maybe I should clean up my digital footprint and throw some things away just in case I do die. I mean, yikes. Then again, I'll be dead, so it'll be quite difficult to be embarrassed.

My biggest regret was . . . I don't fucking know. I tried my best. Shit never worked out. Whatever. Make the most of this bullshit while you have it? Or don't. It doesn't matter. I'm about to die.

Enjoy every moment. Love hard. Take chances.

My own live, laugh, love.

Ha!

More like drink, write, fuck.

The order matters.

Oh, one last thing . . . don't spend a lot of money on my funeral. Don't dress me up and have people gawking at my dead corpse for hours. I hate when people comment "how good" the body looks. Motherfucker is dead. He's never looked worse. Burn my ass to ashes. And if you disregard my wishes and do what you want, which I fucking imagine you will do anyway, don't bury me in or with any Eagles shit. Why the fuck would you burden me in the afterlife with their fucking bullshit?

If you really want to do something special, make some creepy necklaces or bracelets and fill them with my ashes. Shit. That could be a great business idea. Corpse Jewelry (working title). Too bad I can't capitalize on it. Maybe one of you can take advantage of my death and get rich. Boom! There's my parting gift.

Hopefully, I'll see you on the other side.

Probably not, though.

Don't blame the drugs. Or the people. Or California.

I just don't know what the fuck I'm doing.

Just like everyone else.

—Wyatt

November 11, 2019

Monday morning.
I had no job.
No leads on work.
And the California government hadn't sent me a dime.
But I wasn't dead.
I swore to lay off the hard drugs.
And to spend less time with Nikki.
At least for a little while.

Dessert Mac and Cheese

November 17, 2019

It was way past the California courtesy when I showed up. There must have been thirty people sitting along a long white fold-up table in Noah and Summer's driveway.

"Did you drive here from New Jersey?" a man in his forties asked.

He must have noticed my car parked across the street. There was no fooling this member of the neighborhood watch.

"Just haven't had the time to blow at the DMV," I said.

Inside, more people sat around the couple's dining room table, wearing fancy clothes and eating desserts. I recognized Julian and Leah at the table. Tony was nowhere to be found. The rest of the crowd must have been the couple's new neighbors.

I took the tinfoil off the dish I carried.

"Hope everyone likes buffalo mac and cheese for dessert."

"You're late," Summer said.

She got up from the candlelit table and helped me heat the mac and cheese. She made me a plate of leftovers.

By the time I sat down, half the party had cleared out.

"Why are you so late?" Leah asked.

"The Birds," Summer said.

"Did they win?" Leah asked.

"You see how drunk I am?"

"Huh?" Leah said.

I inhaled some food.

"That means they lost," Summer said. "He's wasted."

"How did you get so drunk?" Julian asked

"The Birds lost a close one to the Patriots. I drowned the pain with beer."

"Just you?" Summer asked.

"Paige was my sister in arms."

"I don't get it," someone I didn't know said.

I didn't bother explaining my philosophy.

"Did I tell you what I'm doing with the place?" Noah asked. "Eventually, a deck. It'll shoot out of the bedroom window. Overlook the pool."

"Are you building it?" Julian asked. "That sounds like a lot of work."

"I'll hire professionals for that," Noah said.

Noah walked me and Julian through his house, showing us the new flooring, cabinets, countertops, and accessories, which included a state-of-the-art oven. Noah was proud. He did most of the work himself, and the place looked gorgeous.

We returned to the table to find Leah and Summer drinking another glass of sangria. After Summer and Noah said their goodbyes to their remaining neighbors, Julian, the couple, Leah, and I took a dip in the hot tub.

Julian's new plan was starting his own marketing agency. I told him I'd be more than happy to help out with any copywriting he needed, but I knew the plan was dead in the air.

"You have plans for Thanksgiving?" Julian asked me.

"Nah," I said. "First Thanksgiving away."

"You're more than welcome to come over," he said.

"I appreciate it," I said.

I didn't understand Summer's disdain for Julian.

Sure, he always tried to get rich quick, but who didn't?

Julian looked at Leah.

"You all are more than welcome to come over," he said. "There's always plenty of food. I just got a place in La Jolla."

Fuck Julian.

I never liked him.

"That's sweet," Leah said.

She moved herself closer to Julian.

I needed more booze.

"So, is Julian going to be your best man?" Leah asked.

Summer displayed her empty ring finger.

"There has to be a ring first before we discuss a wedding."

"Yeah, we're not there yet," Noah said.

It wasn't what Summer wanted to hear.

I went home after ten more uncomfortable minutes at the couple's new home.

November 28, 2019

It felt like there were twenty of us jammed into Julian's new condo. There were at least eight dogs. And I didn't even bring Hank, who Julian said could come. I didn't know anyone besides Julian, Summer, and Noah. Everyone else was a member of Julian's family. A beautiful mix of biological and adopted children. The strangers treated me like they knew me my whole life. Even offering to make special cocktails, telling me which sides were the best, and explaining who made what. My plate weighed ten pounds by the time Julian's family finished filling it up.

I couldn't move after I cleared my plate.

There was enough food for everyone to get plenty of helpings. But no one took more than two.

After dinner, everyone sat around the TV with drinks.

Even those under the legal limit.

I didn't have any dessert but watching the Dallas Cowboys blow another Thanksgiving Day game was sweeter than any pie or cake.

The old and young men drank and debated whether football was better now or back in the day. The women drank and made fun of the men for fawning over professional athletes.

On our way out, I thanked Julian for his hospitality.

It was strange that no one took leftovers. No one even bothered to ask. When Summer, Noah and I got into his car, I asked why.

"Julian gives away all the leftovers to the homeless on Black Friday," Noah said. "That's why no one takes anything. This is his eighth year doing it. No. I think it's his ninth."

Some people can really surprise you.

December 1, 2019

The California government declared me ineligible for unemployment benefits for the month of November.

They never gave me a reason why. I collected zero dollars. However, I was awarded unemployment benefits starting in December.

I would collect four-hundred fifty dollars a week.

My rent was eighteen-hundred dollars a month.

My job prospects?

Didn't have a single lead.

And not for a lack of trying.

One company ghosted me after three interviews.

Two of the interviews were in-person.

No one responded to my emails asking what happened.

Most hiring managers lied about the salaries their companies offered. After a phone screening or two, they'd lowball the shit out of the salary. Figured I'd accept the job after being misled.

Yeah, like I'd make that mistake again.

My credit card balances ballooned.

My savings account emptied.

The only thing I had worth anything was Erin's engagement ring. My father recommended I give it to the "next one"—his words. I couldn't explain to him how fucked-up that was. There was no good reason for keeping the ring. Besides the fact I liked reminding myself what California cost. I guess you could say I enjoyed torturing myself.

* * *

Bob's Jewelry was empty when I entered. It looked like one of those "We Buy Gold" stores and not a good one. Then again, did any jewelry store with bars on the windows look safe?

"How can I help ya?" an old man asked me.

He looked exactly how you'd expect an aging jeweler to look. Not exactly healthy. I assumed it was Bob.

I squeezed Erin's ring box one last time.

"I have a diamond to sell."

I put the ring box on the counter.

Bob snatched it.

He pulled the ring out.

"It's a beautiful diamond," he said.

"You should have seen the girl."

He spun the ring around with his fingers.

"The price of diamonds fluctuates. Are you sure you want to sell now?"

"Just give me my money."

He stopped staring at the jewelry and looked at me.

"Kid, I'm telling you."

"My money."

Bob waddled to his office in the back somewhere. I hoped he didn't try to fuck me on the price. He seemed the type.

When he returned, he didn't have a ring, but he held a check. I let out a laugh when I saw the amount.

It was half of what I paid for the ring.

"You could have gotten way more if you waited."

"I don't have much time left."

I left the joint and drove to the beach.

* * *

My skin burned me awake from my beach nap. Coarse sand tangled itself in my wet leg hairs. I brushed off some sand and lathered myself in sunblock.

One of the restaurants behind the beach smelled like a burrito I needed to try. I threw my shirt and towel around my neck, carried my bag, and bought some lunch.

After my meal, I unlocked a rentable bike. I followed the wide path along the coast, maneuvering around rollerbladers, runners, amateur photographers, scooter riders, and cyclists. No one paid attention to what they were doing as they moved. The ocean hypnotized us all.

The path led toward the bay and away from the beach. I pushed my legs a little faster. Boats filled the water, and a few Jet Skis splashed after each lift in the air.

I pedaled farther until I was parallel to a jammed highway. People honked and swore profanities as they inched toward their destinations. I sped past all the stuck cars. Smiling as I did. The highway dumped me into the heart of the city. Only a block away from The Palace. I didn't mean to ride so far, but I guess that's the magic of California.

I thought about heading to my apartment, but I wanted to watch a sunset on the beach. I took my time riding back. Following the same path that led me to the city. When I made it to the ocean, I ditched the bike.

A dozen photographers frantically clicked their cameras in front of happy couples, families, and near-naked models standing right where the water kissed the beach. All hoping to capture a moment with a fading sun. I found a spot in the sand to sit and watch the models. I mean, sunset. The sky turned lavender, red, orange, and yellow. I watched in amazed silence as the sun peacefully fell into the horizon.

When it grew dark, I left the beach.

Leah texted me on my drive home.

I broke up with Tony.

The Bar with the Monster

December 7, 2019

Leah was already drunk when I showed up at her place. She took a long swig from a bottle of red that sat on her kitchen counter. She handed me the wine on her way to the bathroom.

"Catch up."

Chugging wine wasn't exactly something I enjoyed.

But I did it.

I texted Nikki while I waited for Leah.

She's wasted already. It's worse than last time.

Nikki responded.

Fuck. I'll see you soon.

For weeks Nikki and I texted about Leah.

According to Nikki, Leah was spiraling worse than usual for this time of year. The holidays hit Leah hard. Whenever I talked with Leah, I'd let Nikki know how I thought Leah was doing.

When Leah came out of the bathroom, she took the wine from my hands and finished it. I called a ride.

* * *

The floors weren't sticky. Everyone wore suits and revealing but fashionable tops. Groups posed for photos. The joint didn't even serve wings. The bar was clean and offered beer in chalices instead of cheap, clear plastic cups, but Leah told me it was a dive bar.

Julian, Nikki, and Summer stood with Noah at the bar.

"How is she?" Nikki whispered.

Leah's eyes barely stayed open.

"Not well."

Nikki passed me a beer.

"She hasn't gone to work in four days."

"What about school?"

"She didn't tell you?" Nikki asked. "She dropped all but one class. It was too much for her."

"What should we do?" I asked.

"Keep watching her. I may have to do something."

I didn't know what Nikki was thinking.

But I had a feeling I wasn't going to like it.

"I need to think about it," Nikki said. "Come on. Let's keep an eye on her but have a good night."

We walked to the rest of the group. The popcorn machine held Leah up. Julian and Noah talked about the housing market. Nikki and Summer complained about work. I leaned against the bar. Bored.

Leah found me there. She forced herself into a hug and laid her head on my chest.

"I just want love."

"You have it," I said.

"Real love." Leah looked up at me. "Tony didn't love me."

Leah never told me what happened with her and Tony.

Even when I asked.

"The next guy will love you," I said.

"You love me."

"You'll always be the girl I chased to California."

The joint erupted in cheers.

Leah broke away from me.

"What the?"

Kitchen doors swung open in the back of the joint. A crowd followed a cross-eyed creature as he danced past the four booths in the back of the place. Human hands shot out of hairy blue arms. The blue beast carried a giant plate overflowing with chocolate chip cookies as he twirled towards us.

"Is this real life?" Leah asked.

I did a double take.

There was a cheap imitation Cookie Monster giving out warm chocolate chip cookies to drunk people.

"How fucked-up are we?" I asked.

Leah took two cookies off the monster's plate.

"These feel real."

I took a bite of one. "They taste real."

"Cookie Monster comes out every Saturday night," Julian said.

Nikki waited at the bar with another round for everyone. After one sip, Leah handed me her drink.

"I'm tired. I need to go home."

She stumbled out of the joint.

I chugged my drink and handed Leah's to Nikki. "I'm going to make sure she gets home."

"Intervention," Nikki said.

"What?"

"That's what I'm thinking of doing."

This was bad.

I jogged out of the bar, searching for Leah.

She tripped into a brand-new white SUV across the street.

I hopped in with her as she asked the driver to close the door for her.

"Wyatt," she said. "Love. You found me. I love you." Leah rambled nonsense. "My ride. White SUV."

"She will not puke?" the driver asked.

Leah giggled at nothing.

"She does this all the time," I said.

I carried Leah into her apartment, all the way to her bed. I turned on the Bob Dylan playlist on her phone and kissed her on the forehead. Leah stirred awake.

"Are you coming back?" she asked.

"I'm going back out," I said.

"Are you coming back to California?"

I wanted to lie.

"Definitely."

So, I did.

The Best Things

December 15, 2019

Paige and I were especially drunk after a huge win against the Washington Football Team. Yeah, that's a professional sports team's name. When they weren't being greedy assholes, football team owners, which they called themselves, loved showing off their creativity. Then again, I would watch the California Ass Clowns if it meant more football.

Rather than head to Pacific Beach like we usually did on Sundays, Paige convinced me to keep drinking in her neck of the woods. It was called Ocean Beach.

We met her friend Wendy at a joint that reeked of stale beer. There wasn't a suit or pair of khakis in sight. The floor was sticky. A few Sunday drinkers were smoking cigarettes around the horseshoe-shaped bar.

After a pitcher of beer, Wendy wanted to check out another joint. I didn't want to. Neither did Paige. But Wendy complained until we left.

We stopped at a convenience store on our way.

Paige needed a pack of cigarettes.

"I didn't know she smoked," I said to Wendy.

"She doesn't," Wendy said. "She and Bernard ended things."

Turns out December was breakup season in California.

Paige walked out of the store to a homeless man sitting on the curb. He was dirty, with black smears all over his stomach, his face included. His shoes, pants, and shirt torn apart, hanging on by mere threads. His shirt frayed, barely covering his burned and inked skin. Paige gave him a few cigarettes, five bucks, and some crackers. She sat with the guy and talked. Wendy and I could smell him from the corner where we waited. Paige and the homeless guy each smoked a cigarette before she rejoined us.

The bar was only lit up by black lights. There were just five people, excluding us, in the joint. Paige went to the bathroom.

"Make a move," Wendy said. "Paige needs a distraction."

Wendy left.

She didn't even order a beer.

Paige hid in the bathroom.

I had two PBRs while I waited.

She was in there for a long time.

Maybe she climbed through a window and bailed on me.

Ha.

That would be quite the story.

Maybe she passed out in the bathroom.

A better story.

For my ego, at least.

But then Paige appeared full of energy. She had made a friend inside the bathroom. The two shared heartbreak stories, and then cocaine.

"I usually don't do that, but I needed a fucking release," Paige said. "Just need to feel a little better."

"What happened?" I asked.

"I don't know. I just don't."

"Not knowing is knowing," I said.

We had another PBR before Paige wanted to walk to the beach. The sunset was approaching, and she didn't want to miss it. She pulled a joint from her pocket, and we sat in the sand.

The weed was great, but the sunset was better.

In the distance, a car blared music.

"Dancing in the Moonlight" by King Harvest.

I grabbed Paige by the hands and pulled her up.

"We gotta dance," I said. "I love this song."

I moved one hand down to the small of her back and my other held her hand. I leaned into Paige's ear and started singing her the words. We kicked sand and moved out of rhythm as I misremembered the lyrics, but I kept singing, anyway. I twirled Paige around.

When she spun back and faced me, she kissed me.

I kissed her back.

For a while.

But this wasn't right.

It wasn't fair.

I pulled away from Paige.

"I can't," I said. "This isn't a good idea."

"What?"

I took a deep breath. "I'm moving back to Jersey."

Saying the words aloud crushed my soul.

It made them real.

"I had no idea."

"My life has been falling apart out here."

"I'm sorry," Paige said. "When are you going back?"

"When my lease expires. Before that if I get a job."

"You're not going to change your mind?"

I shook my head.

"I can't find a job out here. I ran out of jobs to apply for. Figured I'd just enjoy what little time I had left."

"I'm not going to deal with this. Not right now. The Birds won. It's been a good day." Paige caressed my leg. "And right now, I'm stoned, drunk, fresh off a breakup, and in a giving mood."

I laughed.

"I still don't think this is a good idea."

"The best things rarely are."

She kissed me.

I kissed her back.

And didn't stop.

We sat on the beach, talking and making out until it got dark. We found a secluded spot to continue the fun.

The Lewis Family Tradition
December 25, 2019

My grandmother handed me an envelope. I knew what was inside. It was the same thing as every year. A crisp hundred-dollar bill.

I leaned down and gave her a hug.

"Merry Christmas. And thank you."

My grandmother grabbed my wrist.

"When are you going back to California?"

California.

Just hearing the word broke my heart.

"After the holidays."

Uncle Jeremy overheard the conversation.

"Staying out there?" he asked.

I'd stay until my lease expired.

After that I'd be moving back to Jersey.

"I can't leave paradise. It's always seventy and sunny."

"And I bet the women are wonderful."

Uncle Jeremy, who not only swindled my college savings from my parents on a bad investment deal, but who encouraged a cheating spree when my father decided he didn't want to be married to my mother anymore.

"There's nothing like them," I said. "At least anywhere I've been."

Uncle Jeremy let out a deep laugh.

"There's a song about them for a reason."

"I can't wait to get back."

It wasn't a lie.

My father came over to say goodbye to his mother. She hurried out of her seat, the fastest I've seen her move in a decade, and power walked to the oven. My grandmother pulled out a tinfoil-wrapped dessert and gave it to my father.

"I left it in the oven to keep it warm," she said.

"He always gets his pie," Uncle Jeremy said.

"That's because he's the favorite," Aunt Beth said.

"Mom's perfect son," Aunt Darla said. "Always gets his dessert when he visits."

Aunt Darla was a complete stranger who I knew through photos and forced family interactions on holidays and birthdays. Hell, the only other times I'd see her is when she stopped by my parents' house on her way to cheat on her husband.

"His incentive to come back," Uncle Jeremy said.

"You hear this, Mom?" my father asked. "This is why I never share."

"Be nice," my grandmother said.

My father, Kayla, Zane, and I wished everyone a merry Christmas as we made our way through my uncle's full house.

Mike wasn't there.

He always skipped family events.

No one ever said anything to him about it, either.

The perfect son.

But if Kayla and I tried to skip a family gathering, we'd get berated.

Kayla and Zane left together.

I walked to my father's car.

No one deserved to be alone on Christmas.

"That was nice," my father said. "Thanks for coming."

"No problem."

We drove past lit-up houses filled with Christmas cheer. I hated the commercialization of the holiday, but I loved looking at decorated homes. Especially when families went all out.

"Think the Eagles can make the playoffs?" my father asked.

Common ground.

"They just need to win out. If they get it in, they can do some damage."

There's something beautiful about being in control of your destiny.

"I heard what you were saying to everyone," my father said.

I stopped gazing out the window.

"What?"

"I see you're not ready to deal with the reality of California."

"Can we not do this now?" I asked.

"We're worried."

"It's Christmas."

"We want to know what you're going to do."

"I haven't figured out the exact plan."

"You need to," my father said. "You don't have time to waste."

"Time is a construct made by man."

My father peeled his eyes off the road.

"Stop smoking so much pot."

"It's legal there."

"Not here," he said.

"It will be soon."

My father ignored the comment.

"Your lease expires in June?"

"May."

"Even better. Are you looking for work?"

I debated another lie.

"I'm applying for jobs in San Diego and Jersey," I lied.

Fuck Jersey.

I'd stay in California as long as I could.

"You need to give it up," my father said. "Are you taking Hank back with you?"

"He's staying," I said. "Poor guy almost had a heart attack on the plane. If I get a job out there, I'll take a week off in the summer and drive him back out to California."

It was a lie.

California would be over in May.

But I enjoyed annoying my father.

I always did.

"Give it a rest," he said.

We crossed a bridge that returned us to New Jersey.

One more hour until we were back at my mom's place.

It couldn't come sooner.

The apple pie in my lap seduced me with its smell. I unwrapped the tinfoil and tried to sneak a pinch of pie. My father slapped my hand before I could rip off some crust.

"What's the deal with this fucking thing?" I asked.

"My mom likes me the best."

"Obviously," I said. "But why?"

"I used to be a good kid."

I covered the pie with the tinfoil.

There was no use in trying to steal any.

"I find that hard to believe," I said.

"You don't want to know."

"Why?"

My father pressed down on the gas.

"I don't want to tell you."

I didn't hide my annoyance.

"You need to."

My father took a few moments before he spoke.

"I'm not going to talk bad about the dead."

"You can't just say something like that," I said.

He looked me in the eyes.

"I don't want you to hate anyone else in this family."

Always secrets with this fucking family.

"Tell me."

My father paused.

"Your grandfather used to come home drunk from work. Almost every day. Working his life away in a factory wasn't how he imagined his life playing out, I guess." He let out a deep breath. "Your grandfather took out his frustrations with life on your grandmother. He'd beat the hell out of her. I couldn't stand it. But I wasn't strong enough to do anything. I just had to watch. At eight, I intervened."

I didn't know how to feel.

"How?"

"I'd fight. Fist to fist. He'd beat the shit out of me. For years. Hammering away at me. It made me tough. It made him tired. He'd pass out on the couch. Drunk and exhausted. Your grandmother would hide in her bedroom. I'd sleep outside her door. That way, if my old man got up, I could stop him."

Another horrific secret.

My family was full of them.

"It took me years to beat him," my father said. "He stopped drinking after the second time I whooped his ass."

Boxing matches with his drunk father.

Welcome to the Lewis family.

"How old were you when you beat him?" I asked.

"Twelve."

The world shattered around me.

My despair turned to rage.

"Why haven't you ever told me this?"

"I don't know," he said. "No one knows. Your aunt and uncles weren't born yet. They only knew your grandfather sober."

I didn't know what to think.

There was nothing I could say.

My father was a monster.

Now I knew why.

"I'm sorry," I said.

I pulled my wallet from my back pocket and removed the last piece of the postcard I had left. I squeezed it in my palm.

California was where I belonged.

Wayward Sun

January 22, 2020

I stepped through the airport's automatic sliding glass doors with my luggage in tow. The palm trees let me know I was home.

"Look at all the palms," an older man in a Hawaiian shirt said.

"Of course, that's the first thing you see in California," his wife said.

California.

Just hearing the word made me smile.

I waited an hour at the airport.

That's when Leah's car finally pulled up to the curb.

She bolted out of her SUV. I caught Leah when she lurched toward me. She planted kisses all over my face. Vodka poured out of her breath.

"I didn't think you were coming back."

"There was a week where the temperature didn't leave the teens," I said.

She jumped off me.

"Didn't mean you'd come back."

"California ruins a man." I threw my luggage in her back seat. "Want me to drive?"

"Why?"

I didn't have an excuse.

Leah peeled out of the airport.

"I can't believe the size of Summer's ring?"

"Huge," I said.

"Noah did a good job. I was surprised."

"You got to give the guy more credit than that."

"He's not the most romantic."

"Most people aren't," I said.

Leah giggled.

"You hang with me too much."

The car went silent.

Neither one of us wanted to talk about it.

But we had to.

Nikki showed Leah the text messages I sent her about Leah. It was nothing bad, mostly worries and concerns. And stupid shit Leah said drunk. Leah texted me about a dozen of the messages I sent Nikki. She said we needed to talk. But in person. It's why she volunteered to pick me up from the airport.

"I didn't mean to hurt you," I said.

Leah pulled over on the highway's shoulder.

"Why did you say those things to Nikki?"

"I was worried about you," I said. "I didn't say anything I wouldn't say to you right now."

"It gets me so pissed off when people ask me if I'm okay. And worry about me. I'm fine. I'm a grown ass woman. I have my own place. I work full-time. I'm in school. The holidays just get to me. And I just broke up with Tony."

Cars flew past us, causing the SUV to shake.

"I care about you. I was worried."

"I promise. I'm fine."

I wanted to believe her.

So, I did.

"Just don't talk about me behind my back. Especially not to Nikki. She always starts shit. You can be friends with her. I won't say you can't. But don't talk about me."

I agreed.

But I'd avoid Nikki.

"Thanks for waiting to talk about this," Leah said. "I hate text conversations. Everything always gets lost." Leah leaned across the seat and kissed my cheek. "I missed you too much to be mad at you."

"I missed you, too."

Leah pulled back onto the road.

Without her turn signal.

Or looking behind her.

"Are you staying in California?" Leah asked.

"Depends."

"On what?"

"If I can get hired," I said.

More like if I hit the lottery.

"You better. I want to get over this whole thing, but it's going to take time. So, you need to stay, yeah?"

"Sounds like you're just using me," I said.

Leah smiled.

She parked on the street outside my apartment. Leah got out of her car to hug me good night.

"I'm glad you're home."

I loved when she called California home.

Leah waited until I entered the building to drive off.

The worst part of returning to California was leaving Hank behind. I wasn't sure how long I'd last in San Diego and didn't want to force him on another plane ride. I nearly killed the poor guy flying back to Jersey.

If I could make California work, I'd go back for him.

Or see him when I returned back to Jersey.

I opened my apartment door.

The smell of moldy death welcomed me. I took a couple of sniffs of the air. Not death. Shit. My place smelled like a septic tank. Dirt, mold, and water overflowed from the kitchen sink. I took photos with my phone, grabbed two of the six towels I owned, and cleaned the wet mold. Foul-smelling water puddled underneath the sink, ruining trash bags and all my cleaning supplies. I sent an angry email to the building manager, but I knew I wouldn't get a response. I sprayed an air freshener throughout the entire apartment.

I couldn't stop laughing as I crawled into bed.

Things seemed status quo for California.

The Gang's All Here

January 25, 2020

L eah and I strolled into a joint named after a moon phase.
Julian waited at the bar. Summer and Noah, who held hands,
sat on the stools next to him. The couple kissed when Noah
headed for the bathroom.

"Let me see it, girlfriend!" Leah said.

Summer flicked her wrist, displaying a gigantic clear jewel
surrounded by large white diamonds. "Ta-da!"

"Oh my god! It's gorgeous," Leah said. "And huge!"

"Thank you!" Summer said.

I hugged Summer.

"Congrats. In person."

She flashed her diamond to everyone at the bar.

Even those who didn't ask.

It was Summer's moment.

And she deserved every second of it.

Noah returned from the bathroom. Julian ordered the couple a
bottle of champagne. The booze cost more than the government
paid in a month.

We toasted to the newly engaged couple.

For a few rounds.

"Wyatt's back," Leah said. "Summer's engaged. This is going
to be our year."

"No doubt," Summer said.

Noah caught me up on the stock market and his new house
renovations. Julian updated me on his career. For once, he didn't
try to sell me on some job or marketing scheme.

Maybe it was going to be a good year.

Leah walked across the bar and started talking to a salt-and-
pepper business executive wearing a perfectly tailored suit. She
laughed too loud at something he said. He flirted back. I walked
into another room with a glass of champagne.

"The fuck you doing?" Summer asked.

She must have followed me.

"Is she doing better than when I left?"

"This is the first time I've seen her," Summer said. "What the fuck happened between you two?"

"Nikki shared screenshots of our text conversations with Leah. Things I texted Nikki in confidence. Mostly concerns about Leah. Leah got pissed at me.

"Was it anything bad?"

"Nothing I can't fix."

"Nikki shouldn't have done that to you," Summer said.

"Lesson learned."

"Are you applying for jobs back East?"

I laughed.

"Fuck no. I'm staying out here until my lease expires. Longer if I can find a well-paying job."

"Any leads?"

"I've gotten a lot of interviews, but it's been bullshit," I said. "One looks promising. It's an event company for breweries."

"You better get some samples."

"If I get the job, I'll be able to afford beer again."

"I told you it's not easy out here," Summer said. "I really struggled my first year. Shit, my first two years."

"It's definitely not going how I imagined."

"How did you think it would go?

"Get the job. Move to California. Sweep the girl off her feet. And live happily ever after," I said. "But instead, my life somehow got worse."

"I was afraid you were going back for good."

"California is going to save me."

"Only you can save you, Wyatt."

"I'm trying," I said. "I joined a gym."

"You can afford that?"

"I can't afford not to work out."

"The way your brain works, I'll never understand."

"Here's a tip," I said. "I only came back here because I was jealous of all the attention you were getting for your engagement. I couldn't stand it."

Summer smiled.

"That's what I figured. I mean, I get it. I'd do the same to you. But can we go back so I can show off my diamond? I mean look at this thing."

Summer stuck out her hand and twirled her ring finger.

"It's literally blinding me," I said.

We rejoined the group at the bar. The mature man Leah was crushing on came too. The champagne bottle didn't last long. Leah left with her new man. Julian went back to his downtown apartment. Summer and Noah returned to their new Palace. I thought about texting Paige, but I wasn't sure what to say. I wasn't even sure how long I'd last in California. It seemed silly to bother her.

I went home and wrote some words.

Skintight Zebra Pants

February 2, 2020

I felt the bouncer's eyes staring at me as I entered the bar. He nodded at me. After two quick steps inside, the giant tattooed animal yanked me back toward the door.

"I said let me see your fucking ID," the bouncer growled.

Oh.

That's what he meant with his affirmation nod.

"I thought when you nodded that meant go through."

I handed him my ID.

He studied it.

He kept looking at the ID, then at me.

ID. Me. Me. ID. ID. Me. Me. ID.

He tossed my driver's license at me.

"Cute pants."

I wanted to make a smart-ass remark, but I knew this Neanderthal would throw me out if I did. I couldn't say something and blend into the crowded bar either. Not in my skintight Tommy Lee zebra pants.

Julian had a drink waiting for me at the bar.

"What was that about?" Julian asked.

"I think he hated my pants."

"I can't believe you're wearing those out," Julian said.

After a drink, a cute blonde woman in her thirties, I guessed, asked if she could sit with us at the bar. Julian introduced himself and pulled out a barstool.

"I'm Annie," she waved. "How did you guys meet?"

"By chance, I guess," I said.

"That's so adorable."

"What?" Julian asked.

"How long have you two been together?"

Julian wanted to interject, but I cut him off. "It'll be two months next week."

"Oh my gosh! That's so cute."

Why was a man dating another man cute?

Couldn't a man just fuck another man without everyone needing to make a big deal about it?

"Whatever they want," she told the bartender. "I got your next drink."

An ignorant person was a bad excuse to turn down free booze.

"We like to get out and meet new people . . .," Julian said.

I cut him off.

"Spice it up, you know?"

"Like, to join you?" Annie asked.

"Quite the dirty mind on this one," Julian said.

A woman with lots of eye makeup and a worn face moved next to us. Her name was Carly. She reeked of old-lady perfume. I bought a round of beers.

Julian bought a round of shots.

Annie asked for cinnamon whiskey.

Carly asked for Irish whiskey.

The old hag was my kind of woman.

"Well, can I ask who . . . um . . . pitches?" Annie asked. "Who catches?"

Carly laughed.

"Who do you think?"

I stared down and pleaded with my pants.

It couldn't be them.

"I think you're the pitcher," she said to Julian.

The fucking zebra pants.

"We never actually said we dated," Julian said.

Annie examined Julian and me. "I knew it! I knew it all along! I wanted to see how far you'd take it."

There was no way she knew it.

I gave quite the performance.

Carly started talking to an older man who was leaning on the bar next to her. Annie and Julian were at the handsy stage.

I strolled toward the back of the joint.

There were three young women talking to a tattooed, dark-haired woman who stood behind a stool-less bar. She was slim, with her lack of curves giving her subtle sex appeal.

"You want to buy my friends a shot?" the bartender asked.

"Not really."

She poured five.

"To new friends," she said and handed me a shot.

We cheered and slammed them back.

Tequila.

I swallowed a gag after the shot.

Her friends didn't make eye contact while they gossiped with one another. They scrolled mindlessly on their phones in a language that sounded like English, but it was nothing but acronyms.

"You're the black sheep?" I asked the bartender.

"What do you mean?"

I pointed at her friends, who were glued to their screens. Unaware of anything but the digital world.

"First, you're rude," she said. "Now you're insulting my friends."

"Let me make it up to you. I'll buy everyone a round."

"Even my lame friends?"

They didn't even hear her.

But they heard her when she then offered free shots.

The bartender's name was Jenna. She flunked out of college. She never wanted to go in the first place. That was her parents' dream. It was always art school that she wanted. But her parents didn't believe in that sort of thing. She moved out. Started bartending all over Pacific Beach. She lived in a small apartment and enrolled part-time in school. Only a few classes at a time. It was all she could afford.

The phone zombies, Jenna, and I took another shot.

"We have to go. Gina has to meet Daniel at his place," said the blonde in the black jumpsuit.

Jenna poured me another shot after her friends left.

"I'm thinking about getting my tits done."

"Moving a little fast, huh?" I asked. "But why?"

"Bigger tits. Bigger tips."

"What about paying for art school?"

Jenna handed me a beer that I didn't ask for.

"I can take a few semesters off and save enough to enroll full-time. Bigger boobs will help me earn more."

"The magic of breasts," I said.

"No one knows that I want to get them done." Jenna motioned for me to go to the other side of the bar, so her back would be to everyone in the joint. Besides me. "Tell me what you think." She pulled up her black tank top and flashed me.

I've done enough research into the subject to know they were A cups. And these were beautiful ones.

"Those are great. I'd even call them wonderful."

"Wouldn't they be better bigger?" Jenna asked.

The world was full of people who hated themselves. Myself included. But California was the worst. It was overpopulated with cyborg women created with Botox, silicone body parts, and excessive elective surgeries. Some were vain. But most hated their bodies. And themselves.

"You shouldn't get them done," I said.

"You're the first man to say that."

Man was the worst of our species.

And it wasn't even close.

"Forget that fake shit," I said.

She leaned in and put her hand on top of mine. She smiled at me. A genuine smile. Not the one a bartender uses to secure a bigger tip.

"Do you really believe that?" Jenna asked.

"It's impossible to make those tits look any better than they do right now."

"Oh yeah?"

"Can you show me them again? To confirm?"

Jenna pulled her hand away from mine. She turned her back and tallied up my order on her register, then threw the bill at me without saying a word. She charged me only for two rounds of shots and a single beer.

I wasn't sure what I said.

But I was wasted.

I left a big tip.

Which might have been Jenna's plan all along.

Tired, drunk, and exhausted, I headed for the exit. Annie tapped me on my shoulder when I walked across the dance floor. Julian was nowhere to be found.

"Your friend is a jerk," Annie said.

"Sorry about that."

"No. That's not—"

I kept walking as Annie called for me.

Three steps to freedom.

The outside world.

I didn't make it.

Right in front of the door, something yanked me back into the bar. I turned around to meet the ogre guarding the bar's entrance. He handed me a card.

"I wanted you to have my number."

It had to be the fucking pants.

"Thanks."

"Our secret," he said.

"I appreciate the offer, but I'm straight."

"There's nothing gay about a blowjob."

"What about the view?" I asked.

"Close your eyes," he said.

He had it all covered.

Something told me this wasn't his first time.

"It's a preference thing."

"Dude." It was a familiar female voice. Paige hooked me by the arm and walked me away from the bar. "Stop flirting with men for attention. I can't take you anywhere."

"What are you doing in PB?" I asked.

"It's Sunday."

She led us toward the beach.

"I thought that was only a football thing."

"Sundays are always for the beach." Paige inspected my outfit. "When did you get back?"

"Not too long ago."

"Bullshit," she said. "Where was my phone call?"

"I've been trying to settle in."

"Are you avoiding me?"

"What? No."

Paige kicked off her sandals when we reached the sand.

"Sure."

I took off my shoes.

"Why do you think I don't want to see you?"

"Haven't seen you since I saw you naked," Paige said. "Thought you might be feeling embarrassed."

"Embarrassed?"

She looked down at my junk.

I swallowed the little piece of pride I had.

"It wasn't the biggest," she said. "But I need to see it again to confirm."

She laughed before she parked in the cold, damp sand a few feet from the tide.

"What's up with the Halloween costume?" Paige asked.

"The country peaked in the eighties. The drugs were better, everyone felt rich, and technology didn't trap us. Trying to cultivate some of that energy."

"And the fashion was fire," she said.

"Obviously."

"Don't forget about the movies," Paige said. "Eighties action is cinematic gold."

"*Running Man?*" I asked.

"Duh."

"*Rambo?*"

"Fuck yes."

"*Total Recall?*"

"Get your ass to Mars." She said it in an Austrian accent.

"*Die Hard?*"

"The best Christmas movie of all time."

"*RoboCop?*"

"That's my favorite!"

"Did you know it's a trilogy?" I asked.

"Shut the fuck up," she said. "I've only seen the first one."

"I've got all three on a DVD."

Paige stood up and grabbed her sandals.

"When can we watch them?"

"Whenever you want."

She pulled me to my feet.

"Right now."

"It's late."

"And?"

"It's Sunday," I said.

"When has that ever stopped you?"

Paige rubbed her cold hands underneath my shirt. She pressed her lips against mine. We kissed. And we didn't stop. Her fingers worked their way down my stomach. I let out a moan when she reached down into my zebra pants. Paige stopped kissing me. She gripped my pants from the inside and pulled them down to my ankles. My boxers fell. And so did I.

My bare ass hit the sand.

Paige sprinted away from me.

"There's some weird pervert flashing his dick on the beach! What the fuck!" Paige yelled.

There were only a few people around.

Thankfully.

I fumbled with my clothes.

Got dressed.

And ran after Paige.

All-Night Eighties Action
February 2, 2020

Besides the tan trim along the counters and cabinets, the entire kitchen was tiled white. Magnets of cities, nature, old logos, nineties cartoon characters, superheroes, and pop culture references covered her fridge. Little figures, bobbleheads, and action figures were displayed on top.

"I dig these little figures," I said.

"I switch them all around every so often," Paige said.

"Why?" I asked.

"Gotta make sure everyone has their moment to shine."

Paige packed a bong.

"Want me to show you a cool trick to get really high?"

Paige lit the bong and sucked. She held the smoke in. She put her shirt over her face and inhaled and exhaled quickly for a few seconds. She popped her head back out. "Looks crazy, but it'll get you real fucked up."

She handed me the bong. I burned the fresh weed while sucking smoke into my lungs. When I couldn't hold my breath anymore, I buried my face in my shirt. I inhaled and exhaled as fast as I could. Inhaled and exhaled. I emerged from my shirt to see Paige, who was wide-eyed and smiling. I coughed a hard one. I wiped my watering eyes and cleared my throat.

"I think it worked," I said.

"I'm ripped."

Her dog, Ralph, a medium white fluff ball, licked and bit at my fingers when we fell onto her gray couch.

"What should we throw on?" I asked.

"*RoboCop.*"

"We never went to my place to get the DVD."

"Let's see if it's on anything."

Paige searched all fifty streaming services, but *RoboCop* wasn't free on any of them. I pulled some of my fingers out of Ralph's mouth.

"Have you ever seen *Demolition Man*? It wasn't made in the eighties, but it's an eighties action movie."

Paige watched *Demolition Man* for the first time. She scolded Ralph every so often during the movie, but she was too gentle to get angry at the poor pup. Paige barely raised her voice when she yelled at him. She'd pull Ralph to her and pet him. He'd try to bite her fingers. She'd stroke his fur harder. He'd calm down. Eventually. Long enough that Paige would forget he was there. That's when he'd pounce on me. And after a few licks, the biting would start again.

"That might be a top five for me," Paige said when the movie ended. "Especially with how hot Wesley Snipes looked. That blond hair on his black skin. Fuck yes."

"I see the sex appeal."

"Want to eat?" Paige asked.

"I need some hot cheese curls."

"I'm so munchie-munch."

"What are you gonna make?"

"Chicky nuggs and mac and cheese," she said. "You're helping."

"What kind of mac and cheese do you got? Because it's Velveeta or bust for me."

"I love Velveeta."

"I know the secret to perfect mac and cheese."

"Extra Velv. Please." She paused. "Wait. What's the secret?"

"The secret is to follow the directions," I said. "Set a timer. Don't guesstimate the eight to ten minutes the pasta needs to boil. Make sure it's exactly eight to ten minutes."

"I love that's the secret."

"Did you expect anything less?"

I pulled Paige on top of my lap.

We ripped each other's shirts.

Tossing them anywhere.

I threw Paige on her back.

I ripped off her pants and panties in one pull.

We never made it to the kitchen.

* * *

Afterward, we ate chips, using the calories we burned as our excuse to finish the bag. Paige put on my T-shirt, which barely covered her ass. She made her way to the kitchen where she grabbed a full and tied trash bag.

I followed behind her.

"Want me to do that?" I asked.

"I'm perfectly capable of taking out the trash."

Paige squealed when she opened her back door. She took a step into the alley behind her apartment, flicking her hand at something on the door behind her.

I laughed. "You could just ask me to get rid of the spider."

Paige dropped the trash into the can and met me at her back door. "I enjoy playing you men. Especially getting you to do what I want by making you feel a little powerful."

I scooped the spider into a napkin before letting the spider free in the alley. Paige rubbed my arm and slid past me, back into her apartment.

"Why didn't you just kill him?"

"I don't like to hurt anything," I said. "Besides, spiders eat annoying insects, like bloodsucking mosquitoes."

"Hippie."

I pinched Paige's arm.

"That hurt!"

"Too bad there wasn't a spider to kill that mosquito."

Paige pinched me back. "You're such a fucking dork."

Ralph deserted us for Paige's bed. Paige rolled a joint, which we smoked, and we threw on another eighties action flick. This time it was *The Running Man*.

The movie finished.

The light from the sun reflected off the blank screen.

"What time is it?" I asked.

"It's almost six."

"Might as well finish her out."

"Sure, invite yourself to stay."

Paige never asked me to leave.

She texted out of work around seven.

We crawled into her bed.

I pulled her to my chest.

"Kiss me one more time, baby. I've got an interview later and I need some luck."

"Don't get any ideas. This is a one-time thing."

I cleared my throat.

"It's at least the fifth, but who's counting?"

"Shut up and fuck me before I change my mind."

Back to Work

February 11, 2020

Red Bull vodka and White Claw slushies. It was a new menu item at the joint where I did molly for the first time with Leah.

"Are Summer and Noah coming?" Paige asked.

"They said they were," Leah said.

"It's a long drive from suburbia," I said. "For married people."

Paige sipped her water. "They're not married yet."

"It's just nothing but a government formality now," I said.

"I wanted to see her ring," Paige said.

"It's huge," Leah said. "I'm kinda jealous."

A waiter dropped off the next round of booze slushies.

"A toast to gainful employment," Paige said.

"Why thank you," I said.

"When do you start?" Leah asked.

"Tomorrow."

We lifted our drinks.

"What are you doing again?" Leah asked.

"Writing copy for an event planning business that specializes in beer tastings," I said. "That's not even the best part. It's a mile from my apartment. I can walk to work."

"It's a good thing you came back," Paige said.

"Walking to work. What a luxury," I said.

The staff shut the windows as the wind howled and the moon lit up the beach. It was one of the coldest nights in San Diego.

Another round of drinks went down.

Some of Paige's friends showed up. They didn't get along with Leah, so Paige sat with them at a different table. Paige laughed. She was the life of her friends. Making everyone laugh, and constantly wearing a smile.

She really was something.

"I have such a weak spot for him," Leah said.

"Who?" I asked.

"The guy I've been telling you about."

Shit.

I missed everything Leah said.

"What's his name again?" I asked. "Sorry."

"Chase."

"Chase. Yeah."

"We talked for a bit. Hooked up a few times. And then it kinda died off. You know how that goes."

"Yeah." Leah wanted more from me. "Such a shame."

I ordered two beers. Had to be a little responsible. I had work in the morning. Leah had other ideas.

"He's having a party tonight. Maybe we can check it out."

She went on and on about Chase who lived a few blocks away. During her entire beer, she fawned over him.

Paige returned to the table.

"Want to go to this party a few blocks away?" Leah asked.

"I'm down to rage," Paige said.

"I'm going to get another beer," I said.

"What about the party?" Leah asked.

"After another beer," I said. "But I can't be out late."

Leah stormed out of the joint.

And down the steps to the street.

I went to get a drink.

From the window, I saw Leah standing at the bottom of the steps with her arms folded. She scowled as she waited for Paige and me.

I showed her my full beer.

I swore I heard her scream.

"Come on," Paige said.

"Let's just hang here."

Paige laughed when she saw my full beer.

"She's leaving. We should go."

I took a sip of my brew.

"As soon as I'm done with this."

I couldn't see Leah outside anymore.

Paige took my beer while I was distracted.

She chugged it, slammed the empty glass on the bar, and pulled me out onto the street.

"You know how she gets," Paige said.

We caught up with Leah a few blocks from the bar.

"What took so long?" she demanded.

"I had to pee," I said.

Leah didn't buy it.

She walked ahead of Paige and me until we reached the guy's house. The three of us went up a staircase to a kitchen filled with cigar smoke and eight drunk jacked dudes playing cards and drinking whiskey.

All the men were just as surprised to see me.

Leah must have not told her she was bringing another male. She disappeared with Chase after introductions. Paige and I drank a shot of whiskey. All the guys took turns hitting on Paige. Some tried to talk to me. Mostly to gauge if I was a threat. Tension filled the air. They didn't want me there. One guy offered to deal me into their poker game. I declined. Phil, who seemed to be the leader, offered to split a blunt with Paige and me on his deck.

Phil ignored me outside.

He talked to Paige.

She flirted back.

As she did, she made sure I got extra puffs of the blunt.

We smoked all the weed.

Rather quickly.

Phil went inside after Paige gave him her number.

"Phil's kinda hot," Paige said.

"I'm getting out of here," I said.

"I was kidding," she said. "Come home with me."

"I thought this was only a five-time thing."

Paige grabbed my hand.

"Don't blow your chance at six."

We didn't bother to look for Leah before we left.

Leap Weekend
February 28, 2020

You can tell everything you need to know about a person by how they act in a grocery store.

Paige hopped, twirled, and inspected every weird or mildly interesting food she passed. As she did, she sang Guns N' Roses. She used a banana as a microphone.

She found the most expensive steak, a few broccoli bunches, a bag of potatoes, a package of bacon, and shredded cheese. I grabbed a nice bottle of red to pair with the meal. By nice, I meant a bottle that was more than twelve dollars.

We dropped the groceries off at my apartment and checked on Ralph. Paige brought him over, so she could spend the weekend at my place. It made things easier.

We walked to a brewery for dinner and drinks.

It was a longer walk than Paige expected.

We tried to find some live music after we ate but had no luck. There was a club that played house music Paige wanted to check out, but there was a special event at the joint and it was sold out.

"Want to just head back?" Paige asked.

"You sure?"

"I'm not walking, though."

"I'll call a ride."

Paige walked toward a scooter on the sidewalk.

"I want to try riding one of these."

"You haven't tried them yet?" I asked.

"Too scared."

I lifted up the scooter near Paige.

"Being tipsy is the perfect time to try driving a quick-moving, unbalanced machine."

"I'm not tipsy."

She kicked the stand and gripped the scooter, causing the alarm to go off. The obnoxious beeping noise startled her. Paige tossed the scooter to the ground.

"The fuck," Paige said.

I picked up the scooter.

"You have to unlock it first." I activated the machine with my phone. "Your chariot awaits, milady."

"Are you going to ride one?"

"One scooter per phone, unless you want to download the app."

"No."

Paige jumped back on the scooter. She hit the accelerator. The scooter jumped. She slammed the brakes as a reaction.

Too hard.

Paige flew off the machine.

I caught her as the scooter drove itself into a building.

"How about you drive?" she asked.

I retrieved the machine and rode it back to Paige.

She jumped onto the back of the scooter, holding on to my hips for balance.

She kissed my cheek. "For good luck."

"You just hold on," I said. "I'll do the rest."

"Does that count for when we get home?"

I pulled the accelerator as hard as I could.

February 29, 2020

Ralph woke us up in the morning. Paige got up to shower. She invited me to join. But we couldn't fit in the shower together. We had sex after she finished. Then Paige and I took Ralph to the dog park. I showered when we got back. We fucked again.

We spent the rest of the day getting high and watching cult kids' movies from our childhood. Mostly weird Disney movies. With no windows in my living area, the place was dark, like a movie theater. We kissed. We smoked. We napped. We fucked.

Life was perfect.

Around six, Paige poured me a glass of wine and told me to relax. She charred some expensive steak and cooked caramelized onion and bacon chunks to put on top. She roasted garlic and broccoli and cooked twice-baked cheesy bacon potatoes in the oven.

My apartment smelled the best it ever had.

The food didn't last long on my plate.

It was the best meal of my life.

And not because Paige made it.

"If I'm ever on death row," I said, "I'm ordering this."

"Stop. But thank you."

"I never want to eat anything again."

Paige seductively smiled as she looked down past her stomach. Then slowly back up at me.

"That's a shame," she said.

It didn't take long for me to undress my dessert.

March 1, 2020

We woke up on my little couch. After a nap in my bed, I cleaned last night's dishes and cooked Paige pancakes for breakfast.

"That was really hot when you just got out of the way and let me do my thing last night," she said.

"You're the chef in this house."

Paige grabbed me below the waist. "That's right."

She twirled away and started singing Mötley Crüe to her dog. I joined in when Paige hit the chorus.

And we spent the rest of the day playing house.

The Worst Bronchitis Ever Seen

March 4, 2020

Every day I refused to drink beers with the man who signed my paychecks. Cody, the CEO at Sudz & Crew, asked to go to happy hour every morning when I went to get a cup of "keep my eyes open" flavored water. Sure, his company was interesting. I got paid to write about beer. My bosses weren't up my ass. They listened to my suggestions. There were fewer meetings, but there were still way too many. Cody offered more collaborations than demands. And I could walk to work every day. There were worse ways to make a living. But hanging out with my boss wasn't exactly how I wanted to spend my time away from work. Especially if the CEO was a grown man who named his company Sudz & Crew.

After I fended him off, Paige texted me.

I'm feeling like poo. My friend told me I have the worst case of bronchitis she's ever seen. So, that's looking mighty good for you.

No doubt that a severe case of bronchitis was in my future.

After a few meetings and some of my best work, I went to leave the office. But Cody stopped me.

"Beers? We can talk about some projects," Cody said.

"I can't tonight," I said.

"You never can," he said. "Another workout session?"

Sudz & Crew offered a discount on gym memberships.

So, I started working out again.

Three times a week.

But not today.

"I'm feeling under the weather," I said. "Beer won't help."

"Oh. Okay."

On my way home, I stopped at the liquor store around the corner from my place for electrolytes and cans of chicken noodle soup.

It wasn't even seven when I fell asleep.

I woke up freezing and soaked around midnight.
For the next few hours, I repeated the same cycle.
Wake up.
Cough.
Drink some water.
Cough.
Wrap myself back in my blanket.
Cough.
Fall back asleep.
Cough myself awake.
All night.

March 5, 2020

I forced myself out of bed later than usual. I couldn't stop coughing. Deep, dry coughs that made my brain hurt. I crawled to the bathroom and took a long, hot shower.

I couldn't call out of work. Not with our mandatory team meeting that morning. I threw on my clown suit.

On my walk to the office, I picked up two sports drinks, cough drops, and a bunch of legal drugs. I paused at every block to catch my breath. When I got to work, it was taking all my strength to keep my head raised. My skull weighed a ton.

Thank God our mandatory team meeting was at ten.

It went smoothly.

The company was expanding.

Great.

The meeting should have been a fucking email.

The team wanted to go out for lunch and beers to celebrate, but I told them I was headed to an urgent care.

"You think it's corona?" Cody asked.

There was no way it was corona.

"Just a cold," I said.

"The state called a state of emergency over the virus."

"Really?"

"Yeah," he said. "There's a cruise ship being kept at shore because a bunch of the passengers have the virus. Someone died, too. I'm sure you're fine. You know how it is out here, always over cautious. Just let us know what the doctor says."

Cody was an East Coaster like me.

But a state of emergency wasn't a good sign.

At all.

"I better get going," I said.

Ten blocks to the emergency care center.

After walking one block, I panted. I chugged the last of my sports drink. I felt a burst of energy. It lasted a block. I had a small window before I was going to pass the fuck out on the side of the street.

Five more blocks.

Shit.

These fucking hills.

Why was my neighborhood so goddamn hilly?

By the time I reached flat roads, I was exhausted.

Three more blocks.

A busy intersection with no streetlights or stop signs separated me from the protection of tree shade across the street. A small black car sped down the road.

I can make it.

Shit.

I'm slower than I remember.

The car sped faster.

My legs refused to accelerate.

Fuck it.

Let him run me over.

I'll be rich or dead.

A poor man's gamble.

The car swerved.

He laid on his horn.

The asshole wasn't even close to hitting me.

I had no energy to lift a finger.

That's when I knew I was really sick.

Two blocks left.

Inside the emergency care, a few hypochondriacs wore masks. I took the elevator upstairs and met with the emergency care receptionist. "Do you have shortness of breath, a cough, and a fever?" The receptionist handed me a mask when I said yes. Before I could fill out the questionnaire she gave me, a nurse escorted me back to the examination room.

She took my temperature. "The doctor will be right in."

It was a lie.

A group of medical professionals chatted outside my door as I waited. "This guy walked right in. No mask. Nothing."

This guy was me.

"He wasn't the only one today either," a female voice said.

"We need to get people asking the three standard questions outside the door. We need to be handing out masks before people come in. We can't let people stroll on in here," a male said.

I pressed my ear to the door.

"You think this guy has it?" a female voice asked.

"Doubtful," the male said. "It's not here in San Diego."

The conversation stopped.

Someone touched the door handle.

I retreated back into my seat.

The doctor entered.

He jammed a rod down my throat after pleasantries.

I gagged as he examined my throat.

He told me to lie down before pressing his cold hands on my abdomen.

"Relax."

He pushed down harder on my vital organs.

The doctor needed to relax.

I sat up.

"What do you think, Doc?"

"It's tough to say. We can run some tests on you, but we're not sure if they'll show us anything. You seem like a healthy guy. It could be the flu, or it could be a nasty cold." He jotted something on his phone. "If things get worse before the weekend, pick this up."

That was his nice way of letting me know that because I didn't have health insurance, the tests to determine my illness would put me in a financial crisis. If only Sudz & Crew, and practically all of Corporate America, didn't force their employees to wait ninety days for something as silly as health insurance.

"Could it be bronchitis?" I asked.

"I don't think so," he said.

"Could it be anything else?"

"Don't worry about COVID, if that's where your mind is going." The doctor handed me a mask. "Take precautions, though."

He texted me a prescription.

A basic antibiotic.

I put on the mask the doctor gave me when I left the examination room. Without insurance, my emergency care visit cost me three hundred bucks.

The mask made breathing impossible.

How did doctors complete surgeries with these damn things on?

I tore off the mask as soon as I left the building.

My pocket shook.

Seven missed calls and six text messages.

All from Cody.

I called him.

"What time are you coming back to the office?" he asked.

I was too exhausted for corporate niceties.

"I need to go home and rest."

"Oh." Cody paused. "When can you give us an update on the Brewfest project?"

"I don't know, man. I need some fucking rest."

"Oh . . . yeah. Okay. Feel better. I'll look for your update."

Click.

I grabbed my prescription from the pharmacy near my apartment. A hundred bucks. When I got home, I went straight to bed.

March 6, 2020

I awoke fourteen hours later drenched like I had just gotten out of a pool. My clothes, which I fell asleep in, were stuck to my skin. I stood up and stripped. I chugged a random water bottle, wrapped myself in my blanket, and shivered myself back to sleep.

Somehow, I felt worse when I woke up. I struggled to walk the six feet from my bed to my bathroom to piss. I used the hallway wall to guide me to the fridge for more water bottles. I fell asleep within minutes of lying back down in bed.

Some sunlight peeked through my not-shut-all-the-way blackout curtains. My chest felt tighter. I coughed a deep one. It was one of those coughs that feels great but also hurts. I pulled out my phone and ordered pho. My nostrils must have been clogged. The spicy soup would only help my sinuses. It took most of my strength, but I carried my blanket and pillow to my living room. I lay on the couch and turned on the TV. I avoided the news like the plague. My pho finally came. I didn't have the strength to walk downstairs, so I rang the guy in. The driver dropped my food at my apartment door.

The pho tasted bland. I drowned the broth in sriracha. My nostrils drooled, but I couldn't taste a fucking thing. No flavor. Nothing.

I went to sleep for a few more hours before I shivered awake. Another cold sweat. My couch made an uncomfortable squeal when I rolled over. I wrapped my blanket around my drenched body and closed my eyes. A coughing fit woke me up. I drank the rest of all the remaining liquids around me and sucked on some flavorless cough drops.

Back to sleep.

March 7, 2020

E very so often, I'd wake up with tightening chest pain. After a couple of bad coughs and some liquid medicine, I'd fall back asleep.

When I awoke again, I crawled to the fridge for more water. I swallowed another prescription pill. I warmed up the day-old glass bowl of pho that sat on my floor.

I scarfed it all down without tasting a thing.

I slept for the rest of the weekend.

Cough
March 10, 2020

Never in a million years, did I imagine a clean asshole would be a real concern in my life. I never stocked up on toilet paper. I was a bachelor who bought TP on an as needed basis. I'd run low and go to the liquor store on the corner for more. But the liquor was sold out. And had been for a few days.

No business within thirty miles had any.

I couldn't justify traveling further than that for ass paper.

My poor shower drain.

I ordered six rolls of organic forest TP for eighty bucks to ensure I could wipe. It was an extra twenty for "super-fast" shipping. Supply and price gouging. I mean, demand.

That's how capitalism works.

Then again, it was the softest TP my bum has ever felt.

On my first day back in the office, Rose, who sat across from my desk, called out of work. Whatever I had, I assumed she got. I felt drained, but I couldn't afford another day off. Working sick showed courage. Missing work? Unacceptable. Especially in your first ninety days.

Meghan, the vice president of Sudz & Crew, met with me in her office when I returned to work. Cody joined the meeting too, but they both kept their distance from me.

"Was it coronavirus?" Meghan asked.

Cody laughed nervously.

"They didn't test me for anything. Gave me some antibiotics. Recommended rest," I said.

"What do you have?" Cody asked.

"The doc said he thinks it was the flu," I said.

The two changed the subject and caught me up on the office happenings. It was all very boring.

My colleagues kept their distance.

Elaine, a graphic designer, worked in the conference room for the entire day.

March 11, 2020

My colleagues no longer feared me.
In fact, they pestered me all day.
"Did you get tested for COVID?" Brandon asked.
"You survived COVID, bro. What's it like?" Robert asked.
"I sanitized the entire office," Elaine said. "Doorknobs, chairs, floors, desks, computers. Every nook and cranny."
I wonder how many billable hours that wasted.
I didn't have the energy to work out after work.
By the time I got to my apartment, the NBA season was canceled. Because of coronavirus.
My father called me.
"You're not planning on staying out there, right? Your lease is up, in what, June? You don't have to stay out there until then."
"May."
"You're coming home."
"If things get worse, yeah. It all depends. We've got great doctors and scientists. We can handle this. It's what America does, right?"
It was a lie.
I knew I was coming home.
"Don't be an idiot. But these fucking Chinese," my father said. "Nasty people."
"What?"
"They're assholes. The lot of them. They did this shit."
I let out a few coughs.
"What are you talking about?"
"Don't order Chinese food. I never will again. A bunch of people at work are doing the same. Fuck them. I don't want their virus shit."
It's like the Japanese prison camps during World War II were erased from history books.
"I'm getting tired," I said.
"How do you think the virus is getting here, Wyatt?"

"I'm not a scientist," I said. "But I do have to get going. I have a date."

It wasn't a lie.

"Don't get attached. You need to get your ass home. This is serious."

The conversation ended after that.

When I got home, I invited Paige over for Chinese food. I ordered enough takeout to feed six people. Paige and I got high enough to eat most of it. She walked the leftovers outside and gave it to one of the homeless men who lived on my street.

Paige really was something special.

But I teased her for giving away tomorrow's lunch.

March 12, 2020

A young boy coughed outside the open door to my work's office.

"He needs to get out of here," Elaine said to me across her desk.

"Not cool, little dude," Robert said, who's desk sat next to mine.

Deep, painful coughs came from the boy's chest.

I felt bad for the kid, but he needed to leave.

Now.

"It looks like they're trying to get next door," Meghan said. "There's a government agency or division for immigrants there."

She came out of her office and huddled next to my and Amy's desks.

The boy coughed some more.

Cody approached the boy and his mother.

The team stopped working, and half the employees at Sudz & Crew huddled around the desk closest to the door.

Mine.

"I ain't trying to get the coronavirus," Greg said.

"The China virus?" Robert said.

Meghan glared at him.

"That's not appropriate."

Robert put his arms in the air.

"I'm quoting the president. He said it."

The boy coughed one more time.

Cody convinced the family to leave.

"Thank god," Robert said.

"Seriously," Amy said.

Meghan stood up.

"Everyone in the conference room. I can sense that we're all on edge."

The entire staff crammed into the largest conference room. Twelve more people stood around the glass table.

"Everything is fine," Meghan said. "We understand there are some things going on in the world out of our control. We're mindful of that. We get it. But when you're in the office, be in the office. Work is a great distraction."

The world is ending.

Don't forget to clock out.

"Things are going on as normal. Nothing to worry about," Meghan said again.

"What about the NBA canceling their season?" Robert asked.

"The NBA season is an interesting case, but sports leagues have to be cautious. Lots of travel and personnel. They're going to be overly careful," Meghan said.

Rich, white billionaires stabling their prized horses.

Shit was serious.

"Let's be sensitive to the virus when we talk with clients," Cody said.

The team spent the next hour brainstorming ideas to keep our clients from firing us in a pandemic panic. We came to the conclusion to convince our clients to send a COVID statement to their customers to thank them for their support. Just a touch point to let customers know their favorite business is still open. It wasn't a smart, sinister, or original idea. Every writer, content creator, public relations professional, advertising executive, or marketing guru made the same suggestion. It was hive-mind income preservation.

And that's what every company in America did.

Spammed the nation's inboxes, begging for business as a virus outbreak infected the world.

March 13, 2020

Cody and Meghan forced the team to happy hour at noon. We sat around a bunch of tables pushed together. No one wanted to be there. Except for the weirdo fucking owner.

"Everyone stocked up on toilet paper?" Cody asked.

Some people laughed, but only because the boss said it.

"We're going to be fine," Meghan said.

"What about a potential lockdown?" Robert asked.

Everyone shared their pandemic plans. Food and video games for the graphic designers. Prayers and booze for the rest of us. We drank beers, shared hand sanitizer, and made jokes about the run on toilet paper. Nervous jokes about our impending doom.

"You think it's a bad omen?" Cody drank his dark beer. "It's Friday the thirteenth."

"We have enough to worry about with no toilet paper at the stores than to even think about ghosts and demons," Meghan said. "Am I right?"

We needed a fucking plague.

I bailed on the noon happy hour when it was appropriate. I stopped at one of the corner liquor stores by my apartment on my way home. The place was a lockdown gold mine. Noodles. Beans. Canned veggies. Canned soup. Toilet paper. Pasta sauce. Booze. I loaded up as much as I could carry. I made two more trips.

Worst-case scenario?

Trapped in my apartment for months.

At least I had ramen.

An Empty Speakeasy
March 14, 2020

It was an old-time shop with a black-and-white-checkered floor that sold expensive whiskey and liquor. The register and counter were relics from the past. A young, fit man working the joint wore a bow tie and vest. A fireplace with two seats on each side was to the right of the sales counter. Paige and I sat down while Noah and Summer stood next to us. The man working behind the counter hit a button, and we spun around slowly into a dimly lit room.

Raised By Wolves was straight from the Roaring Twenties. The room had a dark-red domed ceiling, beautiful booths, antique chairs, and vintage decor. The bar sat in the middle of the place. A server took us to a booth in the corner.

"Leah should be here soon, but you know her," Summer said.

"Let's do a round of old-fashioneds," Noah told the black-haired waitress.

"This place is usually packed. We never can find a reservation," Summer said.

"Everyone is acting scared," Noah said. "This could be the last time we're all together in public."

"Don't say that," Summer said. "But if it's true, I'm glad I'm spending the last days on earth with you assholes."

Paige squirmed next to me.

"To one last night," Noah said.

"Noah!" Summer said.

Paige put down her drink.

She headed for the bar.

I went after her.

"What's wrong?" I asked.

"We shouldn't be out," she said. "Not like this."

"It'll be okay."

"Will it?"

I rubbed her arms.

"I hope so."

"What's your plan?"

"Plan?"

"What if we get locked down?"

"I'll handle it," I said.

"You can't live like that. Who the fuck knows what's going to happen? We can't keep avoiding this conversation."

"Let's try to enjoy this. At least for now."

"You think the world is going to end?"

I ordered us beer.

"There ain't a damn thing I can do about it if it does."

"What if you lose your job?"

"I'll write."

"What will you write about, Hemingway?" Paige asked.

"A world more fucked-up than me."

The bartender handed me two cold beers.

I handed Paige hers.

"For real," Paige said. "What's your plan?"

I wasn't meant for California.

No matter how bad I wanted it.

"Why extend my lease if we're going to be stuck inside? My job isn't going to survive a lockdown either. Considering it's all about event planning. In a pandemic. Jersey makes the most sense. I hate it, but it's the right move."

"Yeah."

"I'm drowning out here. I need to cut my losses," I said.

"What if you stayed with Summer and Noah?"

Back at the table, Summer waved her hands violently at Noah. He sipped his drink and tried to calm her down.

"I'm not gonna cockblock Noah like that. He's probably getting a ton of engagement sex."

Paige laughed.

"I'm going to come back," I said. "As long as humanity doesn't go extinct."

"I don't want you to leave."

"Me either." I held Paige's hand. "Let's hope it doesn't come to that."

Going back to Jersey was going to happen.

But I didn't want to think about leaving Paige.

We made our way back to the table. Leah was sitting between Noah and Summer, wearing a long, tight red dress. She must have come alone to the speakeasy. She stared at Paige and my hands clasped together.

"Whoa," Leah said. "How long has this been a thing?"

Paige and I looked at each other.

"Holy shit." Paige ripped her hand away from mine. "I didn't even realize he was trying to make a move. Thanks, Leah. Can't trust any man these days."

Paige slid along the puffy red cushion into the wraparound booth. She sat next to Leah. I put my hand on Paige's knee.

"Is this officially a thing?" Summer asked.

"Wyatt only holds hands with women he's fucked," Noah said.

Summer hit his arm. "Don't be fresh."

"He held my hand," Leah said. "All the time."

"Did you guys fuck?" Noah asked.

"You can't ask that!" Summer yelled.

"Did you have sexual relations?" Noah asked.

"Not like that either."

"Go ahead." Paige sipped her beer. "Answer it."

The look on Leah's face told me she wasn't sure.

"Never," I said.

"He's lying," Paige said. "You should see the videos he sent of him and Leah."

"Fuck," Leah said. "He sent you those? He promised not to send them to anyone."

"Send what?" Noah asked.

"I never knew you were into some of that freaky shit," Paige said. "We should hang out. Leave Wyatt at home."

"What freaky shit?" Noah asked.

"Noah!" Summer yelled.

Paige couldn't stop laughing.

"I knew that you two would be a thing," Leah said. "That night you two met. I knew it."

We all raised our glasses.

After another round, Summer and Noah returned home. Leah went to meet up with her work friends. And I spent the night at Paige's.

Escape from San Diego

March 15, 2020

Fear consumed me when the California governor ordered all nonessential businesses to close. Bars. Wineries. Restaurants that didn't serve takeout. All shut down. I thought there would be a sequel to the "Toilet Paper Panic" with the "Great Beer Panic."

Not long after the governor's shut down order, Meghan emailed the entire company. She gave everyone permission to work from home, as long as we called, texted, emailed, or sent a smoke signal to let her know whether or not we were coming into the office.

With the option to work remotely, there was no reason to stay in California. At least financially. If I left after work on Friday, I could make it back to Jersey before work started on Monday. With the time zones, I'd have a three-hour buffer.

I could do it.

Back to Jersey.

It was official.

I called Paige.

We canceled our Saint Patrick's Day plans.

And I told her my next move.

"I'm leaving Friday," I said. "I think I can make it back to Jersey before work on Monday."

"I've been thinking about going home," Paige said.

If Paige came with me, I wouldn't have to leave her.

"Really?"

"Might be nice to spend time with my parents."

"What about your job?"

"I can work from anywhere."

"I don't think things are going to get better," I said.

"You're definitely leaving this weekend?"

"Yeah," I said.

"I might see if you want to stop in Philly. If that's cool. I don't know yet. I'm still debating."

"Let me know before Friday morning," I said. "I want to see you before I leave."

"Duh."

I called Kayla and let her know I'd be packing my things and coming back to Jersey on Friday. I could hear her smile through the phone. She told my mother and Mike. I texted my father the news. He was very happy to hear that I'd be moving back to the East Coast.

March 16, 2020

Most of the Sudz & Crew staff worked from home on Monday. Some went into the office to escape their spouses.

I texted Paige a picture of me in a dress shirt and boxers with the caption, *Work uniform.*

She wrote back.

Welcome to the club!

Paige sent a picture.

She was pantless.

More photos followed.

From every possible angle.

Meghan interrupted Paige's digital show with an email announcing a mandatory staff video chat. Half of my colleagues were missing from my screen, and they never joined the meeting.

"Welcome to our new coffee chat," Meghan said. "We'll be doing this every morning until things clear up. Everything is fine. Things will be fine. With the ability to work remotely, we wanted to make sure we saw all the smiling faces of the team each and every morning.

"Before we dive into the business of things, we want everyone to get a coffee or a beverage and meet back in five minutes. We're going to do a little exercise. We're going to implement this new activity in our morning calls."

I made an Irish coffee.

My hand was heavy.

"I'm grateful to work with such an incredible team," Meghan said.

"I'm thankful to have a flexible group of talented individuals I get to call my employees," Cody said.

He can't say that. Meghan just said that.

"I'm grateful that I can work in shorts," I said.

"Or without pants," Robert said.

"Robert," Meghan said.

"I wasn't going there," I said.

Cue the fake laugh.

Elaine went next. "I'm grateful for my boyfriend, Rick, my dog, Ruffles, my parents, my friends, but especially my best friend, who is also my boyfriend . . ."

Fuck it.

Inject me with the virus.

"I'm thankful for our Lord and Savior, Jesus Christ," Greg said. "Especially now in our time of most desperate need."

"How about you go next, Oscar," Meghan said before Greg finished.

People sharing generic facts with their stranger coworkers via video chat. This is how the world ends.

The meeting went on and on.

"At the end of the day send me an email of everything you did while you worked," Meghan said. "Attach or link whatever documents you worked on. We're adjusting to the new normal and want to make sure we're still holding our team accountable."

Please more work during a fucking epidemic.

Meghan didn't want to do the work of seeing which staff were worth staying on the payroll.

She'd have employees justify their own firing.

Via email.

Maybe Chuck wasn't the problem.

Corporate America was a parasite.

"Because of the worldwide crisis, we needed to lay off some staff," Cody said. "That's why some faces are missing this morning. We aren't expecting any more cuts, but it's a fluid situation. Please email, text, or call me if you have any staffing questions."

No one had Cody's phone number.

Besides Meghan.

"What Cody meant to say was, your jobs are safe. We're going to make it through this," Meghan said. "Let's have a great workday!"

Cody called me an hour after the morning video call. Robert, who had been with the company since it was founded, joined us. Robert planned beer tastings for corporate events, festivals, conferences, and any type of occasion imaginable. With conferences and traveling grinding to a halt, his job was expendable. Robert was taskless. He had nothing to send Meghan when he completed his work for the day. That's why he went after the new guy's job, with the approval of the chief executive officer.

"I know this client and what they expect in their writing," Robert said. "What you're doing isn't what they need. Especially in this time of crisis."

It was bullshit.

Everyone on the call knew it.

But no one said a fucking thing.

"I'm going to add Robert to your accounts. That way you two can collaborate," Cody said.

After the call, I organized everything in my apartment that wasn't a necessity. I emptied my dresser and closet, folding my clothes neatly into my suitcases.

My career at Sudz & Crew was over.

I should have gone to happy hour with Cody.

March 17, 2020

I made myself a double Irish coffee for the holiday. Cody and Meghan informed the team during our morning call that they laid off more staff members. Only eight people remained employed by Sudz & Crew. Half the staff overcompensated for their fear of losing their jobs by being overzealous. The other four, like me, checked out. We knew what was going to happen. We didn't know who was next to go, but we knew more layoffs were coming.

Mike called me at noon.

"When are you leaving?" he asked.

"Friday."

"Leave sooner. Do you have an emergency kit?"

"Yeah," I lied.

"Get one. What about a route home?"

"I'll use my GPS."

"Wyatt. No. Think ahead. What if shit goes bonkers? Think about the worst case. Memorize a route. I'll do some research and send you one."

"Thanks."

"I sent you a thousand bucks," Mike said.

My phone lit up with a deposit.

"Take out five hundred. Keep it on you. Just in case. Be ready to leave at a moment's notice. Can you pack your car? Or are you parked on the streets?"

"Streets."

"Can you stay anywhere? What about Summer's place?"

"Relax."

"The lockdowns are coming. Whether you accept it or not. If you're coming back, you have to do it sooner rather than later."

Mike was right.

"Alright," I said. "Tell me what I need to do to get back to Jersey."

* * *

I dropped my car off at a mechanic in the morning for routine maintenance. The car was in good shape, but I wanted to make sure it was in perfect condition before my cross-country road trip.

I packed an emergency bag filled with batteries, a radio, a first aid kit, a blanket, a gallon of water, snacks, a portable phone charger, a flashlight, and lighters. I'd leave the big stuff. Couch. Mattress. Bed frame. I'd give Noah and Summer the illegal copy of my apartment key I made and have them try to sell the furniture before my move-out date. If not, whatever. I'd let them keep the money for selling the stuff. Or I'd pay the penalty on my security deposit when my lease expired in May.

My mother and Kayla called and texted me constantly, begging me to come home. They suggested I abandon all my things and catch a flight to Jersey. It was a little extreme to leave my car and all my stuff two thousand miles away. During a fucking pandemic, and all. Between calming my family down with texts and calls, I packed. Somehow, I always forget how terrible packing is. Until I'm in the middle of packing.

My apartment was nearly boxed up before the day ended.

At least the things I didn't use every day.

All my projects for Sudz & Crew went on hold, except for the two richest breweries that were now Robert's clients. I did an hour's worth of work and sent it to Robert via email. Robert forwarded my email to Cody, calling it his own.

That's how Robert and I collaborated at work.

California Goodbye
March 18, 2020

I dialed into the Sudz & Crew morning video call. That's all I did for work that day.

I tore down the two shelves my father screwed into the wall and removed the one piece of art in my entire place. It was a replica Banksy portrait of two children on top of a dumpster, peeing, with their asses out. On the brick wall in front of them read the words "Life Is Short. Chill the Out!" Between "the" and "Out" was a picture of a duck, but that wasn't the word it meant. It was weird, but it made me laugh. I tossed it in the dumpster in my building's parking garage.

At the end of the workday, I didn't even bother to send a recap email to Meghan. Or Robert.

Paige called.

"Plans on Friday?"

"Road-tripping across the country during a pandemic. How about you?"

"How about this? We get high and watch the last two *RoboCop* movies. You can sleep over. But only if you promise to behave. I figure dog beach Saturday. Get In-N-Out for dinner. See one last sunset. Then head back east."

"What do you mean 'behave'?"

"How did I know that's all you'd get from that?" Paige asked.

"Thanks for including me in your plans for my road trip."

Paige laughed.

"I'll wait this out with my folks. I think. I have a few days to decide. It's a maybe. If you can drop me off in Philly, that would be much appreciated, dude. If you have the room."

"Of course, I do."

"It's not definite. I have to think about some things," she said. "Quick question. Maybe it's a concern. Do we have items to protect ourselves?"

"If you mean weapons, yeah. We have those."

"Zombie-proof weapons?"

"My weapons are good for zombies, humans, and small animals. Maybe even large ones, with the right strike."

"Last question. Again, don't judge. Do you think the cops or whatever will stop us from traveling out of state?"

"Not with my Jersey license plates."

"You never went to the DMV?"

"Fuck the government."

She laughed.

"I'm hungry, dude," Paige said. "Want to get dinner? I'm craving some In-N-Out."

"Aren't we going Saturday?"

"Dude," Paige said. "We're leaving California. We may never get In-N-Out again."

* * *

She picked me up from my apartment, and we drove to the closest burger joint. With more eateries closing by the day, the drive-through line was especially long. Even for In-N-Out.

"It might be quicker to go inside," I said.

Paige shook her head.

"Hell no. I don't know if we're even allowed inside. And if we are, I ain't risking getting sick."

"I just hate drive-throughs."

"What do you have against drive-throughs?"

"Memories."

"Stop being so mysterious."

I took a deep breath.

"It's a trigger for me. For whatever reason I can't let it go."

"A trigger for what?"

"My father took my brother and me for fast food at this new joint. He pulled us out of school early. My father always did this after a long night of arguing with my mother. I thanked my father as we entered the parking lot. He didn't say a word. Not a you're welcome. Nothing. He didn't ask what I wanted when we got to the menu. He didn't order me a thing. But he and Mike each got burgers and fries. 'Never thank anyone for anything until you get it' is what he told me. No lunch for me that day. Haven't been a fan of drive-throughs since."

"That's fucked up."

"That's nothing," I said.

"I'm sorry."

"It's a silly reason to avoid drive-throughs."

Paige pulled her car closer to the ordering box.

"Trauma makes for the best people."

"Or the worst."

Paige looked me in the eye.

"What happened?"

"What if I don't want to tell you?"

Paige caressed my leg, working her way up my thigh.

"Then this won't work. I want to know you, Wyatt."

"I'm not sure you do."

Paige moved her car forward.

Four more cars until we could order our food.

"Tell me."

I closed my eyes and took another deep breath.

"My father is an angry, violent, and abusive son of a bitch. He beat the shit out of me, called me an idiot and countless other horrible things every single fucking day of my life. He threatened me with violence and made me live my entire childhood in fear."

"Dude."

"That's not the worst part." I paused. "I'm afraid I'm going to become him. Maybe I already am."

Paige grabbed my hand.

"I doubt you're like him."

"The night before I left Erin, I fucked up. Bad."

"Your ex?" Paige asked.

"Yeah. Erin and I had been fighting for days. The same fights we'd have every few months. Shit boiled over. Late nights. Headaches. Sore faces. Red, dry eyes all day at work. After four days of nonstop fighting, I snapped."

"What do you mean?"

I closed my eyes.

It was time to tell the truth.

"I don't even know what she said, but next thing I knew, Erin threw her hands up to protect herself. And she had this look on her face. A look I knew all too well. Absolute terror. Erin was staring up at my hand. It was cocked back with an open palm. Ready to strike. I didn't even realize my hand was raised. I dropped to my knees. I couldn't stop crying. Erin got on her knees to console me, but I couldn't calm down."

"I don't know what to even say," Paige said.

"I spent my whole life trying to avoid becoming my father, but I'm no better than him. The next day, I packed my things and left. Erin didn't deserve that. No one does."

Paige moved the car closer to the drive-through menu.

"For Christ's sake, Wyatt, you're only human. Is it bad? Definitely. But give yourself a break for once in your life. You got pissed. We've all been there. Shit happens, but you restrained yourself. You didn't hit her."

"My father learned that from his father. His father probably learned it from his father. Who knows how far it goes back? Or maybe it was the alcoholism? A family full of angry, violent alcoholic men making the same mistakes as their fathers. I had to try something different."

"California?"

"Yeah."

"I'm sorry," Paige said. "Have you told anyone this? Like a therapist?"

"No one."

Paige rubbed my hand.

"I don't even know what to say."

The car behind us honked.

"Calm the fuck down, dude!" Paige yelled.

Paige pulled the car up the line.

"I'm sorry," I said. "I'm not a good man."

"Stop. I'm glad you told me, dude. It took a lot of courage."

She pulled her hand off mine to steady her steering wheel.

One more car until dinner.

Paige put her hand back on mine after we stopped.

I gripped Paige's hand tighter.

"My biggest fear is becoming him."

"You won't. We'll get you there."

"I'm glad you said we."

We pulled up the menu.

Paige stroked my hand while she ordered.

She kissed me when she finished.

"I'm here for you," she said. "And I care about you. A lot. But if you ever disrespect me, I'll knock you out, dude."

"I know."

"I'm not even joking."

I smiled.

"That's the best part."

March 19, 2020

I skipped my morning meeting. Paige wouldn't let me out of bed. She and Ralph went back to her apartment around eleven to spend the day packing. She figured she'd spend a few months in Philly. Just until things settled down.

After she left, I parked my car in the loading zone outside my apartment. I had work to do. For the first time since I went remote, I skipped my Irish coffee.

Boxes and boxes went into my car. Up and down two stories of stairs. My glutes burned while my laptop stayed dark. Books, journals, and odd-shaped things went in the trunk. Dishes, decor, and things I didn't care for went into suitcases. I'd tie the three suitcases to the roof of my car, like I'd done when I drove out here.

I called Kayla as I emptied the apartment. We didn't talk about the virus, potential travel restrictions, or the rumors of lockdowns. Not thinking about what I was doing or why I was doing it helped me stay focused.

Well, for most of the conversation.

"Just fly home," Kayla said.

It was the third day in a row she advised this.

"What about my car?"

"This is serious."

I taped shut my last box. "I'll be heading home Saturday."

"I thought it was Friday."

"Change of plans."

Kayla huffed. "You should leave now."

"I know what I'm doing."

"Stop being so stubborn," Kayla said. "I don't want you to fucking die."

"There are worse things."

"I can't do this shit with you!"

"I have to get back to loading my car. It'll be alright. Trust me. I love you."

"Get home!"

The last box fit in my car and still left plenty of room for Paige, Ralph, and a giant suitcase.

The rope holding the suitcases to the top of my car didn't seem tight enough. I pulled it down, but the rope stayed loose. Jimmy, from the halfway house, saw me.

"Heading out of here?" he asked.

"Back to Jersey."

"Are you taking everything?"

He tugged on one side of the rope while I pulled on the other.

"What I can fit. There's a bunch of shit I can't bring. You can look through it."

Jimmy followed me to my apartment, where he placed some cleaning supplies and food into a box. He and I carried my small TV, its stand, and my dresser down two flights of stairs, across the street, and up more stairs to his place.

"They make me rent furniture here. Charging me for the TV, the mattress, the TV stand, and the dresser. Over a hundred bucks every month. I appreciate this," Jimmy said.

Giving back a bit before the world ended felt good.

The hundred bucks he paid me felt better.

Jimmy agreed to watch my car while I hopped in the shower. One last shower in the smallest stall I'd ever known. The water spit out. Barely. At least it was hot.

I dried myself off with an old towel. The steam fogged up my entire bathroom. Texts and calls exploded out of my phone when I wiped the moisture off it. Before I could read any message, a news alert invaded my screen: *Governor Newsom Announces Statewide Lockdown in California.*

Lockdown

March 19, 2020

I called Paige.

"Lockdown starts tonight," I said. "Midnight."

"Dude. It'll be alright. Relax."

"I can't risk waiting. I won't get stuck here."

With the looming lockdown, I feared being trapped inside without a window.

"We can still leave Saturday."

I put the phone on speaker and threw on a black T-shirt.

"I've got to go tonight."

"What?"

I picked the phone back up.

"I'm leaving tonight."

There was a long, uncomfortable silence.

"I can't do this right now," she said. "It's too much."

I needed to get the hell out of California.

"I'm leaving at nine."

Paige paused.

"I'll call you in a bit. I need time to think."

She hung up.

I found the piece of paper with the route back to Jersey written on it. I-10 to I-20 to I-30 to I-40 to I-81 to I-95. I repeated it a few times before shoving the folded directions into my back pocket before I went to my car.

Jimmy smoked panic cigarettes on the sidewalk.

I called Summer as he paced around me.

"I'm getting the hell out of here."

"Want to stay with us?" she asked.

"I'm going back to Jersey."

"It's not going to last long."

I locked my car.

"I'm already packed."

"I think you're overreacting," Noah yelled in the distance.

"I'm leaving."

"It won't be bad," Summer said.

I ran up the steps to my apartment.

"I can't take any more chances out here."

"I get it," Summer said. "You—"

My phone beeped and cut Summer off.

It was Paige.

"I've got to get on the road."

"Are you going to be okay?" Summer asked.

"I'll be fine."

"You better not die on me. I need you at my wedding."

"If the world is still standing, I'll be there."

I switched the call.

I knew what Paige was going to say before she said it.

It didn't make hearing the words hurt any less.

"I can't leave. My life is here. Everything. My career. All my stuff. My friends. I'm sorry. I can't. I can't do it. There's not enough time. I can't rush out like this."

I walked around my apartment, searching for anything important I might have forgotten.

"Are you sure?" I asked.

"I can't."

There was a moment of silence.

"Alright."

"What if we bring the virus back? And what if I get my parents sick? Oh god. I can't even imagine. I couldn't handle that. I can't leave."

It was selfish to convince her to come with me.

"You know what's best for you," I said. "Trust that."

"Are you sure you don't want to wait until Saturday to leave? If I have more time to think, maybe I'll change my mind. It's too much. Too quickly. I can't do it right now."

"After the year I had, I have to get out of here.

"I get it, dude."

"I feel like I'm abandoning you," I said.

"Don't think like that."

"But I am."

"Don't worry about me," Paige said. "Focus on the trip."

"Yeah."

"I don't know what this is between us, but I hope you don't disappear."

Tears streamed down my face.

"I'll call you from the road."

I hated saying goodbye.

"Be safe, dude."

I hung up and put on a pair of sunglasses. It was dark, but I wanted to hide my watering eyes. Two big boxes I planned to leave behind in my apartment fit into the space that I'd left for Paige and Ralph. I checked the rope holding the suitcases one last time before sliding into my car.

Sunshine Highway
March 19, 2020

The cool California breeze whipped through my hair one last time. Leah's number flashed across my phone's screen.
I-10 to I-20 to I-30 to I-40 to I-81 to I-95.
I pressed harder on the gas.
My phone finally stopped shaking.
Leah left a voicemail.
I couldn't handle listening to it.
I-10 to I-20 to I-30 to I-40 to I-81 to I-95.
There were a billion reasons to go back to Jersey. All of them pretty damn compelling. It was a matter of when, not if, I'd be fired from Sudz & Crew. Living alone in a windowless apartment without an income while the world shut down wasn't something I could afford. A pandemic and financial crisis would be my death sentence.
But what about Paige?
I-10 to I-20 to I-30 to I-40 to I-81 to I-95.
What if I stayed?
No.
It was suicide.
Crazy talk.
Insane.
Stupid.
Probably the dumbest thing I could do.
I-10 to I-20 to I-30 to I-40 to I-81 to I-95.
I never allowed myself to think about leaving Paige until I was speeding down a highway with my shit racing against a spreading plague. It was something I couldn't do.
I called my father.
"Figured you'd call back," my father said. "Are you calm now?"
"I'm staying."

"What?"

"I'm staying in California."

"Are you insane?" my father asked. "What are you talking about? This isn't a game. This is life or death."

"Exactly."

"Why? What? Who have you talked to? Have you told your mother?"

"I'm not asking."

"You can't stay out there."

"I can't go back either. Now, can I?"

There was a pause.

"Wyatt."

"If you knew anything about me, you'd understand."

"Don't punish yourself for what I did."

"This isn't about you," I said.

My father struggled to find his words.

"Why do you want to stay?"

"I'm in love."

It wasn't a lie.

I loved Paige.

"This is over a woman?" my father yelled. "What are you fucking doing?"

"Probably something stupid," I said.

"You're going to die. It's fucking insane out there."

"And awful back there," I said.

There was a pause.

"Your mother is going to worry. You can't stay in California."

"I can't control that."

"This isn't a game! This is life. There are consequences. You're not going to make it out there."

"There was only one way to find out," I said. "We can talk later. When you're calm."

"Don't you dare hang up on me!"

"Bye."

The call ended.

I powered off my phone.

No distractions.

I reached into my back pocket, pulled out my wallet and grabbed my piece of California postcard. I held it tight one last time. I tossed it out the window. I didn't need it anymore.

The palm trees flew by me faster.

My car roared across two lanes.

A Range Rover blared its horn after I nearly clipped it.

I turned up the radio.

A soft, familiar voice sang faintly over my speakers.

Bob fucking Dylan.

When I found the first exit west back to San Diego, I smashed the pedal to the floor.

Last Chance
March 19, 2020

S he wasn't how I imagined. Her hair wasn't blonde. Her smile wasn't orthodontist approved. And she wasn't even born in California.

Paige opened the front door with her hair pulled up in a messy bun, wearing a sleeveless, oversized T-shirt. Her nose was red, and her eyes dripping with tears. Before she could say a word, I revealed my *RoboCop* DVD from behind my back.

"I couldn't leave without showing you the trilogy."

Paige smiled.

There was no doubt about it.

She belonged in the California sun.

"What if I have other plans?" she asked.

"Plans? In a lockdown?" I asked.

She pulled a joint from her ear.

"I was about to smoke this. Alone. Now I have to share. Hence ruining my plans."

"I'm always good for fucking things up," I said.

I followed Paige to her couch, where Ralph pounced on top of me. He gnawed my fingers after a few welcome licks.

Paige and I smoked the blunt too fast.

We ignored our impending doom by snuggling up and watching the sequel to an over-the-top action movie filled with awful one-liners by a robot cop with an itchy trigger finger.

"That was so fucking terrible," Paige said when *RoboCop* 2 ended. "I loved every minute."

"It gets worse."

Before I could leave the couch and put on *RoboCop* 3, Paige grabbed my wrist. "Do you think it's a good idea?"

"*RoboCop* 3? Definitely not. A total cash grab."

"This." Paige pointed at herself and then to me. "You think this is a good idea?"

"The best things rarely are."

Paige's green eyes grew warm, and her face grew bright. I pressed my lips against her forehead. She pushed me down and climbed on top of me.

* * *

The lockdown curfew came and went.

I was trapped in California.

"How about we get more high before *RoboCop 3*?" Paige asked.

"The answer is always yes."

She put on her thong and disappeared into the kitchen.

I pulled my jeans off the floor and grabbed my phone.

It rebooted back to life.

Thirty missed calls.

Twenty text messages.

Most from my father.

I silenced my phone and tossed it out of reach.

Paige returned to the living room with a packed bong. She dimmed the lights and turned on her galaxy lamp, which transformed the ceiling into our own miniature universe filled with stars, planets, and space portals.

"Let's have a little fun," Paige said.

She stopped at her record player and rummaged through her vinyl collection, searching for the perfect playlist.

"You got any Dylan?" I asked.

"Bob Dylan? You serious?"

"Not a fan?"

"Listen, dude. I respect the guy. What he stood for and why. But I don't have any of his music. His voice is so fucking plain. And so goddamn whiny."

I couldn't help but let out a laugh.

AC/DC played in the background as Paige swiveled her hips, dancing her way to the couch.

I didn't know if we'd last.

Or if we'd survive this.

But there was nowhere else I wanted to be.
And it didn't have a thing to do with California.

About the Author

Brian Price worked in the marketing and communications industry for nine years. The Public Relations Society of America, American Business Awards, and Association of Marketing and Communication Professionals are a few of the organizations that awarded his work.

Sick of bookshelves being stuffed with bureaucrats' memoirs and snake-oil entrepreneurs using books as sales funnels, Brian wrote a novel, *Last Chance California*.

If he isn't reading or writing, Brian is probably playing with his rescue pup, Bucky, or ranting about the government.

You can follow him at brianvstheworld.com

Brian's second novel, *Once Upon a Subway* will be released on September 5, 2022.